VOYAGE OF FURY & FATE

Vampires of Charleston
Book 2

Madalyn Rae

As with most vampire stories, there are quite a few mentions of death, dismemberment, and blood. Please be aware that this book contains discussions of child abuse, sexual abuse, and young children being turned into vampires, as well as immortal children's (child vampires) deaths.

eudora

TWO MONTHS HAVE PASSED since meeting Marnie, the supposed daughter of Kragen, the ancient vampire who is both my maker and chief asshole, and Eudora, a powerful sea witch. The two months we've bounced between Charleston and New Orleans have been the longest I've stayed in one location for two centuries. Thorne, the ship captain responsible for carrying my family across the Atlantic three hundred years ago, has been by my side this entire time, and I'm eternally grateful. Since reuniting, our time together has been riddled with heartache and pain, making our time together more stressful than it should be.

Even though I know Kragen is hiding in the swamps of New Orleans, I can't stop looking over my shoulder, expecting him to be there, ready to drag me back to the bottom of his ship at any given moment.

The distant sound of a door squeaking brings me back to the present. Sitting in an upscale office building in downtown Charleston was not how I planned on spending my day. Who am I kidding? I didn't have any plans, other than to continue the Netflix series I started last night. I keep that to myself. Thorne needs all the support he can get as he discusses his great-great-great-granddaughter's estate. Even though they didn't know each other long, he watched over her throughout her lifetime. Watching her die and not being able to do anything about it was difficult, and he needs all the strength he can get right now.

I sigh, flipping through the *Better Homes and Gardens Magazine* for the third time, not paying attention to anything in front of me. My mind rambles through the insanity of everything that's happened, ending with the sadness that came with Francis's death.

"Excuse me, Miss Abernathy?" the young woman behind the welcome desk calls to me.

I look up, having forgotten she's in the room. "I hope you don't mind, but I took the liberty of looking your name up in our system. It sounded...familiar."

Shit. Is there some sort of a paranormal database that lists every vampire and lycan in the city? I open my eyes wide, urging her to continue.

She clears her throat. "Are you by any chance related to Aaron Abernathy?" I stare at the young woman, not sure how to respond. "It's such an unusual name around here. I thought maybe you were related. Please forgive me for intruding."

My father was named Aaron, but he never came to America with us. I called the infant my mother refused to name, Aaron. Could he be the same?

I smile, hoping to ease the woman's mind. "I've researched my family history in the past, and there was an Aaron once. He was alive centuries ago, and I'm not sure he ever made it to America."

She taps a few buttons on her computer. "Aaron Abernathy. Born June 1710 in Crail, Scotland. It doesn't seem to list anything else about his birth or death."

June of 1710 would be my youngest sibling. I fight the tears at the thought of Mama keeping the nickname I called him and naming him after my father. "Why do you ask?"

The door to the office opens before she responds, and Thorne exits with a man wearing a three-piece suit and perfectly coiffed hair following close behind.

"I'll be in touch, Mr. Rex, should we need anything else from you." The two men shake hands.

The young woman hands me a business card with her phone number scribbled messily across the back. Is this normal protocol for a law office? Taking the card, I follow Thorne onto Broad Street, where the tourists are covering the paved road. "What happened?" I ask, once we are out of earshot.

"Francis left me everything," Thorne answers. His voice is full of sadness.

"How is that possible?"

He shrugs. "She must have made the arrangements the day we went to the Outer Banks looking for Kragen." He stops walking, turning to face me. "I don't have any need for the money, but it feels wrong to not take it. She worked her entire life for what she had."

"Aye, I understand. Maybe you can donate it to charity?"

"Maybe." He wraps a long arm around my shoulders, and we continue to the house we're *borrowing* after a bomb destroyed the three-hundred-year-old home he built and Francis resided in.

My phone vibrates, pulling my attention back to the present with a text from Luna.

> Can you guys come to The Claw?

I sigh after reading the lycanthrope's text. Luna has quickly become the only friend I've ever had. I'm excited to see her, but now doesn't feel like a great time for us to visit. "Luna asked if we could come to the bar." I hold my phone up for Thorne to read. "If you don't feel like going, I can tell her no."

He shakes his head. "No, I could use a distraction." Luckily, the bar isn't far from the law office, and it doesn't take long to get there.

Luna is working behind the counter when we walk in. Since she insists on keeping tabs on Thorne, Connor put her to work in the bar, which is the perfect job for her. Her short blonde bob is pulled up in messy pigtails, making her look even cuter than she already is. "Elsie! Thorne! Look who the bat dragged in." She laughs at her joke. "Get it? Bat dragged in? Because you're vampires?"

I return her smile. "We just came from a meeting with Francis's lawyer."

Her eyes open wide, understanding. "Connor's in his office."

The moment Thorne opens the door, the smell of sulfur hits me in the gut. I freeze, refusing to move any further. "What is it?" Thorne whispers.

"It's me," a young voice says from the chair in front of Connor's desk. The woman we haven't seen in two months stands with a smile.

"What's she doing here?" I ask the Alpha of Charleston.

"Marnie is here to help with your search for Kragen," Connor answers.

"And why would she help us?"

"Because my father is a piece of shit who no longer deserves to be allowed to breathe," she answers.

"I think we can all agree with that," Thorne answers.

"Why should we believe anything she says?" I ask the room.

"Because she's here, offering to help," Conner answers.

I move closer. "You announced you were the child of

Eudora and Kragen on a crowded New Orleans street, then disappeared instantly. I don't trust you."

Marnie smiles. "I get that."

"Then why are you here?"

"Because you never visited my mother."

I shift from one foot to the other. "No, we didn't. Going on a wild goose chase wasn't exactly a top priority." My tone sounds just as rude as I intended.

She stands, moving toward the door. "The Alpha has the address. I don't recommend you ignore her request a second time." She's gone in a heartbeat, taking the sulfur smell with her.

"Connor, you can't believe her. She's leading us on a wild goose chase."

The Alpha leans back in his office chair and props his long legs on the messy desk in front of him. "I do."

Thorne asks the logical question. "What if Kragen is there, waiting for us?"

"I don't believe it's a setup," Connor answers. "She was here a while before you arrived. I'm a good judge of character. She feels legit to me."

"Nothing personal, Connor, but Marnie's energy feels ancient. She's had plenty of years to perfect her ability to lie." I prop my hands on my hips.

"What has Amelia discovered about Eudora?" Connor changes the subject.

"Not much. We researched both of her libraries until there was nothing left to research. Other than a few mentions of Eudora along with a few weaker sea witches, there was nothing."

"What does Amelia think?"

Thorne sits in the chair Marnie was in moments earlier. "She thinks that the story of my men killing Eudora was a lie and that she's still alive." His words bring memories of the night Kragen took me from the ship. The night he changed my life forever. Claiming he took me in payment for Eudora's death was nothing more than a huge pile of shit. That bastard thinks of no one but himself. Sensing my energy, Thorne lays his hand on top of mine, bringing me back to the present.

Connor pulls a piece of paper out of his shirt pocket. He throws the paper on the desk in front of him. An address is scribbled in messy handwriting.

"This is in Charleston," I announce, picking the paper up.

"It is. Only a few blocks from here."

"What are we waiting on?" I move toward the door.

The three of us leave Connor's office, heading into the main bar. "Where are y'all off to?" Luna asks, wiping down the rims of glasses with the cloth she has thrown over her shoulder.

"To see Eudora," I answer.

"Trace, you have the bar," she yells toward an older man seemingly doing inventory. "I'll be back when I get back." She joins our small crew and follows us outside.

The few-block walk takes longer than usual as we push our way through the barrage of tourists. The number of women who stop what they're doing and stare at the vampire and lycanthrope leading the way is comedic. I understand. Thorne and Connor are undeniably gorgeous in otherworldly ways. They draw attention everywhere they go. Luna seems oblivious to the stares as she stays by my side.

Connor stops in front of an older colonial-style home, similar to the one I rented before staying with Francis. The gate is standing open, and tourists are taking pictures of the perfectly decorated structure.

"Is that your home?" a woman asks as we pass through the entrance into the small yard.

"No, ma'am. We're here to visit a friend," Connor answers.

"I would love to look inside," she continues.

"I'm afraid that's not possible."

The woman moves closer to Thorne, placing her hand on his shoulder. "You're so strong and handsome. Especially for a vampire."

Our group stops moving. "Excuse me, ma'am?" Thorne asks, turning on his Southern charm.

"I think you understood me," she answers. I take a few minutes to explore her features. I don't feel any paranormal energy coming from her, but something definitely feels *off*. Beautiful blonde hair hangs halfway down her back, the color reminding me of the morning sun, reflecting off the calm water of the sea. Bright green eyes hold a hint of something I have no words for.

"What are you?" I question.

The woman smiles. "That depends on who you ask. I've been called many things over the years."

"Eudora," Thorne whispers.

"Aye," she answers, using a Scottish brogue. "'Tis I."

"You wanted to meet with us?" Connor stands tall and performs his Alpha duties well.

"You're lycan." She moves in front of the giant man, placing her hand on his thick bicep. "What a handsome specimen you are." Connor's cheeks turn a soft pink hue as she turns toward Luna. "And look at you. You're just the cutest little thing, aren't you?"

"Thanks?" Luna's tone brings a smirk to my face.

She steps closer to Thorne. "Captain." She bows her head slightly. "I can smell the sea on your skin."

"Aye," he answers. "I sailed for many years." She laces her fingers through Thorne's, pulling his hand to her nose and sniffing deeply. "One of my favorite smells."

"What do you want?" I interrupt whatever the hell she's doing.

"Please, come in." She moves to the front of our group, leading us through the courtyard. We follow her onto the first-floor piazza and through the large wooden entry door.

The foyer is furnished to match the colonial style of the home, and the familiar smell of mold fills my sinuses the moment we enter.

"You came," Marnie says, standing from a perfectly coordinated couch.

"They did," Eudora answers. "They're much more handsome than you described, dear. Shame on you for leaving that part out."

The longer this woman speaks, the more annoying she's becoming.

"Thank you for the invitation," Thorne answers, moving to a chair on the other side of the room.

"I don't normally offer two invitations to meet with me." She sits in a straight-back chair, crossing her legs at the knee. Eudora oozes class, sex appeal, and awe as she sits perfectly posed.

"That was my fault," I add. "We've been rather busy."

For the first time, her eyes turn solely on me. "*He's* your maker."

"Not by choice." I know without asking who she's referring to.

Eudora smiles. "Kragen has...a way with women."

"If those ways include kidnapping, torture, abuse in every type of way possible, and starvation, then yes, he has his ways."

"Kragen believes you are dead," Thorne interrupts my tirade.

She turns her attention back to my lover. "Because that's what I wanted him to believe. There was simply no other way."

"That's the reason he took me," I interrupt again. "The reason he turned me into this...this monster."

"I'm sorry about that," Eudora answers. Her voice is void of emotion. "It was necessary."

I stand, moving closer to the sea witch. "*How* was it necessary?"

"Elsbeth," Thorne's calm voice warns. He's right. This woman could kill me in the blink of an eye.

Eudora smiles at the captain. "It's quite alright. The poor dear is frustrated."

"Kragen needed to believe my mother was dead in order to save me," Marnie interrupts my pity party.

Eudora stands, moving toward her daughter. "I'm sorry for what he did to you." She turns back toward me. "I truly am." She crosses her arms across her chest. Her body language says something different than her words. "Marnie is correct. Kragen thinking I was dead was the only way."

"I apologize if this sounds rude, but why is your life more important than mine?" I turn my attention back to Marnie.

Her energy shifts. "Because there is no one else like me in the world."

"Half sea witch and half vampire?"

Eudora laughs. "Dear child, you truly don't know, do you?"

"Please, enlighten me."

The sea witch moves to the center of the room, holding her hands to her side and whispering words in a language that feels older than time. Her skin transforms, becoming translucent and revealing movement that resembles water. Beautiful blonde hair turns dark green and becomes malleable as it floats around her head in a sea of movement.

"No, my child. I am not a sea witch. I am much more than that." A wicked smile covers her face. "I am where the sun meets the sea. I am the land and sea conjoined. I am the power behind the winds. I am Eudora, the Goddess of the Sea."

"Well, shit." Everyone in the room turns toward me with my words.

As quickly as Eudora transformed, she returns to the beautiful woman who greeted us at the gate. "Any questions?" she asks, looking around the room like she's just taught a lesson on long division.

I raise my hand, like the asshole that Kragen turned me into. "I have one." She raises her eyebrows in question. "If you're the 'Goddess of the Sea,'" I use air quotes with her title. "Why didn't you just snap your fingers and tear Kragen's head from his body centuries ago?"

The energy flowing from the men in the room reeks of anxiety as they shift nervously in their seats. *"Elsie,"* Thorne warns through my mind. A talent he hasn't used often.

"That's a fair question," Eudora answers. She turns toward her daughter. "Would you like to clarify that, my child?"

"If she kills Kragen, I die, too," she answers simply.

I look between the two of them. "How exactly does that work?"

"You're quite *spirited*, aren't you?" Eudora asks. "I think it wise you remember who you are speaking with."

"*She's right,*" Thorne says through my mind again. "*Let's leave the attitude out for a minute.*"

I sigh deeply. "I apologize for my tone." It takes everything in me to get the words out.

"Apology accepted," the goddess answers.

"If my mother kills Kragen, I will die, too," Marnie repeats her words from earlier. "Because I carry his blood, if he dies at the hands of my mother or myself or through a direct result of my mother, my life will end with his."

"I could see how that could put a damper on things." And...the attitude is back.

"Thinking I was dead was the only way for us to escape." Eudora smirks. "I'm sure you know how *persistent* he can be."

"Why involve me?"

"Because you're the only one strong enough to kill him," she answers simply. "Other than us, of course."

"I tried that already. It didn't work very well." My mind flashes to Francis and her crumpled body after the explosion.

"That's because you didn't have my help," Eudora adds.

"Wouldn't that be considered a direct result when it comes to his death?" Thorne asks the question everyone in the room is thinking.

"Semantics," she answers, reminding me of Kragen's words not long ago.

"What's in it for us?" I ask, looking around the room.

The goddess crosses her arms in front of her chest and directs her attention directly toward me. "Freedom."

"I'm already free," I lie. I haven't been free from the moment Kragen took me from Thorne's ship.

a horde of what now?

WE LEAVE the house with a promise of more contact and nothing else to go on. No plan, no secret contact method, nothing. In other words, we know nothing more than we did before. Thorne's energy has been off since leaving Eudora and Marnie, and I know why without asking. It's not until we're several streets over that he speaks for the first time, confirming my suspicion.

"What the hell were you thinking, Elsie?" he asks once we're out of earshot of the goddess.

I stop walking, turning toward the man I've loved for three centuries. "What was *I* thinking? I was thinking that she's the bitch who caused all of this to happen. If Kragen hadn't thought she was dead and taken revenge on you, none of this would've happened."

"It did happen," he retorts. "You can't change the past. You can only look toward the future."

"Thank you, Dr. Phil." I continue walking.

A large hand on my arm stops my movement. "Elsie, I understand that you're angry. I'm angry, too. If you can stop Kragen, then you should do it."

"If you think for one minute that woman back there doesn't have ulterior motives, then you're not as smart as I thought you were."

"Damn, Elsbeth," Luna says, moving in front of us. "I'm not sure what's going on with you, but you're not acting like yourself."

"Maybe neither of you has seen the real me." I turn, leaving them standing on the sidewalk. Thorne calls through my mind several times, but I push his words away. Moving toward the river, the smell of blood fills my soul. I've lost track of the last time I ate. The damn goat's blood isn't working for me, which might explain the bitchiness I feel.

The sun is beginning to set over the horizon, casting a colorful glow on the city behind me. I close my eyes, allowing my senses to lead me toward my next meal. The meal I've deprived myself of for the past few months. It doesn't take long to find it. The smell of alcohol hits me before the scent of O negative—my favorite—does.

I turn, finding the source of the smell, staggering his way down the sidewalk. Stepping in front of him, I block his path, stopping him in his tracks.

"Excuse me," he slurs.

"No, excuse me." I make eye contact with him, reaching to touch his shoulder. "Do you need help?"

He burps loudly. "No, thank you. I'm good." He moves around me, nearly falling as he steps off the sidewalk.

Wrapping my arm through his, I pull him close to my side. "Let me help you."

"You're pretty," he stumbles over his words. "You remind me of my daughter."

"That's sweet," I answer, pulling him closer toward the recesses of the riverbank. "How old is she?"

"She was twenty." He immediately starts crying, catching me off guard. "My wife and I are in town for her funeral."

Shit. "I'm sorry," I whisper. "Where are you going?"

"Over there." He points toward the water. "I'm going to join her. Just needed a little liquid courage first."

I look around, hoping to find someone to pawn him off on, and finding no one. "I'm not going to let you do that." I pull him under the streetlight and away from the water. "Are you staying at a hotel?"

He hands me a key card from a building that's only a few blocks away. "My wife is there. She doesn't understand. I just want to be with her. Be with my sweet girl."

With my hunger suddenly gone, I usher the man back to the vintage hotel. The moment we open the large wooden front door, a middle-aged woman rushes to his side. "Marty, are you okay? You scared me when you ran out of the funeral home."

Marty doesn't respond. Instead, he grabs his wife, pulls her close, and cries the kind of tears that are reserved for times like this. I turn, leaving the couple to mourn. Anger and guilt wreak havoc on my stomach as I realize how fucked up I truly am.

Dammit, what's wrong with me? Thorne's right. I'm being a class-A bitch. Closing my eyes, I focus on Thorne's face and try to send a message the same way he does to me—through his mind. I know he's nearby. His energy has stayed close since I stormed away. To his credit, he's left me alone to pout. *"I'm sorry."* I send silently.

"Me, too," he responds immediately. *"You saved that man's life."*

I huff a laugh. *"Yeah, I'm getting soft."*

"You're not a killer," Thorne says, stepping behind me.

"I'm trying," I whisper. "But that goat's blood sucks."

"Let's find you something a little better." He wraps his long fingers through mine, pulling me toward the familiar bar that serves as the lycan's headquarters.

"Hiya!" Luna says the moment we enter. Unlike before, the room is full of lycan and humans, who have no idea they're the minority in the room.

"Am I eating a lycanthrope?" I ask as we make our way to the bar. Several large men turn in my direction.

"I heard that," Luna says as she sets a wine glass full of dark red liquid in front of me. "This is fresh and should help the snarkiness a little." She stares, waiting for me to empty the glass.

I send a glare toward Thorne, wondering if the two of them have had a conversation about my attitude. "Thank you."

"Sure thing." She doesn't move as I pick up the glass, taking a small sip at first and then finishing the contents in one gulp. I feel better the instant it hits my stomach.

I close my eyes, relishing the flavor. "That tasted like a glass of sunshine."

"You're welcome," Luna answers with a smile.

"That...that was your blood?"

"Yep." She picks up the empty glass, wiping underneath it. "You've got a little..." She points at her chin.

I copy her movement, wiping the small amount of blood from my chin. "Is that what all lycan tastes like?"

"I'd like to think no, but truthfully, I have no clue."

"Thank you, Luna." She smiles, turning back to her duties at the bar.

"There's someone here that wants to meet with us," Thorne says, pulling me away from my meal.

I sigh. "Dammit, why is there always something?"

"Because until Kragen is dead, neither of us is free."

He opens the door to Connor's office, revealing a familiar vampire and her Alpha husband.

"Elsie," Amelia says, moving in front of me and hugging me tightly.

"I took the liberty of filling Christopher and Amelia in on the events of this afternoon," Connor says, standing from his desk.

"We were already in the city, so the timing was perfect," Amelia answers.

"I suppose you two think I need to work with Eudora, too?"

They share a look. "I don't think you have a choice," Topher answers for the two of them. "None of us has any experience with someone like Eudora. Hell, she's a goddess. I thought they were the things of movies and fantasy books."

"Did you even read my thesis?" Amelia asks her husband.

He stands, ignoring her question. "We're in the city for reasons besides Eudora."

"What's going on?" Thorne asks.

Connor stands, turning on a television hung high on the wall. A young reporter is standing in front of what looks like a brick home in the suburbs of Anytown, America. Yellow caution tape surrounds the perimeter as police swarm in and out of the house.

"Police say the bodies were placed in what appears to be a ritualistic circle and completely drained of blood," the reporter announces.

"Vampires?" I ask the crowd.

"Sounds that way," Micah, the future Alpha of Charleston and Connor's son, answers, joining the conversation for the first time.

"Out of the twenty students at the party, five are missing from the premises, while the rest were found deceased," the reporter continues.

"Students?" Thorne asks.

"A college frat party," Amelia answers.

"Feeders?" I ask the crowd.

"Most likely. Does anyone think Kragen had anything to do with this?" Thorne asks.

"Common sense says yes, but my spies say he's still in the swamps of south Louisiana," Topher answers.

I look around the room. "Is there a vampire capable of doing something like this, other than Kragen, that's in the area?"

"Not that I'm aware of," Connor answers. "Not unless someone is passing through with a horde of monsters."

"I believe I can help with that," a deep voice answers as the door opens. The vampire energy flowing from him instantly fills the room.

"Thank you for coming, Elijah." Connor moves toward the stranger, greeting the man with a handshake.

"I would like to say it was my pleasure, but we both know that isn't true." His accent holds the typical South Carolina drawl mixed with something I don't recognize.

His ebony skin is the perfect accent to his amber-colored eyes. High cheekbones accentuate his angular face, giving him a mysterious, otherworldly look. He looks around the room, fixing his eyes on Thorne and me. "Who are you?"

"Captain Hawthorne Rex." Thorne moves in front of the man, holding his hand out.

"Elijah Montclair," the man responds, shaking his hand. "Since I don't recognize you, I'm assuming you're friends of Connor's."

"They are," Connor answers for us.

Elijah turns toward me. "And who is this lovely lady?"

"Elsbeth Abernathy." He lifts my hand, bringing it to his lips, and kissing gently. His motions surprisingly bring chills to my skin.

"Elsbeth. What a lovely name." His eyes linger on mine longer than necessary.

Thorne moves protectively to my side. "Do you know anything about the murders?" He nods toward the television.

"I don't. I'm assuming that's why I was asked to join this,"—Elijah looks around the room—"meeting."

"It is," Connor answers. "As the elder vampire in Charleston, I thought you might be privy to information that I am not."

"You think this was done by vampires?" Elijah points at the television behind him.

"The bodies were drained of blood, and five of them

are missing," I repeat the information from the broadcast.

"Nothing else makes sense," Micah states the obvious. "Nothing was stolen, and there was no evidence of a motive."

"What aren't you telling us?" Amelia asks, stepping closer to the vampire.

Elijah's face wrinkles with question as she approaches. "I thought the wolf energy I was feeling was because of this location and the lycan in this room." He smiles, showing a mouthful of snow-white teeth. "You are quite intriguing, young one." He sniffs the air around her.

"Stop, you're going to make me blush." Her voice is laced with sarcasm, making me like her even more.

"Your maker was ancient," he continues.

"*Is* ancient," Amelia interrupts. "She's still alive."

Elijah bows slightly. "Excuse me for my mishap of words." He begins to walk around her, assessing her from all angles. "You have lycan blood as well as vampire?"

Amelia turns, looking at her Alpha husband. He smiles, nodding his head slightly. "I have a splash," she answers with a smirk.

He turns his nose up, sniffing the air in front of him. "Smells like more than a splash."

"My mother was a hybrid. Half human and half lycan," she continues.

"Who would've thought something so perverse was possible?"

She huffs a laugh. "Yeah, who knew?"

The energy in the room feels *thicker* than moments before. Something is about to happen. Instinctively, I move away from the duo.

"Show him, my love," Topher encourages her from his spot on the wall.

"You might want to move, Mr. Montclair." Amelia bounces on her feet slightly, reminding me of an athlete about to run the race of their lifetime. She begins to shake her hands out, and within seconds, the beautiful woman transforms into a larger-than-life red wolf. She moves closer to the vampire until barely any space separates the two of them. In wolf form, Amelia is much larger than her human form. Her shoulders line up with Elijah's eyes. She bends slightly, licking him on the face and covering him in lycanthrope slobber.

"Amelia says you taste like sunshine," Topher interrupts the awkwardness. "She would like to know if she has adequately answered your question as to what she is?"

Elijah steps back, pulling a bright red handkerchief from his suit jacket and dramatically wiping his face. "You have, my dear. Thank you."

The wolf's head bows before she begins shaking, resembling a dog in a bathtub. Standing in the middle of the room is the tiny woman from before. Long red curls cover her breasts as Topher wraps a blanket around her waist.

"Holy shit," Thorne whispers through my mind.

"Agreed," I answer.

"I'll ask you again, Mr. Montclair. What aren't you telling us?" Amelia's words carry more weight than before.

"May I?" Elijah asks, motioning toward an empty chair in front of Connor's desk.

"Please." Connor motions to the chair.

Elijah sighs before speaking. "A few months prior, I was contacted by a woman looking for a safe place for her and her children to rest for a few weeks."

"By children, I'm assuming you mean the vampires she's created," I fill in the blanks.

"She said they were going to be in the area and would require sustenance for the time they're here." Elijah avoids my question.

"What was her name?" Amelia asks.

"Patrice," he answers.

I share a look with Thorne and Amelia. From the looks on their faces, they don't recognize the name either. "What was she doing?" Thorne asks.

Elijah shrugs. "She never said, and I never asked."

"The *children* would explain the drained bodies," Topher says what we're all thinking.

"What was her purpose for coming to Charleston?" Connor asks.

"Again, I never asked. Minding one's business is an excellent way to keep friends."

"You're just full of useful information," I say as bitchy Elsie rears her ugly head.

Elijah stands. "I believe that is my cue to leave." He moves closer to the door and bows to the people in the room. "It's been a pleasure to make your acquaintance." He closes the door behind him.

"A horde of hungry vampires in the vicinity doesn't sound like a good thing," Micah says, crossing his arms in front of him.

"Who is Patrice? Is her name familiar to anyone?" Topher asks.

"I don't know, but I intend to find out." Amelia wraps her blanket tighter.

"It seems we have a much larger problem than Kragen and Eudora at the moment." Connor stands from his desk.

I can't control the laugh that boils up from inside me. "The Goddess of the Sea, a two-thousand-year-old vampire, and their offspring are trumped by a horde of hungry vampires? That was not on my bingo card for today."

Amelia joins my laughter. "I agree." She turns to the men surrounding us. "What are we going to do about it?"

"How long is Eudora willing to wait?" Micah asks.

I shrug. "I have no idea. She doesn't seem like the type of person who shares her plans on a regular basis."

"Then we deal with the horde first," Topher announces, taking the lead.

"We need to get into that house." Micah nods at the television screen. "Something tells me there is more to the story than what they're reporting."

"I'll make some calls." Connor steps out of the room with his phone in hand.

"What are you thinking?" Thorne asks Micah.

He shrugs. "Nothing specific, but something feels off about this entire thing. First, Eudora and her daughter are in town, and now this. There's more to this than the obvious."

Connor steps back into the office. "We have access to the house at midnight."

"Will we be alone?" Micah asks.

"Yes." Connor turns toward Topher. "If you don't mind, I'd like Micah to accompany you four to the house."

"Of course," Topher answers.

house of horrors

A LITTLE BEFORE MIDNIGHT, the five of us load into a black SUV. Topher climbs in the front next to Micah, while Thorne, Amelia, and I slide into the back. "The house is about twenty minutes from here," Micah announces, speeding away from the front of the lycan bar.

"What are we looking for?" Amelia asks.

"Honestly, I don't know. I hope with our heightened senses, we might pick up on something the humans couldn't," he answers.

Twenty minutes later, Micah turns onto a long driveway surrounded by overgrown bushes and stops in front of the house I recognize from the news broadcast. Bright yellow police tape is still wrapped around the porch, blowing in the Atlantic winds.

"It looks haunted," Amelia announces, climbing out of the back seat.

"We don't need any other mythological creatures to join this shit show," Topher adds with a laugh.

The faint smell of sulfur hits me the instant I step out of the SUV. "Does anyone else smell that?"

"That depends on what you're talking about. I smell a plethora of odors." Amelia holds her head high in the air.

"It smells like Kragen," I answer.

"Or Marnie," Thorne adds.

We follow Topher to the back of the ranch-style home. What was once a screened-in porch is nothing more than framing and torn screen blowing in the breeze. A broken sliding glass door sits on its rails, leaving a three-foot gap to enter. "Look. Someone left it unlocked for us," he says, leading us inside.

The smell of sulfur grows as we enter the dark home. Remnants of what was once nice furniture are scattered around the living room, and a large stone fireplace covers the back wall. Dark blood splatters the floors, and from the smell of it, it's human.

"This looks like a Halloween attraction, only it's real," Micah says, staring at the bloodstains.

"We should split up," Amelia announces, looking around the room. "We'll cover more ground that way. I'll take this level."

"Elsie and I will go to the basement." Thorne moves to my side.

"I'll go to the second floor," Micah says, moving toward the base of the stairwell. "Unless anyone else would care to take it." Seeing the future Alpha of Charleston anxious about exploring a murder house strikes me as funny.

"I'll check the yard and outlying buildings," Topher adds.

We split, going our separate ways. I follow Thorne down the squeaky stairs that lead from the kitchen to the basement below. The smell of sulfur is replaced with rotting blood, making my stomach gurgle with memories.

Lining the cinderblock walls are chains. The scene reminds me of my time on Kragen's ship. The ends of the chains have heavy latches made to be attached to a person's arms and legs. "This is a torture chamber for something that wasn't human," I whisper. Why am I whispering?

"Aye."

The faint sounds of animals scurrying through the room bring back memories of the rats I ate to stay alive while on Kragen's ship. "Do you think this was where they found the bodies?" I ask questions, hoping to thwart the memories.

"From the look of the main floor, I think they found the bodies everywhere." Thorne moves past me toward a door on the opposite wall. A heavy logging chain is wrapped several times through the handles and secured with a matching lock.

"Why is this door still locked?" he asks, rattling the metal.

"Maybe the police locked it before they left?" Scuffling from the other side of the door makes the hairs on my arm stand at attention. "Did you hear that?" The sound of something sliding across gritty concrete rings through my ears again.

"Aye. It came from behind the door."

I don't hesitate. Pulling the chain with my hands, I break the lock open easily, letting the metal clatter to the ground.

"Wait." Thorne places his hand protectively over my chest. "We don't know what's in there."

"It could be nothing," I answer.

"Or it could be something."

"Amelia!" I call through the house. She's by our side seconds later.

"It stinks down here," she says, looking around the room.

"I think we found something." The scraping sound echoes once more.

Amelia grabs the handle without hesitation, pulling the heavy door off its rusty hinges. "Hello?" she says into the room.

"Help me," a young voice whispers.

The three of us rush into the room, finding what looks like a child chained to the back wall. Her clothes remind me of a time long ago. Blood covers her face and hands, and tiny fangs protrude from her mouth. "Oh, my God," Amelia says, stepping away from the girl. "An immortal child."

"What's an immortal child?" I ask.

"A child that was turned into a vampire," Thorne answers.

"My maker was an immortal child." Amelia squats in front of the girl, not adding anything extra to her revelation. "What's your name, little one?"

"Gretchen," the young girl answers.

"Why are you tied up, Gretchen?"

"Because I was hungry." She growls slightly. "There wasn't enough food for everyone."

I reach for the silver cuffs wrapped around the young vampire's ankles and wrists. "No!" Amelia touches my shoulder. "You can't free her."

"What the hell kind of logic is that?" Anger fills my voice.

"Immortal children are...unpredictable," Thorne fills in the blank. "They're capable of unsurmountable destruction."

I look between the two vampires. "You...you don't think she did this, do you? She's nothing more than a child."

"She is more than capable," Amelia answers. "Topher's coming." Seconds later, heavy boots make their way downstairs.

"Amelia?" he asks into the darkness.

"In here."

Topher stops at the door we're staring through. "Oh, my God. Is she?"

"Yes," she answers. Sadness fills her voice.

"What is the big deal about an immortal child?" I ask for the second time.

"Because they're young, most lack the ability to control their behavior. They have the same strength and ability as you or I do, but they're children. Most aren't able to control their power. Imagine a four-year-old human having a temper tantrum about something a typical four-year-old does. When an immortal child has a temper tantrum, they can destroy an entire neighborhood, leaving no one alive. They're not only dangerous, they're against the council's rules."

"There is a council and rules?" I ask, generally confused.

"You have much to learn." Amelia turns back to the young girl. "Who is your maker, Gretchen?"

"Mother," the young girl answers, pulling at her bindings.

"Where is *Mother*?"

"They're gone. They left me here."

"Who's gone?" I take over questioning.

"My brothers and sisters."

The four of us share a look. "How many brothers and sisters do you have, Gretchen?" Amelia asks.

The young girl fights against her chains. "He smells good. I'm hungry," she growls, lunging toward Topher. Silver chains attached to the wall are the only thing holding her in place.

"How many brothers and sisters?" Amelia repeats.

"Ten," she answers.

"Are they like you?"

"Yesss." Her words are slurred as she lunges toward the Alpha lycanthrope once more.

"Did Mother put you down here, Gretchen?"

The immortal child lunges towards Topher once more. Perfectly styled blonde curls bounce with her movement as she growls once more, and chill bumps cover my skin with the sound. "No, the other one did."

"The other one? Someone other than your maker?" Amelia asks, kneeling closer to the girl. Gretchen lunges once more, biting the air as she moves and coming remarkably close to Amelia's hand. "Who put you down here?"

"I smell his blood. Set me free."

"I'm sorry, Gretchen. We can't do that," Amelia answers.

"Like hell, we can't," I retort. "She's nothing more than a child."

"Look at her, Elsbeth. She's wearing clothes from another century. She's not a child. She's a killer, trapped in the body of a child for all eternity." Amelia steps between the young girl and me, blocking my view.

"Help me," Gretchen whines. Her voice takes on the timbre of her appearance. "I won't hurt anyone. Please, help me. I'm scared. They...they hurt me." She begins to cry, reminding me of my sister Bonnie from so many years ago.

"Move, Amelia," I demand. "I will not let that child suffer."

Amelia's eyes turn black in an instant. "Elsbeth, I will not set this creature free. Do you understand me?"

"The woman smelled funny," Gretchen says from behind Amelia's legs. "She smelled like fire." She looks at me with her answer. "Hot fire," she adds.

Amelia turns back to the girl. "The one who put you down here smelled like fire?"

"Someone who smells like fire has to be Marnie or Kragen, except Gretchen says it's a woman, which only leaves one of the people in the equation. Am I the only one who knows what that means?" I raise my voice louder than needed.

"Let's not jump to conclusions," Topher says, closing the gap between the child and his wife.

"Jump to conclusions? I spent a hundred years being held captive by that asshole. I know what he smells like. His daughter smells just like him." I don't know why I'm taking my anger out on the only friends I've ever known.

"So do you!" Amelia matches my energy. "*You* smell like sulfur. *You* smell like Kragen *and* Marnie."

I take a step backward. "You don't think I..."

"No," she interrupts. "I don't think you had anything to do with this. I'm simply stating the fact that you smell like Kragen because he was your maker. There are others out there that would carry his smell. Hell, it wouldn't even have to be someone he turned. It could be an old lover. Kragen and Marnie don't hold the patent for smelling like fire." I stare at the hybrid, not sure how to respond. The thought of me carrying around Kragen's smell for three hundred years never even occurred to me.

"What the hell is that?" Micah interrupts the insanity from the bottom of the stairs.

With the combination of Topher and Micah's blood, Gretchen's face transforms from the sweet child she was moments earlier into a monster equal to Kragen in its appearance. "I'm hungry!" she screams. She fights against the chains, pulling with all of her strength. The chains rattle and shake, refusing to give way.

When Gretchen realizes the silver isn't giving way, she begins chewing at her wrist, biting hunks of flesh away, and spitting them across the room.

"Gretchen?" I focus on keeping my voice as calm as possible. "What are you doing?"

"She's doing the only thing she knows," Amelia answers. "She's an animal trying to get her next meal."

"We can't just leave her here." My voice cracks at the realization that it leaves us only one other option.

"We won't," Amelia says. The timbre of her voice tells me what she's going to do without saying the words. "She'll be out of her misery."

I back away from the beautiful girl. "I can't watch," I whisper.

"Take her upstairs," Topher barks an order. Thorne wraps his arms around my shoulders, leading me away from the immortal child. Micah joins us as the three of us leave the basement, and the young girl who never had a chance to live.

"Did you find anything?" Thorne asks Micah, trying to distract my thoughts. I appreciate the effort.

"Nothing out of the ordinary. Three bedrooms and a couple of bathrooms. There was definitely evidence of a massive party, but nothing stood out as unusual," he answers.

"Gretchen said she had ten brothers and sisters. Do you think that means there are ten other immortal children out there?" I ask the two of them. Both men look at the stained flooring, answering with their actions instead of words.

Images of my brothers and sisters sailing across the Atlantic in hopes of a better life flash through my mind. These children were like us—like me.

"It's done," Amelia says, coming up the stairs.

I wipe the tears silently streaming down my cheek. "We can't leave her here. We can't leave her in that... that dungeon."

Amelia sighs. "She was already returning to dust. There's nothing of her left to take."

"Did she feel anything?" I ask, not sure I want to know the answer.

"No. I made sure she didn't." Amelia's eyes are glassy, telling me she's not the big bad wolf she makes herself out to be.

"Thank you."

Topher clears his throat, moving to the center of the room. "I think it's safe to say that Gretchen's brothers and sisters are like her, immortal children."

"That's an army of insanity." Amelia moves to his side, and he wraps an arm around her short frame.

"What would be the purpose for ten immortal children, and why would they leave that one here?" Thorne asks, nudging his head toward the basement door.

"Gretchen. Her name was Gretchen," I interrupt. "She was a real person with feelings and emotions who wanted nothing more than to be normal—marry a nice man and have children of her own. Her hopes and dreams were taken away from her. She had no choice but to become the creature that she was. It was forced on her." Everyone in the room is staring at me, clearly aware that I'm no longer talking about Gretchen.

"It's time to leave," Amelia announces after several awkwardly quiet moments. We load into the SUV in silence, and Micah leads us away from the house of horrors. Thorne's arm stays wrapped protectively around my shoulders, pulling me close to his side. No doubt, he's afraid I'm going to lose my shit and try to kill someone. Truthfully, the only thing I'm on the brink of losing is my sanity.

immortal children

MICAH DROPS us off at the lycan-owned house we've been staying in since Thorne's home was destroyed. My mind won't stop replaying the events of the day, ending with the death of Gretchen. I was that girl at one time. I was Gretchen. The only thing separating the two of us is age.

"Amelia's downstairs," Thorne says softly, entering our shared room.

"I don't feel like company."

He scuffs his heavy boots on the wide plank floors. "I understand. But I think you should talk to her."

Throwing my phone onto the bed, I stand, moving into the hallway. I'm not sure what she would want to talk to me about. Any awe I felt for her left the moment she killed Gretchen. I don't speak as I follow Thorne downstairs and into the room where Amelia is sitting alone on the overstuffed Victorian couch.

"Thorne, would you mind if I speak to Elsbeth alone?"

"Of course not," he answers. He bows his head slightly before leaving us alone.

"I'm sorry about today." I don't respond. I don't trust my words right now. She looks at her hands before continuing. "I understand how you feel. What I had to do today wasn't easy for me either."

"But you did it, anyway."

"I did. I had no choice. *We* had no choice."

"You always have a choice," I retort.

"Not when it comes to immortal children."

I stand, moving toward the fireplace. "You said your maker is an immortal child. What makes her different than Gretchen? Why did she get to live?"

"My maker is nearly eight hundred years old and was protected by a man who loved her more than himself." She pauses at a memory. "Her father had himself turned into a vampire to protect her after she was turned."

"Where is she now?"

Amelia laughs. "She's attending college in Mississippi."

"College? A child?"

"She's no longer a child. That's a story for another day." She slides to the front of the couch. "Celeste isn't normal. Most immortal children are like Gretchen. They lack the ability to control their impulses. They can't control the monster inside of them. I once witnessed

Celeste destroy a horde of strigoi by herself. It was like nothing I'd ever seen before. The difference is that she was able to stop. Most can't."

"You love her?" My words are more of a statement than a question.

"I do. She acts like my mother, but I love her like she's my sister."

"Why are you telling me this?"

"Because I know how painful it is to see something like that. I know the horror that fills you at the thought of children becoming monsters. I understand."

"How can you? Were you taken against your will and forced to become this?" I run my hands down my body, adding extra drama.

"Yes," she answers simply. "Not in the same way you were, but I had no choice in becoming a vampire. Hell, I had no choice in becoming a lycan hybrid. I'm a damn freak of nature." She laughs. "I'm even a freak among the paranormal community. Most are terrified of me, and others want to fuck me."

"I wouldn't have been able to do it." Amelia knows what I mean.

She closes her eyes. "It wasn't easy, but it was necessary." She looks me in the eyes. "We're not so different, you and me."

"Last I checked, I can't turn into a wolf on demand."

Amelia smirks at my words. "That's probably for the best."

The front door opens, revealing two oversized

lycan. Topher moves straight to Amelia, kissing her on the forehead. "I checked with Aunt Susan. Edon is doing great, but she thinks he might be teething."

"My baby is growing teeth, and I'm not there to see it?" Sadness covers her face.

"Don't worry. He'll gain plenty more," Topher says, pulling her to his chest.

"Elijah would like to meet with us," Micah says from the foyer.

"What's the point? He didn't know anything," Amelia asks.

"He's the one who requested a meeting this time. I'm guessing he knows more than he let on before."

"Or he's going to try to kill all of us," Thorne adds, coming into the room. "Sorry, I was eavesdropping. When's the meeting?"

"In half an hour at his home," Micah answers.

"Am I the only one who feels this is a little weird?" I look around the room as I speak. "What could he possibly know that he couldn't tell us earlier?"

"In his defense, he was surrounded by people he didn't know or trust. Maybe he was intimidated." Micah moves into the room. "I've known Elijah since I was a boy. He's worked with my father many times over the years and has always been honest."

Thirty minutes later, we pull in front of a house that rivals vampire homes from B-roll movies. The Gothic Greek design features a two-story turret and a dark, nearly black brick exterior. "This isn't obvious at all," I say, sliding out of the back seat.

"This is something Viktor would do," Amelia laughs.

I turn toward Thorne. "Viktor? The same Viktor that was your maker?"

"Aye," he answers. "It's a long story."

"That's an understatement," Amelia adds, following the lycan to the entrance.

The heavy wooden door opens, revealing a young woman dressed in a French maid's uniform. "Welcome," she says, bowing her head. "My master was expecting you."

Master? This is getting better by the minute. We pile into the elaborately decorated foyer, awaiting our next instructions. Hunter green wallpaper, covered in large bouquets of blue hydrangeas, lines the walls from floor to ceiling, giving the home funeral home vibes.

"Please, have a seat. I'll alert him of your arrival." She turns, leaving us alone in the opulently designed sitting area. A fireplace with a dark wooden mantle is the showpiece of the room. To the right of it sits a chair that reminds me of something you'd find on death row, complete with the straps for ankles and wrists. I half expect to see a coffin in the dining room.

"Welcome," Elijah says, entering the sitting area. "Thank you for taking me up on my invitation." He moves straight for the death chair. He sits, crossing his legs at the knee and laying his hands neatly on top. His body language is screaming asshole.

"Thank you for the invitation," Micah answers for our group.

"Would anyone care for a drink?" He snaps his fingers, bringing the woman from earlier back into the room.

"Cut the shit, Elijah," Amelia interrupts from across the room. "No one wants anything to drink or eat." She looks around the room, holding my eye contact longer than anyone else. "What are you hiding?"

The vampire clears his throat and sits up even straighter. "I'm not hiding anything and don't appreciate the implication that I am."

"No one's implying you are hiding anything." Micah tries to ease the tension filling the room.

"We found a child today," I add, hoping to rescue the conversation. "She couldn't have been older than six or seven when she was turned."

"A child? You mean an immortal child?" Elijah asks.

"Aye," Thorne speaks for the first time. "She told us there were ten more just like her."

"Oh, my." Elijah relaxes his posture with Thorne's words.

"Any information you have on Patrice would be great about now," Amelia continues, calming her tone from earlier.

"A horde of immortal children serves only one purpose," Elijah continues. "Destruction."

"Destruction of what?" I ask.

"Anything and everything." Elijah stands, moving toward the fireplace. "What became of the child?"

"She was...taken care of," Amelia answers. "But there are more just like her."

Elijah sighs deeply before speaking. "Patrice is someone I knew from long ago." He picks up a glass of red liquid and drinks it in one gulp. "Our makers were... acquaintances." None of us speaks, nervous he won't continue. "Patrice was turned a few years before me, and our makers decided it would be best for us to *learn* from each other." He moves toward a cart in the corner, pouring another glass of liquid.

"What do you mean by *learn*?" Topher asks.

"It means just what you think it means." Elijah takes another large gulp. "We were lovers, hunting partners, and more for many years."

"What does this have to do with the immortal children?" Amelia asks.

He sets the empty glass down before facing us. "Because to understand Patrice, you must first know who and what she is." He moves back to the death chair. "Patrice was from Egypt, and I was from what is now known as Ghana. I don't know how she ended up in my country, but it was there that she was *altered*. It wasn't until we'd been together for several decades that she began to change."

"What kind of change?" I interrupt.

"She began talking about wanting a child. She knew

she would never be able to produce an offspring, and that upset her. So much so that it became an obsession. It consumed her thoughts and was all she talked about."

"You knew she was turning children into vampires?" Thorne asks.

"No," Elijah answers quickly. "I left her in Africa before she…before she created an immortal child. Her obsession ruined what was left of our relationship, and I left."

"Did you ever tell anyone about her desires?" Micah asks. He's casually leaning against one of the ornately carved posts in the entryway.

"No. Unlike lycan, vampires don't care about the doings of others. Truthfully, I hadn't thought about her until she contacted me a few months ago."

"What did she want?" Micah continues.

Elijah shrugs. "She asked me to recommend where she could find food for her children when she arrived. I assumed her children were other adults she had transformed through the years. I didn't fathom she actually meant…children."

"Did she say where they were going?" Amelia takes the lead.

"No."

"Dammit." I stand, moving into the grand foyer. "This is the biggest bunch of fuckery I've seen in a while, and believe me, I've seen fuckery."

"Is there anything else you can tell us about Patrice?" Amelia ignores my tirade and continues her questioning.

"She likes to play with her food." He loses his perfect posture, slumping his shoulders slightly. "Young lovers are her favorite. When we were in Africa, she would hunt couples, saying their thoughts of love flavored their blood. She would stalk them for hours, even days at a time. Torturing them. Terrifying them. Often, killing one in front of the other just for the thrill of it."

"So, you're saying, not only is she obsessed with immortal children, she's also a psychopath?" Amelia stands, moving toward the door. "What concerns me is the fact that she hunted couples and murdered them in front of each other isn't what made you decide to leave. It was her obsession with being a mother that sent you over the edge." She moves toward the door. "I think I've heard enough."

"Aye," Thorne answers, wrapping his arm protectively around my shoulders and ushering me toward the door. I have no doubt I could rip Elijah's head from his torso before he noticed my movement, but I appreciate Thorne's attempt either way.

"She's heading south," Elijah says, stopping us at the door.

"How do you know?" Micah asks.

"Let's just call it a hunch," he answers.

The energy in the room changes in an instant as a large red wolf appears seemingly out of nowhere. Amelia steps in front of the Charleston vampire, inches from his face. Saliva drips from her jowls as she snarls a warning.

"Be careful, Elijah," Topher warns. "We're not into playing games when it comes to children."

"I'm not *playing* any sort of game."

"Where down south?" Topher continues.

"The Gulf Coast of Alabama," Elijah answers. "That's all I know."

Amelia snarls one last warning before backing away from the vampire. Whether her warning was perceived as it was meant, I don't know. Elijah looks more bored than nervous. The giant wolf stays in wolf form as we exit the home and climb back into the SUV.

Instead of joining Thorne and me in the back seat, Topher opens the back of the SUV, and Amelia jumps inside.

"Who wants to go to the beach?" Topher asks, climbing into the front seat. He laughs loudly, making me wonder what silent conversation just passed between him and his wife.

The trip back to the house is uneventful, and when the back of the SUV is opened, a petite redheaded woman, wearing a pair of sweatpants and a sweatshirt, hops out. I have no idea when she shifted or dressed.

"That bastard knows more than he's letting on," Amelia says, moving to Topher's side.

"Agreed," he answers, turning toward Micah. "You've worked with Elijah before. Is his information valid enough for us to make the trip?"

Micah shrugs. "I'll talk to my father, but in my experience, he's always been truthful."

"I'll get the jet prepared," Amelia announces, heading toward the front door. Micah steps away, pulling his phone from his pocket.

"Looks like we're heading to Alabama," Thorne says, wrapping his fingers through mine.

"Aye. What about Kragen?" I ask.

"He's busy licking his wounds and building an army. I'm more worried about Eudora and Marnie at this point."

"You can add Patrice to that list, too," I state the obvious, squeezing his hand. "Gretchen said the woman who chained her in the basement smelled like fire. Do you think it was Marnie?"

Micah interrupts before Thorne has a chance to answer. "My father says Elijah has always been truthful to the pack. He has no reason to believe he's not being truthful now." He slides his phone back into his pocket with his words. "He's going to call in a few favors and secure us a place to stay while we're down there."

"The jet will be ready in half an hour." Amelia joins us back on the porch.

I raise my hand, interrupting the flurry of movement. "Does anyone know what we're going to do when we get there?"

"We're going to the beach?" Luna asks, exiting the house and joining our small group. "I'm game! I love the Gulf." My stomach growls at the sight of the blonde lycanthrope, and guilt fills me from the inside.

roll tide!

THE TRIP to the Gulf Coast is uneventful and quick. Less than two hours later, we're on the ground in a small regional airport not far from the emerald green water.

"God, why does it feel like a sauna out here?" Luna asks as she dramatically exits the jet. "My makeup just melted off my face."

"You're still beautiful," Micah announces, making her cheeks turn pink. I can't help but smile at the energy flowing between them.

"So are you," she answers while punching him in the shoulder.

Vampires are immune to temperature changes, but the hot air slaps me in the face, telling me it's even more humid than Charleston. A clone of the black SUV from South Carolina sits on the tarmac and is currently being used as a leaning post for one of the largest people I've ever seen. Long legs are the host of a pair of shorts that are so thin that I can see the palm trees on his boxers. A pale green Jimmy Buffet shirt and a pair of worn flip-flops are the perfect accessories for the lackadaisical lycan energy flowing from him.

"Hey!" He waves as he greets us. "Welcome to the Gulf Coast." He moves in front of Topher, bowing his head slightly. "Christopher."

"It's good to see you again, Fynn," Topher says, patting him on the shoulder.

"You, too, sir." He turns toward the rest of our group. "Fynn Jackson." His eyes lock on Amelia. "Is this your mate?" he asks Topher, sniffing the air in front of him.

"He's *my* mate," she answers with a laugh.

Fynn moves in front of Amelia. The top of her head barely reaches the pecks showing through his too-tight shirt. "I've heard so much about you. It's a pleasure to meet you in person."

"Thank you," she answers. For the first time since meeting her, her energy feels awkward, helping me realize she's not a fan of being the center of attention. She nods around the group, introducing everyone to the tall lycanthrope.

"It's a pleasure." He opens the door to the SUV. "We have a short trip to the beach house."

"Beach house?" Luna asks from the back seat.

"Yeah, it's one of the smaller homes the pack owns.

There are only twelve bedrooms, but it should be perfect for y'all."

"Yeah, that should be plenty," Amelia scoffs.

Less than ten minutes later, Fynn stops in front of a three-story house lifted high on pedestals. To the unsuspecting eye, this house is no different from any of the others nearby. To my eyes and nose, it reeks of lycan.

We follow Fynn through the parking area/game room, up a flight of stairs, to a regular front door. He unlocks it, handing a set of keys to Topher afterward. "It's yours for as long as you need." The door opens, revealing a large open room, ending with a wall of floor-to-ceiling windows facing the clear water of the Gulf.

"This is beautiful," Luna whispers.

Fynn smiles at her admission. "I've taken the liberty of stocking the refrigerator and pantry." He clears his throat. "Several donors are willing to provide nourishment for the vampires if needed."

"That won't be necessary," Amelia and Thorne answer in unison. I shift from foot to foot, thinking about the disgusting taste of the goat's blood they both drink.

"Let me know if you need anything," Fynn says, moving to leave. "If not, I'll be back tomorrow morning, and we will begin the search." He claps his hands, clearly excited about the hunt.

"Anyone else hungry?" Micah asks the lycan in the

room. They collectively agree they're starving as he and Luna head toward the kitchen to start dinner.

Thorne follows me up the next flight of stairs to a long hallway filled with doors on each side. I peek into the rooms, all of which are decorated in the same style, before choosing one that faces the water.

"Do you mind if I stay in here with you?" he asks, following me into the room.

I turn toward the man I love. "Of course not. I assumed you would."

Thorne looks down at my words. "You've felt a little distant the past few days. I thought maybe you could use some space."

I step in front of the captain. "I have had a lot on my mind, but pulling away from you wasn't the catalyst. I'm sorry if it came across that way."

Long arms wrap around my shoulders, pulling me tightly to his chest. "It's understandable. The past few weeks have been a whirlwind of emotion. I know how hard it was to see the immort...to see Gretchen." His words bring tears to my eyes. "That's why we're here. We're going to stop Patrice."

"How?"

"Guys!" Luna's voice echoes through the house. "You need to see this!"

Thorne and I race down the stairs at vampire speed, finding her standing in front of an oversized television set. A ticker runs across the bottom of the screen. "Read that." She points to the screen.

Search teams are still looking for the two missing children. If you have any information on the whereabouts of 10-year-old Jensen Montgomery or 8-year-old Sarah-Beth Olson, please contact the authorities immediately. Both were last seen in the Meeting-Place area of Gulf Shores, Alabama.

"Could that be Patrice?" Micah asks, moving to Luna's side.

"There's no way of knowing, but my gut says yes," Topher answers, as he and Amelia stand side by side on the staircase. "I don't believe in coincidences."

Tears fill my eyes, thinking of the two children she's adding to her collection. "Can we save them before... before she changes them?"

Every pair of eyes in the room looks at the floor in unison, giving me the answer I already know. Turning them into mindless killing machines would have been the first thing on her agenda.

"How do we find them?" Luna asks the next question.

"Fynn's coming back tomorrow morning," Topher answers.

"We can't wait until tomorrow!" I shout at the room of mythological creatures. "Tomorrow morning, she may be gone, or heaven forbid, she'll take another child."

"Elsbeth," Amelia says, moving off the staircase. "The lycan must sleep and eat. The three of us don't need sleep, but they do. If we go out half-cocked and unprepared, we're going to end up making dumb mistakes that will cost a lot more in the long run."

"Two children are missing and most likely monsters by now. What could be worse?" I demand.

"Three children and one of us," she retorts. Dammit, she's right, and it pisses me off. I turn, walking away from the television. "Why don't we go for a walk?" Amelia asks, moving to my side. She wraps her arm through mine, pulling me through the open sliding glass doors onto the deck overlooking the beach without giving me much choice.

We walk down the flight of stairs and past a small swimming pool in silence. The roar of the waves sends calming energy my way. I copy Amelia's movements, taking off my shoes to walk in the white sand and stopping where the water meets the grit.

"I'm sorry," she says, breaking the awkward silence.

"Why are you sorry?"

"I'm sorry you've had to learn how to be a vampire on your own."

I huff a laugh. "It's that obvious, huh?"

"I don't know your story, but you're not the only person who has one."

I stare at the woman, not sure if I should be pissed or listen. "I didn't mean to imply my life was worse than anyone else's."

"You didn't. But you carry a huge chip on your

shoulder. It's obvious in everything you do and, lately, everything you say."

I feel the tears form behind my eyes with her words. My mind flashes to Kragen and the hole I lived in for a century. She's right. I've been an insufferable bitch.

She starts walking, scuffing her bare feet in the water as she moves. "Do you mind if I tell you my story?"

"I'd like that."

"Before I begin, please know that I am in no way saying that one person's story is worse or better than another." She sighs. "I can tell you've been isolated for many years. I think hearing from someone who shares a similar story could be helpful for you."

I nod, not trusting my words.

Amelia takes a deep breath before continuing. "I was born to a single mother and never met my father. She raised me in the toughest neighborhood in New Orleans." She huffs a laugh. "I say raised, but to be honest, she didn't raise me at all. She left when I was thirteen. She would go missing for days at a time until one day, she never came home. I was alone without money to pay for utilities, food, you name it."

"I'm sorry." I don't know why I'm apologizing.

"I'm not looking for sympathy," she reprimands. "Topher's mother was my school nurse, and she saved me. There's a lot more to that story, but she's the one who helped me when no one else would." She stops walking, turning toward the open water. "I was in high school when I first met him. I didn't remember until I was changed into a vampire, but he followed me throughout my life, starting when I was just a child."

"Who?"

"Harrison." Amelia wipes a silent tear. "Harrison Chamberlin. One of the oldest vampires in New Orleans." She pauses and takes a deep breath. "I looked like the woman he was obsessed with. So obsessed, in fact, that he thought I was her reincarnation." She huffs. "Hell, he even had me convinced for a while." She kicks a hole in the sand. "He paid a witch to erase any memories of him and the lycan world, and he left me alone for ten years. During those years, I went to college, got my life on track, had food to eat, a warm bed to sleep in, and I was going somewhere. I was on the fast track to receiving my Ph.D. when my world imploded."

"What happened?"

"Harrison," she repeats the name from earlier. "This time he pretended to be a transfer student in one of my classes, and I fell for it, hook, line, and sinker. So much so that I gave him every part of me." She doesn't have to elaborate on the meaning behind her words. "I trusted him. I was in love with him. When Viktor rescued me from Harrison, I believed he was the bad guy, and Harrison was nothing more than a victim of Viktor's insanity."

"Viktor? Thorne's maker."

Amelia laughs. "Even in death, Viktor is larger than life." She bends down, picking up a broken seashell, and tosses it out to sea. "Viktor wasn't the monster I was groomed to believe he was. Turns out, I was in love with the monster." She throws a second shell into the water. "Viktor was trying to protect me. His methods were a little off kilter, to say the least." She laughs at a silent memory. "Viktor is Celeste's father. Celeste is my maker."

I begin piecing the parts of the puzzle together between Amelia, Thorne, Viktor, and the immortal child, Celeste. "He's the one who became a vampire for his daughter?"

"Yes. There's more to the story, but the details aren't important. By the time I realized who and what Harrison was, it was too late. He'd already killed so many people...so many good people, all to keep his lies and me for himself." She swallows deeply. "He attacked me. I didn't know why for the longest time, but over the years, I've come to realize that in Harrison's mind, if he couldn't have me, no one could." Amelia stands quietly, overlooking the water. "He drained nearly every ounce of blood from my system. The only thing that stopped him from killing me was Violet, another of his creations. She killed him before he could kill me."

"Where is Violet?"

"New Orleans," she answers. "She's strong, rich, and beautiful. Living the life she deserves on her own terms. Living the life that was stripped away from her."

"Celeste?" I ask. "How did she become your maker?"

"I barely had a pulse. Nothing more than a lifeless body. She took my choice away. She turned me into this."

"Are you angry?"

Amelia stares into the Gulf. "Maybe a little at first. I'm not anymore. If it weren't for being transformed into a vampire, I wouldn't be married to the love of my life. I wouldn't have a baby at home, and I wouldn't have ever learned who I truly am."

"My choice was taken away, too."

"Most don't have a choice. Viktor is the only one I've personally known who chose this life." She turns, facing me. "I know you've had a shitty life, and I wish I could take that pain away from you. But you're at a precipice. You can choose to run, hide from your past, and avoid your future, or you can choose to accept what you are and use that pain to make you stronger. Kragen will get what's coming to him. Patrice will get what's coming to her. They always do. Don't let the monster inside of you take over. Don't become something that is feared. Use the pain as your strength. Take back your power, and use it for good. I sense something in you that you may not sense in yourself. I don't know exactly what it is, but there's something inside you, waiting to come out. Use it."

"Can you teach me?"

Amelia smiles. "I'd be honored."

Talking to Amelia eases the tension I've mindlessly carried around for years, hell, centuries. The anger and frustration are still there, but hearing someone else's story, I realize I'm not alone in this fucked-up vampire world. The two of us enter the beach house just as the lycan finish cooking.

"Dinner's ready!" Luna announces from the kitchen. "I hope you like chicken and rice."

"I'd eat just about anything," Topher answers, leaving the couch and heading toward the dining area.

"Our meal should be delivered soon," Amelia says, pulling her phone from her pocket. "Actually, this says it's been delivered." She opens the front door and returns moments later, carrying a large styrofoam cooler.

"Goat's blood?" Thorne asks, taking the box from her.

"Enough for all three of us. I had it shipped from home."

"Yaaay," I answer. The sarcasm in my voice is more than obvious.

"I got you covered," Luna announces from the table. "I can spare a few liters."

"No. I need to learn to drink this stuff. You'll need your strength. Thank you for the offer, but it's time for me to grow up." I take the glass bottle from Amelia's hands and take a deep breath before chugging it like a frat boy during spring break.

The blood hits my stomach, reminding me of my

time aboard Kragen's ship when my two choices were rat blood or nothing. I cough, trying to hold it down.

"It's an acquired taste," Amelia says, copying my drinking style. "You'll get used to it over time."

"I can't wait." I smile, screwing the lid back on the bottle.

forts and princesses

"HELLO!" a voice calls from the foyer of the house. "Are y'all awake?"

The sun is just beginning to crest over the horizon, casting a beautiful glow through the windows of the beach house. "Sounds like Fynn is here." I stretch my legs from the cramped position they've been in for the past six hours. After the lycan went to bed, Thorne and I have been in our room. I found a set of books on the bookshelf downstairs and am in the last chapter of the final book in the series, while Thorne spent the night researching the identity and history of Patrice.

"Find anything?" I ask.

"Nothing substantial. A few possibilities throughout the last few decades of unexplainable attacks on humans, but nothing like what happened in New Orleans." He shrugs. "I get it. Keeping a low profile is part of the vampire culture, but she's either managed to wipe the internet of her name or uses a few different aliases."

"Y'all better hurry. I brought food," Fynn yells from below. The smell of fried flesh, otherwise known as bacon, permeates my nose, making me feel even more nauseous than the goat's blood from last night.

"Good morning," he greets us as we make our way to the kitchen.

"I don't think any of the lycan are awake," Thorne tells the giant wolf.

"Yeah, I figured. I'm an early riser."

"Morning," Amelia greets us, wandering into the kitchen wearing pajamas and messy hair.

"Do you sleep?" I ask, not sure what to make of her appearance.

She wiggles her eyebrows. "Sleep? No. Enjoy my husband when there's no baby around. Yes." I don't know why her words embarrass me. I feel the heat in my cheeks instantly.

Luna and Micah join the group, suspiciously arriving at the same time. Both carry a lustful look on their face. "You brought bacon!" Luna exclaims, heading straight toward the food.

"I thought we might explore some of the more secluded areas today," Fynn says, pulling a container of eggs from the bag.

"You think that's where Patrice could be hiding?" I state the obvious.

"It's the height of tourist season down here. There

aren't many places she could hide a horde of hungry immortal children." Fynn pulls another container from the bag, setting it next to the rest of them on the bar of the kitchen. "I thought we'd start with the fort."

"Aren't forts closed this early?" Amelia asks as Topher wanders into the room. His hair looks as equally messy as Amelia's as he wraps his arm around his wife, kissing her on the top of her head.

"That's the best time to go," Fynn answers. "I managed to ensure that we'd be the only ones there until noon. That should give us plenty of time."

"Sounds like a plan." Amelia smacks Topher on the ass before leaving the rest of us in the kitchen. "I need a shower first!" she yells through the large house.

"Aye, me, too," Thorne adds.

Fynn crosses his long legs at the ankle. He's wearing a *Landshark* T-shirt and brightly colored flowered shorts. "Don't mind me. I'll just be waiting here for you all to shower." His sarcasm brings a smile to my face. He speaks my language.

While Thorne showers, I change into the only pair of shorts I brought, along with the thinnest shirt I own. Pulling my dark curls into a long ponytail, I slap on a little mascara and lip gloss and head downstairs. Vampires don't get hot, but wearing a hoodie and leggings seems out of character for our location.

"How long will it take to get to the fort?" I ask our lycanthrope tour guide. He's cleaned up the mess from breakfast and is staring through the back sliding doors.

"From here, about twenty minutes."

Thirty minutes later, the seven of us load into the black SUV and head away from the water. Fynn's small bursts of road rage ease the tension of what we might find.

"It's seven o'clock in the morning. Where could you possibly be going?" Fynn yells at the car in front of us. "Especially at twenty miles an hour!" He turns toward Micah, beside him in the front seat. "Tourists! They help the economy, but they drive me crazy."

"You mentioned there were only a few places where Patrice would be able to hide her children without being seen. Doesn't the fort receive a lot of visitors?" Luna asks from the back seat.

"Yeah, it does. But some parts are blocked from visitors. Older parts that aren't in as good of condition as the rest." Fynn lays on the horn, sending a few curse words with it. "Sorry, y'all. These drivers bring out the worst in me."

Right on time, we pull through the entrance. Several outlying buildings surround the sprawling walls in front of us. "That's the Gulf on that side." Fynn points out to the water. "That side's the bay."

"This is the perfect location for a fort," Micah announces.

"Yep, amazing that they thought of it." I can't hide the smirk that comes with Fynn's words as he pulls into the visitor parking lot. True to his word, we're the only car around. "Follow me," he announces, leading us through the main entrance, into a large courtyard. We continue moving through the courtyard, into the furthest side of the building.

Fynn leads us through the continually darker rooms until reaching a heavy metal door with a chain and lock still in place. "This is where they'd be."

"That chain and lock haven't been touched for years. The rust is older than me," Topher announces. "Is there another way in?"

"Not by land." Fynn wraps his hands around the rusty lock, breaking it easily.

"I can't see shit," Luna says, following me into the room. Vampire vision allows me to see everything. I reach back, latching my fingers around her arm, and pull her with me.

The smell of mold and mildew floods my senses the moment we enter. "It feels like we're moving underground," Thorne whispers.

"We are," Fynn confirms. "This section was originally built to house prisoners. Later it was used as barracks for officers because of the temperature difference, and toward the end of the Civil War, it was used as an escape route for emergencies." He turns on a flashlight I didn't realize he was carrying, shining it in front of us.

The faint sound of waves crashing against the shore echoes off the concrete walls. "This goes to the Gulf?" I ask.

"That it does. We're almost to the cave," Fynn

answers, shining his light off the walls, which have turned from concrete to brick.

"How is there a cave on the coast of Alabama?" Luna asks. "This land is flatter than my chest."

"It was man-made," he answers with a laugh.

The painted brick walls show obvious signs of wear the further we walk. The whitewash that covered them a century ago is worn and chipped away. The brick floor slowly gives way to sand, a telltale sign we're approaching water.

"You think Patrice is bringing the kids into the fort through this entrance?" Amelia asks as we move single file through the room.

"It's possible." Fynn shines his flashlight ahead, giving light to what looks like stone. Man-made material turns into natural limestone and gritty sand the further we move. "Other than the entrance we came through, the only way in is to swim." Light bounces off a pool of stagnant water in the middle of the dome cave.

"This looks natural and not natural at the same time." I run my fingers along the walls. "It feels like stone, but it's too perfect."

"The stone was quarried near the mountains in North Alabama and brought here to create what is now a cave." Fynn shines his light above us. "We're beneath the beach. This area is thirty feet below the surface."

"How has this stayed hidden for so long?" Micah speaks for the first time in a while.

"The people who need to know about it do." Fynn leads us to the edge of the smooth-surfaced water. "The water down here is nearly toxic to humans. It's been inside the cave long enough to grow stagnant and dangerous to most, still containing chemicals from the war."

"There's no evidence that anyone's been in this area since the war," Amelia says as she runs her hands along the walls. "Other than our footprints, the sand is undisturbed. There are no lingering smells, and zero evidence of anyone being here for hundreds of years."

"Aye," Thorne agrees. "If immortal children had been in here, this place would be destroyed."

"Are there any other places here like this? Places that the average person wouldn't know about?" Topher asks, rubbing sand through his fingers.

"There is another fort twenty miles from here that was used around the same time. As far as I know, there aren't any hidden areas," Fynn answers.

"Why does it have to be a fort?" Amelia asks. "Why not a home in a secluded area? Or an abandoned building? To be honest, a fort seems a little too obvious."

"There aren't a lot of abandoned homes in this area, too many visitors."

"The news station said the two missing children were in the 'The Meeting-Place area.' What is that?" Luna joins the conversation.

Fynn laughs. "It's a restaurant-slash-tourist trap, smack dab in the middle of Gulf Shores."

"Can you take us there?" Amelia asks.

"Sure." He shrugs. "The police have been all over that place with a fine-tooth comb. I don't know what you'll find that they didn't."

"Maybe we'll pick up on clues that humans wouldn't," I answer. Our mismatched group of lycan and vampires follows Fynn back through the cave and into the sunlight and courtyard of the fort.

"Are there ghosts here?" Luna asks, changing the subject.

"Supposedly," Fynn answers. "There are stories of people being touched along with disembodied voices floating all over the internet and ghost shows."

"That's super cool!" she answers with the enthusiasm of a child. We load into the SUV and leave the fort behind.

Ten minutes later, Fynn pulls into an already busy parking lot next to the white sandy beach. Families are filling rolling carts with floats, towels, chairs, and coolers, ready for a day in the sun. "I need a beach day," Luna announces, climbing out of the back seat.

"We should split up," Amelia says. "We can cover more ground and draw less attention that way." She turns toward me. "Luna? Elsie? Why don't you come with me? We'll let the guys do their own thing."

"Sure." I send Thorne an apologetic look. He follows Topher and Micah, heading toward the water and leaving me alone with a hybrid and a lycanthrope.

We move toward the restaurant area. "I thought the

three of us together might draw some attention if you know what I mean." Amelia winks.

"I know what you mean," Luna answers. "I'm gonna shake what my mama gave me."

Being on the run for two centuries, I've never had the opportunity to have a friend. Being with others has always felt awkward, making me feel out of place. Being with Luna and Amelia feels natural and relaxes me slightly.

The three of us enter the restaurant, quickly finding the hostess at the stand. "Are you here for the Pirates and Princess breakfast?" she asks, looking between the three of us.

"We are," Amelia lies.

"You're in luck." The woman smiles. "We have three spots left." We follow her upstairs to an outdoor seating area on the roof overlooking the water. She seats us at a picnic table not far from the stage. "The show is about to begin."

"This is perfect!" Luna says, looking around at the patrons. "There's nothing but kids up here."

"This would certainly be the perfect hunting ground for a new immortal child," Amelia agrees.

"Do you think Patrice is one of the guests?" Luna asks.

"I doubt she'd be dumb enough to hunt in the same place twice. Plus, immortal children are hard to control, especially young ones. If she's already taken two, I doubt she's in the market for more," Amelia answers.

"Ladies and gentlemen," a woman announces from the stage. *"Our pirates and princesses would like to tell you all how much they're enjoying having you here today, and they hope you will eat until you can eat no more."*

Teenagers dressed in cheap Halloween costumes wave from the stage before exiting the sides and moving toward the patrons. "Was that the show?" I ask, not sure what I just witnessed.

"It appears that way," Amelia answers with a laugh.

I watch as the performers make their way around the tables, greeting children and parents alike. A young girl dressed as Princess Anna stops at our table, giving us a strange look. "Are you ladies into pirates and princesses?"

"We are!" Luna answers, wearing a wide smile.

"We'd like to ask you a few questions if you don't mind," Amelia interrupts.

"Sure," Anna answers.

"Were you working the day the two children disappeared?"

The young girl looks down, taking a braid from her wig into her hand and fidgeting with it. "I told the police everything I know."

"Do you mind sharing what you told the police with us?" I ask, plastering a fake smile across my face.

She makes eye contact with all three of us and sighs. "I saw them here, at breakfast. The kids. They were with their families." The timbre of her voice becomes sad at the memory. "The little girl was so sweet and happy to be here. Anna is...was her favorite princess, and she talked to me a lot that morning."

"Do you remember seeing anyone watching the children while they were here?" Amelia continues the questioning.

"No. Nothing out of the ordinary."

"Was there an adult eating alone?" Remembering the description Elijah gave, I describe her hair color to the girl.

She shakes her head. "No one was alone, but there was a woman with dark hair who had a kid with her."

"No offense," Luna prefaces. "With all the people you see daily, what made this woman stand out?"

The girl shrugs. "It wasn't her so much as her kid. He was wearing a sports coat and slacks in the heat. He sat perfectly still and didn't eat a bite. Something about him gave me the creeps."

The three of us share a look. "When I tried to talk to him, his speech was weird, and he kept smiling at me." She huffs a laugh. "This is going to sound crazy, but he looked at me like he wanted to *eat* me."

Amelia stands. "Thank you. You've been very helpful."

"That had to be Patrice," I whisper as the three of us work our way out of the restaurant.

"Why the hell would she bring an immortal child to a breakfast for human children?" Luna asks.

"To choose the next ones?" Amelia says. "Maybe she allows him to pick the kids, like ordering from a menu."

"Damn, that's harsh." Luna takes the words out of my mouth.

"Where do we go from here?" I ask our small group.

"We keep looking and asking questions."

"Find anything?" Topher asks as we approach the male members of our group.

"Yeah," Amelia answers. "We're pretty sure Patrice took one of the immortal children to the same breakfast that the kids that disappeared attended."

"She brought an immortal child out in public?" Thorne asks.

"One of the better-behaved ones, I'm assuming," I answer.

"What about you? Did you find anything?" Luna asks, moving to Micah's side. The energy flowing between them is palpable and makes me happy for the moment.

"We talked to all the lifeguards and beach workers. No one saw anything out of the ordinary," he answers.

"We think Patrice brought the boy to help choose her victims," I say to the crowd.

"If she's coming down here to find children, she can't be too far from the area." Fynn props his hands on his hips as he speaks.

"Too bad we can't send a spy to find out." My words are more of a thought rather than a statement. I look up, realizing the entire group has stopped brainstorming and is staring at me.

"That's actually a great idea." Amelia turns toward

her husband. "Kind of like when I went back to college for a while." The two of them share a laugh at a story that the rest of us aren't privy to.

"How? We don't have a clue where to find her," Luna adds.

"Elijah." Micah pulls his phone out of his pocket. "There's no doubt in my mind that he knows how to contact her."

I hold my hands out to my sides. "Wait, people. What are you suggesting?"

Amelia looks around the group. "I don't know what everyone else is thinking, but I think you had a great idea. One of us needs to infiltrate her group."

"None of us is a child," I state the obvious.

"With the number of immortal children under her control, she's bound to be at her wits' end. She could use *help*." Thorne joins in on this crazy idea.

"Are you all mad?" I ask the group. "Who do you suggest we send in there?" I look at each person. "She's not going to accept Thorne for the basic reason that he's a man. The children would eat the lycan, which means it's either me or you." I stare at Amelia with my last words.

"Amelia?" Topher whispers. "Think about Edon." She closes her eyes in response.

The realization hits me. "It has to be me," I whisper. "I'm expendable."

"You're not expendable," Thorne argues. He turns toward the rest of our group. "No. I won't allow her to do this. She was held captive by a monster for a century. Doing this would be the same thing. No," he repeats.

"It has to be me," I whisper. I reach up, kissing Thorne on the cheek before turning back to the group. "Tell me what to do."

my love is like a red, red rose

NO ONE HAS SAID MUCH since we've returned to the beach house. The thought of infiltrating a horde of immortal children terrifies me. I won't be held captive, but Thorne's right when he says I'll be right back where I started. It's funny how life turns and sends you back to the place you've spent your life trying to escape.

"Are you okay?" Thorne asks as he wraps his arms around my waist. I've been standing on the edge of the deck, staring into the Gulf for the past hour. Why? I have no idea.

"Do you want the truth?"

He turns me around, facing him. "You don't have to do this. We could leave and be back in Charleston by the afternoon."

Tears fill the corners of my eyes. "I can't leave them there."

"Who?"

"The children." My mind flashes back to Gretchen in the basement. "They don't deserve this."

"Aye, they don't. But neither do you."

"I'll be okay," I reassure him.

"You don't know that."

"I'm stronger than I was when I was with Kragen."

Thorne crosses his arms over his chest. "You heard Amelia. Immortal children are unpredictable...out of control. What if one of them overpowers you?"

"It's a chance I have to take," I answer.

"Elsie?" Amelia's voice calls through the door. "Micah has some information for all of us."

I sigh, grabbing Thorne's hands. "You have to let me do this."

"I won't stop you," he whispers. "But I don't have to support the idea."

I open the door, finding Amelia standing against the wall on the opposite side. "I'm sorry to interrupt, but he says it's important."

We follow her downstairs, finding the rest of our crew lounging across the furniture in the living area. Micah stands as we enter.

"Elijah arranged for a meeting," he announces.

"Did he magically find a way to contact her?" Luna's voice is laced with sarcasm.

Micah laughs. "My father can be very *convincing*."

"What's the plan?" I ask, not sure I want to know.

He turns toward me. "Elijah's going to contact

Patrice and tell her he's met someone with the same... the same *taste* as her."

"Same taste? What the hell does that mean?" Luna asks.

"The same taste in children." He won't look me in the eye as he speaks.

I close my eyes, understanding his words. "You mean, someone who wants to turn innocent children into vampires?"

"What is the expected outcome?" Thorne asks.

"Elijah believes that Patrice will jump at the chance to find someone like her. Especially if the recommendation comes from him."

"This is fucked-up," Amelia announces. "I thought this was a good idea, but damn. I...we understand if you don't want to do this."

"No. It was my idea to start with, and it's the only way to save them. I've lived in much worse conditions." I take a deep breath, pushing memories from my mind.

"You can stay here as long as needed," Fynn announces to the group. "If Patrice is in the area, I doubt you'll want to go far."

"Thank you," Micah answers for all of us.

Thorne wraps his fingers around mine protectively. I'm not the only one with memories flashing to mind. I squeeze his hand, hoping to offer comfort. "I'm taking Elsie for a walk," he announces to the group.

I don't argue as he leads me down the deck stairs to the sand. It's not until we're standing side by side, staring into the sea that he speaks. "This is going to sound so selfish." He closes his eyes. "But I don't know if I can do this." He wipes a tear from his cheek. "I just found you."

I turn, facing him. "I have no intention of being lost."

"I know, but what if..."

"No," I interrupt. "We can't do the what ifs." My mind flashes back to Francis's words when we were going after Kragen. "This is my chance to save them. To make up for the humans that I've killed over the years."

"You don't need to make up for that, Elsie."

"Yes, I do. I've killed so many people, Thorne. Innocent humans who did nothing wrong except carry the very thing that sustains me in their veins." It's my turn to wipe a tear. "I turned into the monster I escaped from."

"You're nothing like him," Thorne argues.

"Every human I killed is one step closer to becoming him." My fingers glide softly over his cheek. "I'm going to be okay."

"You don't know that."

"No, I don't. But I have to believe it." I pause. "If I can save a child, it's worth it. If I can save another group of humans from becoming their food, it's worth it."

Thorne closes his eyes, allowing the tears to cover his cheeks. "I love you, acushla."

"I know, and I love you, too."

"We have contact!" Luna yells from the sliding glass window.

"That was quick." I laugh awkwardly.

"I will rip her limb from limb if one hair on your head is damaged." The energy pouring off Thorne is something I've never witnessed, and in any other situation, it would be hot.

"I would expect nothing less," I say, wrapping my arms around his waist and pulling him close. His lips are on mine in an instant. The intensity of the kiss says more than words ever could. His tongue separates my lips, making contact with mine and sending chills down my spine.

I pull away from the kiss, out of breath. "We'd better stop, or this is going to turn into a spectacle for the tourists." Thorne doesn't laugh at my weak attempt at humor.

Lacing my fingers through his, I lead him up the stairs and back into the house. "What has happened?" I ask the crowd staring at me.

"Patrice wants to meet you," Micah answers.

"Where?"

"A home off the bay," he answers. "In an hour."

"Hell no," Thorne answers. "She's not going to be ready in an hour."

"I'll be ready," I lie. I pull Thorne's hand to my lips, kissing the back of it. "We have to make Patrice believe for this to happen. If I truly wanted to join her, I would be ready to jump when she says jump. I wouldn't make her wait."

"The bay is almost an hour away," Fynn says. "We need to leave now to get you there on time."

"You can't come with me." I look around the room. "None of you can. I don't need to be dropped off like a child at daycare. I have to do this on my own."

"I'm coming," Thorne interrupts.

I turn toward the man I've loved for three centuries. "I love you and will always love you, but you can't come with me either. If she senses another vampire, it could destroy any chance we have of saving them."

Thorne turns away from me and punches a fist-sized hole through the drywall. "Shit!" he shouts.

"Elsie, I told you I sense something inside of you. I know what it is." Amelia moves in front of me. "Your strength. Your power lies in your heart and courage. Use it to your advantage." She pulls me into a hug.

Luna lines up behind her, copying her movements. "Take some of my blood before you go." She hands me a water bottle full of red liquid. "You'll need your strength." Before I realize it, everyone, even Fynn, has formed a line, coming in for hugs.

"Thank you, everyone." I turn toward Thorne, who's standing against the wall with a solemn look. "Take care of him," I ask Amelia. She nods at my words. "Don't let him do something stupid."

Without another word, I move to the front steps and the road at vampire speed, stopping at the mailbox to take one last look at the house that holds the only friends I've ever had. I turn, running into the hard chest of my captain.

Without speaking, he pulls me into his arms, holding me tight to his chest. "Check in with me every hour through this." He points at my head. "If I don't hear from you, I will kill every last one of them."

I nod with a silent promise. Thorne is strong but not strong enough to kill a horde of immortal children. "I will."

I turn, leaving the man I love alone on the street, fighting the tears threatening to fall. I continue moving faster than the human eye can track, following the coordinates Micah dropped to my phone. I have to stop several times while the GPS catches up with my speed. Less than thirty minutes later, I'm standing in front of an abandoned building that matches the address. *What the hell?* In front of me is a once beautiful wooden structure with a tall steeple and two columns on the front— a church. It's nestled between several live oak trees covered in Spanish moss that dwarf the dilapidated remains. There's no turning back now. Everyone in that building knows there's a vampire outside.

"I'm here," I send to Thorne through our connection.

"Be safe," he repeats his words from earlier.

I step up on the porch and take a silent breath. "Hello?"

Seagulls caw in the distance, answering my greeting.

The door is slightly ajar, seemingly welcoming me inside. The moment I touch the doorknob, the overwhelming energy of a vampire fills me from head to toe. Whoever or whatever is here is strong. "Hello?" I call again.

I push the door open to a large room. Long wooden pews are still lined up in perfect order as I work my way closer to the front. A large stained glass window colors the room in bright pink and blue hues as the sun lines up perfectly, casting a colorful glow into the room. In any other situation, this room would be beautiful. In this one, it's terrifying.

I move to the stage area in the front. An old pulpit is still standing and holds several pieces of yellowed sheet music that look to have been torn from an old hymnal. Soft movement behind me grabs my attention. I turn, seeing something from nightmares.

"Hello?" a young boy greets me. He's standing in the doorway that leads to another part of the church. "Who are you?"

The dark suit and tie he's wearing accentuate his pale skin perfectly. His dark hair is perfectly combed, and a drop of blood covers the bottom portion of his lip.

"Elsie," I answer. "Who are you?"

"Alexander." He sniffs the air in front of him. "What are you?"

"I'm a woman."

"I know what a woman is. You smell like Mother."

"Where *is* your mother, Alexander?"

He moves closer, bringing the hair on my arms to attention. "I asked you a question." His accent has a hint of another time.

"I'm the same thing as you," I answer truthfully.

"What do you want?" he asks, moving closer still.

"I would like to meet your mother."

He cocks his head, reminding me of a dog at the sound of a squeaky toy. "Why?"

"Because I love children and have dreamed of becoming a mother." I pause, looking at the boy. "Your mother and I have a mutual friend."

"We don't need another mother," Alexander argues.

"I'm not trying to replace your mother. I would love a few children of my own."

"Who's this?" a female voice says from the other side of the room. "I can smell her from here."

I turn, seeing a little girl dressed in clothes from the '50s. She doesn't look any older than nine or ten. "She's mine," the boy answers. "Stay away." He hisses at the girl.

"I'm here to see your mother," I answer.

"Mother?" the girl repeats. "What do you want with Mother?"

"A mutual friend of ours asked me to come." The girl moves completely into the room, giving me a glimpse at her angelic face. The innocent child depicted through her smile is instantly hidden by her eyes...eyes that hold the look of death.

"Tell her I'm here," I say, using a sterner voice. "She's expecting me."

"Mother doesn't accept visitors." The boy is standing next to me in an instant. Even with my vampire eyes, I didn't see his movement. His face changes from the innocent child he was moments earlier to that of a monster. Black eyes replace the blue, and fangs protrude from his mouth.

"Stop!" I demand. "Don't make me punish you."

"Punish? You're not Mother." The girl's face contorts as the two children move even closer.

"Amelia says to sing," Thorne's words echo through my mind. Sing? Was that my imagination? *"Dammit, sing, Elsie!"*

A song I used to sing to my siblings when we lived in Scotland is the only song that comes to mind under pressure. I begin softly, then crescendo as the verse continues.

My love is like a red, red rose
That's newly sprung in June
My love is like the melody
That's sweetly played in tune.

The children freeze in place. Both stare at me.

As fair art thou, my bonnie lass,
So deep in love am I
And I will love thee still, my dear,

Till all the seas gang dry.

Their faces return to normal, and their eyes soften. "That was beautiful," the girl whispers. "Sing more."

Loud clapping echoes off the walls of the wooden church. I turn, finding a woman with dark hair standing in the corner. "Well done, my dear. Well done."

"Patrice?"

She bows grandly. "The one and only."

a hunting we will go...

I STARE at the woman in front of me. While the children are dressed in clothes from what I presume is their era of death. she's wearing a pair of designer leggings and a fitted shirt. Her coal black hair and over-sized dark eyes are a beautiful contrast to her pale skin. If I didn't know better, I'd think she was in her mid-twenties, driving an oversized SUV with three kids in the back, and on the way to a soccer game.

"Why are you here?" Patrice asks, looking me up and down.

"I want to be a mother," I lie.

She sniffs the air in front of me. "You're old. Why now?"

"Before becoming a vampire, I had eight brothers and sisters. I miss them."

Patrice steps closer toward me. "What happened to them?"

I look at the floor. "One was killed by the vampire that changed me, another was changed by the vampire that changed me, and one of my sisters married a lycanthrope." I clear my throat. "I don't know about the rest."

"What happened to the one that was changed?"

"Dead." I don't go into detail.

"Can we play with her, Mother?" Alexander asks.

"Oh, please, Mother. Can we?" the girl joins.

"I believe we have a mutual acquaintance," I interrupt the children's attempt to murder me. "Elijah told me he spoke to you earlier on my behalf."

"He did," Patrice agrees. She begins to walk around me, making me feel like prey. "How old are you?"

"A little over three hundred years old," I answer truthfully.

"Why do you feel older?"

I shrug. "I'm not sure." No one has ever told me that before.

Patrice steps behind me, placing a cold hand on my shoulder. It takes every part of me not to wince with her touch. "If I allow you to stay, what are your intentions?"

"To help with the children."

"I don't need help," she retorts.

"I'm not implying otherwise. Being the eldest of nine, I always helped care for and feed my brothers and sisters. My mother never needed my help, but I was there in case she did. Being with the children would bring back those treasured memories I've lost." I give myself a mental pat on the back for thinking under pressure.

She steps in front of me, pulling her hand away from my skin. "Caring for immortal children is not an easy task. They can be quite...temperamental."

"Aren't we all?" I laugh, hoping to ease the tension.

"Elijah didn't share much information about you." She ignores my attempt to ease the tension. Patrice steps toward an empty pew, sliding into the seat. "Enlighten us."

My mind reels over how much of the truth I should share, and I decide on an abbreviated version. "I was taken from the ship that brought the rest of my family to America in the early 1700s."

Patrice slides back, crossing her arms in front of her chest. "Go on. This has the makings of an interesting story."

"I was kept aboard the vampire's ship for a century until finally escaping."

"I was right! This is going to be good."

"Since escaping, I've been on the run, hiding from everyone and everything." I resist the urge to fidget my hands while speaking. "On a trip to Charleston, I met Elijah, and we became...friends."

"Isn't he handsome?" She claps her hands. "And so well versed in using *every inch* of him, if you know what I mean."

"We weren't that kind of friends," I interrupt.

"Oh, that's a pity. He's quite well-endowed."

I glance at the children, who are listening intently. My first instinct is to speak carefully around them, but with the amount of *life* they've seen, I doubt censoring my comments is needed.

"Maybe I'll change our relationship," I tease.

Patrice stands, moving toward a door on the other side of the room. "Your room is through here."

My stomach jumps into my throat. Does this mean I'm in, or is she setting me up for something far more sinister? I smile, not knowing which. "Thank you, Patrice. I'm looking forward to learning from you."

"The children will decide if you stay." She turns toward the two children in the room. "Come, Alexander. Come, Autumn." They step ahead of her obediently. I follow them through the door into a narrow hallway.

Rooms line each side of the hall, serving as what I would guess are rooms for the rest of the children. She stops in front of a door at the end. "Here's where you'll stay." The door opens, revealing an empty room. The smell of sulfur hits me instantly.

"Elsie?" Thorne questions. *"Are you alright?"*

"Yes," I lie. I step into the room while my mind reels over who has been here before me. The worn carpet and asbestos-covered ceiling welcome me into their womb. "This is perfect, thank you."

"You'll be expected at feeding time," Patrice says, closing me inside. The sound of a heavy lock sliding into place brings memories of the bottom of Kragen's ship to the surface.

"She locked me in a room. I'm safe," I call through our connection.

"Is everything okay?" Even in my head, his voice sounds frantic.

"Aye. I'm fine. I'll be expected at feeding time."

"What does that mean?"

"I have no idea." I slide down the wall, sitting on the filthy floor. *"How did you know I needed help earlier?"*

"I felt you."

"Felt me? How?"

He pauses a while before answering. *"I'm not sure how to explain it. I felt anxious and could tell it wasn't my emotion I was feeling."*

"Singing helped."

"Amelia says we shouldn't be able to communicate like this."

I feel my forehead scrunch in question. *"Through our minds?"*

"Aye. She says that is something that some vampires can only do with their makers."

I scoff. *"You're not my maker."*

"It's also possible through a strong bond. Viktor could apparently speak to Celeste that way even though he wasn't her maker."

I pause. *"We have a strong bond."*

"Aye, we do." Thorne breathes deeply through our connection. *"Stay safe, acushla."*

"I am," I lie. Truthfully, I have no idea what the hell I'm doing.

I lose track of time, sitting alone in the sulfur-filled, moldy room. The smell I've attributed to Kragen all these years, now associates with Marnie, too. Does that mean she's been here? I think back to what Amelia said at the death house. *I smell like sulfur.* Anyone who's had contact with Kragen most likely smells the same. Closing my eyes, I focus on keeping thoughts of the pirate who kidnapped me out of my mind.

The only audible sound in the building is the echo of the water, lapping against the shore not far away. PTSD hits hard as my mind switches into the dissociative mode it spent a century in. I stare at the door, willing it to open. The sound of a key rattling brings memories of Kragen to the surface, causing me to recoil instinctively.

The door creaks open slowly. Standing in the crack is an image from a nightmare. Alexander holds the key in his hand and smiles the smile of a cold, calculating killer.

"Mother would like for you to come with me."

I stand, moving closer to the door, trying to seem unfazed by his behavior. "Where are we going?"

"It's time to eat," he answers, smiling once more. "Follow me, please."

He leads me down the hallway, back into the room I entered earlier. Scattered throughout the room, intermittently filling several pews, are children. Most have silver chains wrapped around their torsos, holding their arms to their sides.

"What is this, Alexander?"

He turns, smiling once more. "I told you. It's time to eat."

I count the number of heads as we enter. Not including my tour guide, there are nine children in the room. Gretchen said she had ten brothers and sisters. That means the two new children are missing.

"Is this everyone?" I ask.

"Nearly," he answers without elaborating.

"Children!" Patrice calls from the stage. "I would like to introduce you to Elsbeth Abernathy." Chill bumps cover my skin at the realization that I never told her my name. Shit. Did Elijah tell her? Does Elijah even know my last name?

The children hiss in my direction.

"Elsbeth is here because she wants to be a mother."

Again, the children hiss. The ones being held with chains begin struggling against their hold, fighting the silver holding them in place. What the hell is happening?

"*Elsbeth?*" Thorne calls.

"*I'm okay. Just not sure what's going on.*"

"You get to choose whether she stays with us," Patrice continues. "Before you vote, she must prove her worth."

Shit, shit, shit. This is going downhill fast.

"Elsbeth! What's going on?" I ignore his call and focus on the children in the room.

Patrice turns toward me. "Prove your worth to them, Mommy."

"How?" I whisper.

"Feed them."

I turn back toward the immortal children. Most of their faces have contorted to the monstrous form I witnessed from Alexander and his friend. "Where do I find food?"

"Anywhere you can," Patrice answers.

"She wants me to feed the children."

"Is there...food there?"

I look around the room, seeing and sensing only vampires. *"No."*

"Alexander will accompany you on the hunt," she continues. "He knows what we need." Oh, my God. I can't do this.

Small fingers lace through mine. "Are you ready, Mommy?" he asks.

"Elsie?"

"Yes, sweetie. Where are we going?" I lie, holding back tears.

"The beach is where Mother finds the best food."

The realization hits me that Patrice didn't take the two missing children to add to her horde. They were food.

"Alexander, make sure Mommy makes good choices." Patrice pats him on the head.

"Yes, Mother." He smiles, pulling me toward the door.

"We'll be waiting for your return." Patrice waves like she's sending us off to camp.

Once outside, I take a deep breath, hoping to clear my mind. *"Elsie, talk to me. What's going on?"*

"We're coming to the beach to hunt," I answer, still holding onto Alexander's hand. I look down at the immortal child. "How are we going to get there?"

He looks confused for a moment. "We run, silly."

"Who's we?" Thorne asks.

"Alexander is coming with me. He's one of the children."

Alexander drops my hand. "Are you ready, Mommy?"

Hell no. "I am. Lead the way."

He takes off at vampire speed, almost faster than I can move, heading south toward the Gulf. It doesn't take long before we're standing in front of the familiar restaurant from this morning. "This is where we found food before."

I look around at the huge crowds, milling around the beach and open area of the restaurant. *"We're back at the same location the children went missing from."*

"We're almost there. Fynn insisted on driving."

"No! He'll feel you."

"Dammit, Elsie. What do you want us to do?"

I sigh as Alexander laces his fingers through mine again. *"I don't know. You didn't see those children, Thorne. I have to see this through."*

"Look, Mommy," Alexander interrupts my silent conversation. He points at a young woman sitting alone at a secluded table. "She wants to die."

"What?" I ask, looking down at the boy.

"She wants to die," he repeats. "I can hear her thoughts."

"You can hear her thoughts? How is that possible?"

He shrugs. "I don't know. Mother says I'm special."

I turn back toward the girl. "Why does she want to die?"

"Because her boyfriend has been fucking her brother." He looks up at me, confused. "What does that mean?"

"It means she's very sad."

"Is that what Mother does? She has you listen to people to choose the best food?"

"Yes," he answers. "I don't like to choose the happy ones."

"Amelia and I will stay back far enough he can't sense us, but the lycan are moving closer."

"Okay," I relent. *"The child has picked out a human for dinner."*

"You can't take the human to them," Thorne states the obvious.

"I know. But what else can I do?"

"Mommy?" Alexander looks up at me. "Who do you keep talking to?"

"What do you mean?"

"I can hear you."

alexander

"I'M TALKING TO MY FRIEND," I admit.

Alexander looks around. "Where is he?"

I kneel face-to-face with the immortal child. "How old are you, Alexander?"

He shrugs, looking away. "I don't remember." It's obvious he's lying.

"How long have you been with Mother?"

"I'm the oldest." He looks behind me. "They smell funny." I turn to find a group of lycan standing on the sidewalk not far away. "What are they?"

I close my eyes, not sure if I should tell the truth. What if he attacks everyone around us? I take a deep breath before deciding not to lie. "They're lycan."

"What's a lycan?"

"We're werewolves," Luna says from behind me. I stand, moving between the immortal child and my friend.

Alexander's eyes turn black. "Mother doesn't like werewolves."

Luna moves to my side. "We're not here to hurt you or any of your brothers and sisters."

"Why are you here?" he asks. The energy flowing from him is powerful and dark.

"To help you."

Alexander cocks his head. "*I* don't need help."

I pull the immortal child away from the crowd of humans toward a more secluded area. *"We need Amelia,"* I send to Thorne. Seconds later, they're both standing in front of us. Alexander hisses, sensing their power.

"Alexander, these are my friends, Thorne and Amelia." He continues to hiss. "They're not going to hurt you."

"I don't like vampires," he continues. The lycan join us, and his teeth become visible. "They smell so good." He pulls slightly against my hold.

"Alexander," Amelia says, sitting on the ground cross-legged. The boy ignores her call. "Alexander," she calls again. "Will you sit and play with me?"

He looks down, calming slightly. "Play what?"

She draws a picture pedestal and a row of lines in the sand. "Hangman. Do you know how to play that game?"

He looks at the lines. "No."

"Good! I get to teach you how." She smiles warmly. "The lines are a word. You guess the letters of the word you think it is, and if you get one right, I add it to the correct line. If you get it wrong, I draw parts of a man. If you figure out the word before I add all the pieces of the hangman, you win."

"R," Alexander says.

"No R's." Amelia draws a circle for a head.

"T," he continues.

"There are two T's." She draws the T's in their correct spot.

"Tarantula," he announces.

Amelia's smile disappears as she fills in the rest of the word. "Excellent. Let's try another one."

His eyes return to their blue hue as Amelia starts another game. This time the word is longer. "S," he says, staring intently into the sand. Amelia fills in four S's. "Mississippi," he announces before she's drawn the last s.

"That's correct!"

"He's smart," Thorne says.

"Aye. Maybe that's why he's able to control the vampire side of him."

"Alexander," Amelia says after three games. "I have a ton of games back at the beach house. Would you like to see them?"

The boy stands up straight. "Mother wouldn't want me to go." He turns back toward me. "Mommy and I are here to find food."

"We can take them food." She turns toward the crew of otherworldly creatures behind her. "Can't we?"

"Sure," Thorne agrees. "I'm sure your mother won't mind."

What we're doing feels wrong on so many levels. What *are* we doing? Alexander looks up at me. "What do you think, Mommy?"

"I think you would love the games at the beach house. Maybe we could stop by for a quick minute, then come back and hunt."

Alexander pulls back slightly. "No. Mother won't approve. We need to feed my family." He straightens his already perfect sports coat. "If you'll excuse us." He laces his fingers back through mine. "Please don't talk to Mommy in her head anymore."

Thorne's eyes open wide. I shake my head, silently begging him to stay quiet.

Alexander points at an older man standing against the wooden fence. His arms are crossed in front of him, and his boot is propped on the pickets behind him. "He just shot his wife and children."

"What?" Luna and Micah ask in unison.

"That man, he killed his family," Alexander repeats. He sighs. "He says his wife was a cheating whore, and the kids weren't his." He stares at the man a few minutes longer. "He's planning on taking that woman." He points at a young woman dancing with a group of friends. "He's going to rape and kill her."

Hearing those words from what appears to be a child is hard to accept. "Are you sure?" Amelia asks.

"Yes. He keeps replaying the images of her screaming in his mind."

"You're not seriously considering this?" I ask the group around me.

"It wouldn't be a great loss," Topher answers for the group. He moves toward the human, with Micah in tow. The lycan tower over the man, and the three of them speak for a few minutes.

"What are they doing?" Alexander asks.

"Searching for the truth," I answer.

Movement happens quickly as Topher pulls the man's hands behind his back. The human fights back, not getting very far with the two lycan holding him in place.

"Where are they taking him?" Alexander asks.

"I'm not sure." His hand is still wrapped inside of mine as we follow them out of the crowded area, into a more secluded part of the beach.

"What the fuck, man? Let me go," the man argues.

"My friend asked you a question," Topher spews inches from his face. "What did you do to your family?"

"Fuck you." He spits in Topher's face, hitting him right in the eye.

Amelia's face transforms into something similar to Kragen's. She moves between the men. "My husband asked you a question." Her eyes are dark, and her face has contorted into a monstrous form.

"What the fuck, bitch. What are you?"

"Your worst nightmare." Fangs protrude from her face as she moves even closer.

"I killed them," he whispers. "She was a lying whore and had it coming. Damn kids, too."

"He'll do," Alexander says, looking up at me. "I don't like to take the good ones. That's what Mother does. She takes the good ones."

"Are you talking about the children?"

He looks down, kicking the sand in front of him. "I... I couldn't eat from them. I refused the food. They were just kids."

I pull Alexander away from the spectacle in front of us. "What if I can help you to stop killing?"

Large tears well in his eyes. "You can't." His moment of weakness has passed as he puts the stoic killer back on the throne. "I'm a killer. It's what I'm made to do."

"Alexander, you don't have to be." I soften my voice, hoping to break through his wall of protection.

"Mother will be expecting us." He straightens his perfect coat once more, signifying that he's finished with our conversation.

Squatting to his level, I put both hands on his shoulders. "There is another way. We can survive on animal blood."

He wrinkles his nose. "No, thank you. I don't eat rats."

I laugh. "Me neither." Just thinking about drinking

from a rat makes my stomach boil. "My friends drink goat's blood."

"Goat? Is it good?"

I focus on not making a disgusting face as I speak. "It's drinkable, and it keeps them alive and strong."

Alexander looks at the sand surrounding us. "What about my family? I can't leave them."

"There's enough for everyone."

"What about Mother?" He wipes a silent tear. "I can't leave her alone with the others. She needs me."

"Are there others like you?" I ask.

"What do you mean?"

I sigh, not sure how to ask what I'm asking. "Others that don't have to be chained in silver."

He nods. "Autumn and Everly. The rest are..."

"I know."

"I can't leave them there." He looks past me at the human man attempting to fight off the lycan holding him. "I don't want to go back," he whispers. "I want to go to the beach house."

"Okay," I agree. "We'll go to the beach house."

Behind us, Topher has the disgusting human man in a choke hold, leading him away from the crowd, while the rest of our group is in deep discussion about how to feed Patrice and her horde of immortal children. I take Alexander's hand into mine and lead him back to my friends. "I'm taking Alexander to the beach house."

I look into each of their eyes, begging them to

understand. Amelia smiles. "That's a great idea." She looks at our group. "I'll come with you."

"What about..." Fynn starts.

"We'll figure it out," she answers with a smile.

Minutes later, the three of us are standing in front of the stilted home. "It's lifted to protect the house from the hurricanes," Alexander says, staring up at the large house. "Is this where the games are?" he asks Amelia.

"It is. Would you like to come inside?"

He nods, moving up the stairs at vampire speed. Amelia gives me a look that I'm not sure how to interpret. We move behind him, opening the door, and the three of us enter the opulent home.

"This is nice," Alexander says, looking around the room. Thorne walks in behind us, startling the young boy. "Why is he here?"

"He's staying here with us. So are the lycan," I add.

"I don't like the lycan," Alexander hisses slightly as he speaks.

"No one here will harm you."

"I know," he answers, moving toward the television. "I've seen these before. How does it work?"

I push the button on the remote, filling the large screen with a game show. Alexander walks behind the TV with a puzzled look on his face. "Are they inside there?"

"No. It's been recorded."

He lifts his nose in the air. "The lycan are here."

"Alexander, how long have you been with Mother?" Amelia changes the subject.

He shrugs, running his hands along the television screen. "I was the first."

"How did Mother find you?" I ask.

He's so quiet, I decide he's not going to answer. "At the circus. I was lost." His words are soft.

"Did she hurt you?" Thorne joins our conversation.

"I don't want to talk about it," he answers, moving toward the kitchen. "What happens in here?"

"That's where the magic happens," Luna answers, coming inside the house. "We use that room to cook our food."

"Are we eating from you?" he asks.

Luna's eyes grow several sizes. "No. At least I hope not. That's where we cook for the lycan."

Alexander nods in understanding. "I don't need to be chained."

"No one is going to chain you up," Amelia says.

"He's thinking about chaining me in one of the bedrooms on the third floor." Alexander nods toward Topher.

"It's for our safety," Topher says softly. "I would never hurt you."

The immortal child stops moving and turns toward Topher. "You couldn't hurt me, even if you tried."

"No one is going to try," I interrupt. "We want to help you."

"My maker was like you. An immortal child," Amelia distracts him.

"Was?" he asks. "Did he kill her?" He nods toward Topher once more.

"No. He loves her. She's still alive, but no longer an immortal child."

Alexander fully turns his attention toward Amelia. "Tell me how."

"I will. I promise. But first, we have to stop Mother. She cannot take any more children."

"I know." He sighs. "We have to save my sisters."

"Autumn and Everly?" I ask, remembering the names he told me earlier.

"They're like me. The others aren't."

"What do you mean, the others aren't?" Thorne asks.

"They're killing machines." Alexander's words are far more mature than his body appears. "They can't survive on their own. Autumn and Everly can."

"We'll save them," I promise, receiving confused glances from everyone in the room.

"Mother will not let us go," Alexander says, straightening his coat for the tenth time.

"How do we get to them?" Micah asks.

"I have a plan." Alexander moves to the television, staring at *Wheel of Fortune*. "Pick a peck of peppers," he says, solving the puzzle with one letter exposed. He turns toward me. "I'll take some of that goat's blood now, Mommy."

TEN

what have i done?

ALEXANDER DRINKS two bottles of goat's blood before moving to one of the couches in the living area.

"Did you like the taste?" I ask, sitting next to him.

"It was...drinkable," he repeats my words from earlier.

No one in the house is speaking, no doubt terrified Alexander will hear. Not speaking aloud doesn't make any difference. He can hear our thoughts. I work on keeping my mind clear of thoughts that aren't about what's happening at the moment.

"Would you like to play a game?" Amelia asks.

Alexander turns toward me. "Would you care to hear my plan?"

Every head in the house turns in our direction. "I would."

"Please turn off the television. I find it distracting."

Alexander stands, moving away from the couch and me.

"Mother will have realized we're not coming back by now."

"Does that upset you?" Amelia asks.

"Not as much as it will upset her." He clasps his hands behind his back, standing perfectly still. "Mother doesn't think...rationally at times. She enjoys hurting others and my siblings."

"You don't?" Topher whispers.

"No. That's why I choose the ones that want to die or have done something bad to feed us."

"Like the man tonight?" Luna asks.

"Yes, like the man tonight." He looks at his feet. "When Mother took them, she crossed the line." The lycan share a look.

"The children from the restaurant?" I confirm.

He nods. "I suggested we take the old man who was having sexual thoughts about one of the princesses and several of the younger girls. She didn't listen. She wanted them."

"What happened to *them*?" Micah asks.

Alexander clears his throat. "They were disposed of."

Tears well in my eyes with his words. The thought of those terrified children and the last thing they saw before dying breaks my heart.

"My sisters and I refused to eat from them."

"Did Mother notice?" Amelia asks.

"She was angry. She tried to force us to eat." He looks at me. "That's why she sent me with you tonight. As punishment. I was supposed to kill you before returning home with our meal."

"Why didn't you?" she continues.

"Because Mother is wrong. The vampire children... they're not natural. *I'm* not natural."

"We found Gretchen," I say without thinking.

Alexander closes his eyes. "Gretchen needed to die." He looks at Amelia. "You killed her." His words are more of a statement, than a question.

"She didn't feel any pain."

"Thank you," he answers. His words surprise me. "She's not the only one who needs to die."

"What's your plan?" Fynn interrupts.

"We go back to the church and take her with us." He nods toward Luna.

"Me?" Luna asks.

"Mother will think she's our meal."

"Patrice will recognize that Luna's a lycan," Topher interrupts. "I will not put a member of my pack in danger."

"I won't let Mother have her," Alexander says. "I'm stronger than her."

"Are you stronger than the immortal children who you described as monsters?" Anger sounds through Topher's words.

"Most," he answers honestly. "Autumn and Everly will help."

"Look, little man," Fynn says, moving closer to the boy. "I realize you think you're all big and bad, but Patrice is an old vam..." Faster than the blink of an eye, Alexander has Fynn against the wall of the house with his teeth inches away from the lycanthrope's neck.

"And you are a six-foot-five-inch lycanthrope who a *child* just overtook," Alexander slowly pulls away from Fynn's neck. "I am stronger than her and most of my siblings. With your help." He turns toward me. "My sisters and I will be able to kill them all."

I stare at the immortal child, both in awe and terror. No wonder immortal children are against the rules. This kid is terrifying.

"I'm terrifying?" he asks. His voice loses the threatening tone.

Shit. Shit. Shit. "Your power is terrifying. I'm in awe of your abilities." I stare at the young vampire, hoping my words are adequate.

"Thank you, Mommy," he answers. "Mother never feeds the children the same day we receive the food. She likes to let them sit for a few days. She says the terror they feel makes their blood taste better."

"Sick bitch," Thorne mumbles.

"While we wait to eat, I'll talk to Autumn and Everly and fill them in on the plan."

"This is the plan?" Topher asks.

"While you leave me locked in a room, waiting to become...to become food for immortal children vampires, you're going to recruit your friends?" Luna asks.

"Yes," he answers simply.

"What if Patrice changes the plan and decides to feed me to her children tonight?"

"She won't. Mother likes to keep certain things the same. This is one rule she won't change."

"What's the plan after you get your sisters on board?" I ask.

Alexander smiles, and chill bumps cover my skin. "We will kill them all."

"This isn't a game, Alexander," Amelia scolds. Her boldness brings chill bumps to the surface.

"I'm not playing a game. There is simply no other way." He moves closer to Luna. "Are you ready, lycanthrope?" he asks Luna. "The longer we wait, the angrier she will become."

"How will you explain the fact that we're late? You said she will have already figured out we're not returning?" I slide away from the immortal child as I speak.

"Leave that to me." He turns toward Luna and repeats his words from earlier. "Are you ready?"

"I...I don't know if I want to be bait." Terror sounds through her voice. She turns toward the rest of the group. "I'm sorry."

"Don't apologize." Topher wraps his arm around her protectively.

"I'll go," Amelia interrupts. "I'm part lycan. My blood might fool her."

"It won't," Alexander answers plainly. "You smell like a vampire, not like her." He nods at Luna. "It has to be the girl."

"What if we get the man from the beach?" I ask, hoping to spare Luna from the terror.

"Why are you questioning my plan, Mommy?"

"I'm not. It's just that Luna is my friend. I don't want anything to happen to her."

He sighs. "They all can come, but they have to stay far enough away that Mother won't sense them."

Luna's eyes close. "Okay," she whispers.

"You don't have to do this," Topher repeats his words from earlier.

"I know." She wipes a stray tear.

"Will Mother be upset that you didn't follow her orders? You're supposed to kill me."

Alexander shrugs. "I'll simply explain that there wasn't an opportunity and that I will take care of it after we eat."

"How do we get there?" Luna asks.

"We run of course." Alexander smiles with his answer. "I'll carry you."

"Give us a head start," Topher interrupts. "It'll take longer to drive there."

"I understand," Alexander answers. "Will ten minutes be adequate?"

"Not really," Fynn answers honestly.

"I'll go with you and wait for the lycan at a

distance." Amelia stands, moving closer to her husband.

"Aye, me, too," Thorne agrees.

"That will be fine," Alexander agrees. I'm not sure who put him in charge, but no one is questioning his control.

"If something happens to any of them…" Topher doesn't finish his statement directed toward the immortal child. He follows Micah and Fynn to the awaiting SUV. They speed out of the driveway, heading toward the abandoned church.

We sit in silence, waiting for the second hand to move slowly on the clock. Exactly ten minutes later, Alexander moves toward the door. "Are you ready?"

"Is no, an acceptable answer?" Luna says, with an awkward laugh.

"You will be safe," he says, as Luna approaches.

"No offense, but you're half my size. Are you sure you can carry me?"

He lifts her and throws her over his shoulder like she weighs nothing. "Are we ready?"

"After you." I motion to the stairs, and the rest of us follow the boy down the stairs. Once we're on the road, we begin moving at vampire speed, heading toward the worst plan ever.

Several miles away from the church, Alexander stops in the middle of the tree-lined road. "This is as far as you can go," he warns Amelia and Thorne. "She'll sense you if you come any closer."

"Oh, dear God, I feel sick. Is this how you people move all the time?" Luna dry heaves from Alexander's shoulder. "Set me down, please." He follows her request, and Luna falls to the ground. She sits cross-legged on the grass, lowering her head to her ankles. "If the immortal children don't kill me, the mode of transportation will."

"We must go," he reminds everyone. "There is no time to waste."

Luna stands, wobbling slightly. "Okay. I'm ready."

Alexander pulls a piece of rope from his coat pocket, wrapping it around the lycanthrope's wrists, along with a piece of fabric, covering her eyes before picking her back up and moving quickly to the church. "She knows we're here," he announces. "Stay by my side. Act scared," he whispers to Luna.

"That won't be a stretch," Luna whispers back.

He opens the door to an empty room. "Where is everyone?" I ask.

"In their rooms." We move through the remnants of the sanctuary to the hallway door. Patrice is standing at the end of the hallway.

"What took so long?" she asks with her arms crossed over her chest.

"Hello, Mother. The one we found got away," Alexander answers. "We found this one in his place."

Patrice sniffs the air. "It's not a human."

"I know." He smiles.

"We thought you might enjoy the blood of a lycan-thrope," I answer for him.

Patrice smiles. "It's been ages since I've tasted lycan blood. Where did you find this one?" She moves closer.

"At the beach," he answers. "It took a while to catch her."

"She smells *wonderful*."

I can feel Luna's fear from here.

"You know where to put her." Patrice claps her hands. "She'll marinate well. I'll forgive you for your *indiscretion*, Alexander."

"Thank you, Mother." He opens a door to our right. The smell of rotting flesh and mold slaps me in the face. He begins moving down a set of stairs with Luna still thrown over his shoulder. *"Alexander!"* I scream through my mind. He stops, turning toward me. *"We can't leave her down here."* He nods and continues moving, ignoring my words. Damp soil makes up the floor of the basement. Four freshly dug mounds of dirt are in the back corner. No doubt, they hold the bodies of previous victims.

He moves to the corner on the opposite side, setting Luna on the only dry ground in the basement. *"She won't have to be here long,"* he speaks through my mind like it's something we've done all along.

"One minute is too long." Tears stream down Luna's cheeks, and I fight the urge to free her.

Alexander moves to a shelf, pulling out an antique lantern and lighting it. He sets it next to Luna and draws a line in the soil surrounding her. *"Take her blindfold off,"* he demands.

I follow directions and move in front of her. "Don't react," I whisper into her ear. She takes a deep breath and nods. Lifting the blindfold, I make sure she sees my face before anything else in the basement. I mouth the words in silence that I whispered seconds earlier. Her eyes close as tears drip from them. Slowly, I step away from my lycan friend, allowing her to see the horror of the space she's in.

Luna sucks in a breath, biting her lip to hold in her reaction. Alexander points at the hastily drawn line and then motions the room around her. I don't understand what he's trying to tell her, but Luna nods in understanding.

"What does this line mean?" I ask.

"She's safe if she stays inside." He holds a finger to his lips, warning Luna to stay quiet before he turns, moving to the stairs. I link my fingers through Luna's and squeeze before following him. Once the door is closed, Luna's silent whimpers pound through my mind. She's terrified. If anything happens to her, I'm responsible.

"If something happens to her, I will make sure everyone in this building is dead," I warn. *"Everyone."*

"I understand."

"Is our meal marinating?" Patrice asks, standing in the same spot as earlier.

"She is, Mother. Where are my sisters?"

Patrice looks down. "In their rooms, where you should be."

"*The lycan are here,*" Thorne says through our connection. "*Is Luna okay?*"

"*Physically, yes. Mentally, I don't know.*"

"*Amelia and I are closer than the lycan. We can be inside in less than a second.*" He pauses. "*I love you, acushla.*"

"*I love you, too.*"

"It's time to go into your room, Mommy," Alexander says.

"Yes, it is. Thank you, Alexander. I enjoyed hunting with you today."

The vampire boy turns, entering a door not far from the basement.

"He is such a sweet boy," Patrice says, moving into a room next to where she's standing.

"He is," I whisper before going to the room I spent several hours in earlier. The smell of sulfur slaps me in the face, reminding me of the never-ending connection between Kragen and the insanity of my life.

Sliding to the floor, my mind won't stop thinking of my friend, tied up in the basement. Did I just sacrifice her to a horde of immortal children? Is Alexander playing a game, tricking all of us? Holy shit, this is a nightmare.

"*Rest, Mommy. I'm not playing a game.*" Alexander's voice echoes through my mind. Now, my thoughts aren't even my own.

suppertime

THE BUILDING around me is silent. Not even the rustling of a mouse can be heard through the stillness. The thoughts of Luna, alone in the basement, are filling my every thought. I haven't heard from Alexander for a while and have lost track of the time. Silence can be deafening.

One skill I learned while on Kragen's ship was how to move in total silence. Vampires are intrinsically silent, but while there, I acquired the ability to be even more so. Pulling on the skills I learned, I stand, moving to the hallway door. I'm thankful for silent hinges as I move down the hall and in front of the door leading to the basement.

Moving down the stairs, I'm standing on the floor of the basement before Luna notices my movement. Her legs are curled to her chest, and she's staring into the emptiness of the room. I'm in front of her seconds later. Her eyes blink, holding back tears.

Sitting in front of her, I hold my finger in front of my lips, issuing a silent warning. She nods, understanding.

Taking her hands into mine, I lace our fingers together, hoping to offer comfort through our silent connection. The bright pink tips of her blonde hair look faded in the dim light of the lantern. I've never seen her look so weak. I move beside her, and she lays her head on my shoulder. It's not until soft movement resonates through the building that I move. I don't know what I'm hearing, but I need to return to my room before someone discovers I'm missing.

I squeeze her hand, and Luna raises her head. Silently, I work my way back up the stairs and into the hallway. Entering the room that's supposed to be my own, I open the door to find Mother.

"Patrice," I greet the woman with a fake smile.

"Where have you been?" she asks.

"I…I went to check on the lycanthrope," I admit. Instinct tells me not to lie.

"Why?"

"Her ties were loose last night. I wanted to make sure she wasn't able to shift."

"Why are you truly here?" she asks. Every part of me is on alert. I don't know where this conversation is going, and I'm not sure I want to find out.

"I told you. I've always wanted to be a mother."

She moves closer to me. "I smell that lycanthrope on you, *in* you. You drank from her."

Shit. She's right. Luna gave me her blood before I arrived. "I did. I only took a tiny amount. It's been weeks since I've eaten."

"There won't be enough for all the children now," she reprimands. "Part of being a mother is the willingness to sacrifice for the sake of your children."

"I apologize. My hunger overtook me. It won't happen again."

Patrice closes her eyes. "I'm going to allow you to plead ignorance this time. However, if you make another mistake, I will kill you." She moves toward the door. "You'll need to find more food to replace what you took." Less than a second passes before the woman is gone.

"Mommy? What did you do?" Alexander asks.

"Patrice thinks I drank from Luna."

"Did you?"

"She gave me some of her blood yesterday. Patrice smelled it." He doesn't respond. *"Patrice is demanding I get more food."*

The sun peeks through the cracks of the boarded-up windows, which means that Luna's been alone in the basement for over eight hours. I can't leave her down there while Patrice sends me out after more *food*.

"Good morning, Mommy," Alexander says, opening the door to my room. "I wanted to introduce you to my sisters."

He opens the door fully, revealing two small girls. One of them is the girl I met when I first entered the abandoned church. The other one I recognize from the large room.

"These are my sisters, Autumn and Everly."

"It's nice to meet you, Autumn and Everly."

The girl I met before steps forward. Her dress is perfectly creased and looks brand new. Dark brown curls hang to her shoulders, held together with a calico-flowered bow. She holds her hand toward me. "I'm Autumn." I shake her small hand. "I'm Elsie."

"Hello," the second girl greets me. She's wearing a pair of modern blue jeans and a *Hello Kitty* sweatshirt. Her ebony skin is flawless, along with large brown eyes and dark hair. She smiles, copying the movement of her sister and holding her hand toward me. "My name is Everly. It's nice to meet you as well."

"I've informed my sisters," Alexander says.

"*What about your mother?*" I ask through my mind.

"She's gone," he answers out loud. "She'll be back momentarily."

"Then we should go." I move toward the door. "You've got your sisters. Let's get Luna and leave."

"I'm afraid we can't allow that," Autumn interrupts.

"What do you mean?"

"My sister means, we can't allow you to leave with the food," Everly adds.

"*The food* is not staying here and will not be food." I focus my energy on the children.

"We're not going to eat her, silly," Autumn says with a giggle. "But if we take her now, Mother will know, and she will not let any of us leave."

"She will hunt us down," Everly adds.

"What are you suggesting?" I ask the evil trio.

"We have to kill her," Alexander answers for the group. "It's the only way."

I know what it's like to be hunted. "I will not leave my friend in the basement any longer."

"You have to," Autumn answers. "If Mother discovers she's missing, she'll figure out what we're doing."

"What the hell *are* we doing?" I ask.

"We're going to kill them all," Everly smiles with her words, making my stomach turn.

I look into each child's eyes. "Are you sure this is what you want to do?"

"Yes," Alexander answers simply, with no tone in his voice.

"What about your other siblings?"

"They're monsters," Autumn answers. "They're not capable of living in the world."

"And you are?" I ask.

They look at each other. "Yes." Autumn steps closer to me. "Alexander told us about the goat's blood. My sister and I are willing to try it."

What is the correct answer to this? I don't know that there is one. "I can help you," I tell them.

"How many are outside?" Everly asks.

"Two vampires and three lycan," I answer truthfully.

"Are they strong?" Autumn asks.

"Yes." I have no idea if they're strong enough to fight a horde of immortal children, but they're strong.

"Mother will be back momentarily," Alexander repeats. "Tell your friends to stay hidden until we give them notice."

"Alexander? What is the notice? What is the plan?"

"Mother's home." He smiles. "That was a funny joke, Mommy," Alexander laughs just as Patrice enters the hallway.

"Is Mommy telling jokes now?" she asks, rubbing her hand gently through Autumn's curls.

"She is," Autumn agrees. "It was about a chicken and a road." The three immortal children share another laugh.

"I've got more where those came from." I join the insanity.

"Mommy has jokes. I have food." Patrice sends a judgmental look in my direction.

"More food?" Everly asks. "You spoil us, Mother."

"It's in the meeting room. Do be a dear, Alexander, and go get it."

He bows his head slightly, leaving us alone in the hallway. Seconds later, he returns with a familiar figure thrown over his shoulder. Fynn's long arms and legs drag on the floor as he's carried by the child vampire.

"You found another one?" Autumn asks, sniffing the air.

Patrice looks at me. "This one was close by. Imagine my surprise when I found such a large specimen lounging a few miles away."

"It would make sense that she wasn't alone." I nod my head toward the basement door.

Fynn appears asleep, although I know it's much more than that. His heart is still beating, but his energy feels weak. I don't know what she did to him, and anger fills me thinking of the possibilities. "Put him with the girl," Patrice orders her tiny minions.

"Yes, Mother." Alexander opens the door, carrying the giant man to the basement below. Luna's sobs fill my ears the moment his body is thrown on the ground.

"When will you be feeding the children?" I ask the insane vampire in front of me.

"*We* will be feeding them. Isn't that what you wanted?"

I close my eyes. "Yes. That's what I want." I plaster a fake smile across my face, hoping she falls for it. "When will we be feeding the children?"

"Tonight," she answers.

"*Thorne,*" I call through our connection. "*What the hell happened? How did she get Fynn?*"

"*Topher and Micah were running reconnaissance around the area, while Fynn rested.*"

"*Dammit! She's going to feed the immortal children tonight.*"

"We can't allow that to happen," Thorne answers.

"The man is next to the woman," Alexander says through my mind, interrupting my communication with Thorne.

"We have to do this today."

"Okay," he answers like I'm announcing we're making a trip to the store later.

"Elsie?" Thorne's voice overpowers Alexander's. *"Tell us when. We'll be there."*

"If I didn't know better, I'd swear you were talking to someone," Patrice interrupts, drawing me back to the narrow hallway.

"I'm sorry. I have a tendency to zone out every once in a while," I lie.

"He's with the woman," Alexander says, as the three of them exit the basement door.

"Good. Gather your brothers and sisters, and begin preparing them to eat."

"You said we'd feed them tonight," I interrupt.

"Did I? I must have gotten my times mixed up." She claps her hands. "Get busy, children."

"Alexander?"

"I know, Mommy. My sisters and I will get the children ready to feed. Mother will ask you to help with the lycan. Bring them into the room, and we'll take it from there."

"What am I supposed to tell my friends?"

"Tell them to wait for the signal then come inside with guns blaring." He giggles at his words. *"I heard that on the television at the beach house."*

"Get the lycan ready for our meal," Patrice orders, before turning heel and leaving. I don't wait to be told twice. I'm standing in front of Fynn and Luna seconds later. Fynn is awake but weak. Tear stains cover Luna's cheeks.

I quickly loosen the ties around her wrists and pull her to a standing position. "I'm so sorry," I whisper.

"What the hell, Elsie?" Fynn whispers. "What did that bitch do to me?"

I move as close to Luna's ear as I can get, whispering the ridiculous plan. She nods. I do the same to Fynn. I give them a few minutes to understand before uttering words for Patrice only. "I'm taking you filthy dogs upstairs. Don't fight me, or you will die now."

Luna closes her eyes, fighting back more tears. Tying the rope back around Luna's wrists, I grab both of them, pushing them up the stairs.

"This is about to go down," I send to Thorne.

"We're ready. Topher and Micah are with us now."

I push the lycan into the hallway and toward the entrance of what was the sanctuary. The irony of the word doesn't slip past me. What's about to happen in there will be the total opposite of a sanctuary. I take a deep breath before opening the door and pushing the lycan through.

Spread throughout the room are the immortal children. All of them except three, Alexander, Autumn, and Everly are chained in silver. They begin hissing the moment we enter.

"Children, it looks like our food has arrived," Patrice says from the stage. The spectacle she's putting on makes me even more sick than before.

I push the lycan next to her, refusing to let them out of my grip.

Alexander moves to my side. "Mother, may I do the honors?"

Patrice smiles. "Of course, my love."

He turns toward the audience. "Bow your heads." The children obey his demand, bowing their heads. "Mother is good. Mother is great. Let us thank her for our food. Amen." The children erupt in roars. Alexander turns toward me. "Are you ready, Mommy?" I stare at the boy, not sure what's about to happen. Is he going to betray me or his family? Is this the signal? "Everly, Autumn, please stand with me."

The girls join their brother instantly, and the three of them hold hands, forming a tiny line of terror. They turn toward their siblings. *"This is the signal,"* he says through my mind, and the three of them transform into monsters.

"Now!" I scream to Thorne as all hell breaks loose.

blood and bubble baths

WHILE THE TRIO of death moves toward the rest of the immortal children, I move to my friends tied up on stage. Ripping their blindfolds and bindings loose, I help them to their feet. "If you two want to shift, now is the perfect time."

"My pleasure," Luna says, wiping her stained cheeks. Seconds later, she transforms into a beautiful blonde wolf, while Fynn transforms into a giant brown wolf.

"Don't hurt Alexander or the two girls helping him," I warn. "Everyone else is free game." The lycan nod, moving toward the fight in front of them. The three immortal children have already killed four of their siblings. They're working as a team and watching them is terrifying.

"My children!" Patrice screams from the back of the stage. "What have you done?"

The door to the church bursts open, revealing three more wolves and Thorne. *"Don't hurt Alexander or the girls helping him,"* I send to Thorne through our connection.

"You bitch!" Patrice says, moving in front of me. "This is all your doing." She jumps through the air, landing on the corner of the ceiling. "Stop them!"

"They can't live," I warn her. "Turning a child into a vampire is cruel and sadistic."

"They're my children, my babies," she cries from the rafters.

"Your children have to die," Amelia says, standing in the middle of the chaos shifted into human form.

"You!" Patrice sniffs the air. "You're the hybrid."

"In the flesh. Seems my reputation precedes me." She bows dramatically.

Patrice lands in front of Amelia, staring into her eyes. "I've heard of you."

"Then you should know that you aren't going to survive this." Amelia stands her ground as Patrice recesses to the rafters once more.

I look around the room at the carnage that remains. Blood is spattered throughout the room, covering what's left of the wooden pews. Alexander and his sisters are surrounding the last remaining immortal child who doesn't look any older than four or five. He's wearing a pair of pajamas with Bugs Bunny printed all over them. Silver chains are still tied around his wrists, but he's managed to pull his hands far enough apart that he's using the chains as a weapon for his benefit. The lycan are standing behind the vampire trio, allowing them to take the lead.

"Walter, we won't hurt you," Autumn says as they continue circling the young boy.

Walter growls in response. The sound sends chills down my spine. He swings his chain, striking Everly in the face. The silver from the metal burns into her skin, exposing her skull through the flesh.

"Walter. You're not being a very nice boy," she scolds, wiping her cheek with her hand. "That almost hurt."

The boy growls once more before swinging the chain again. This time, Alexander catches it in mid-air. "That's not nice, Walter. It's time to stop playing now."

Patrice takes advantage of the distraction and leaps to the trio's side. "Mother is very angry with you," she warns. "It's time to go." She grabs Alexander's wrist, forcing him to drop Walter's chain.

"We're not going with you, Mother," Autumn answers. "We're going to live with Mommy at the beach, watch television, and drink goat's blood."

Patrice looks at me with hatred in her eyes. Sensing what's about to happen, Amelia and Thorne flank either side of me, along with the three lycan. We stand as a team, awaiting whatever Patrice is about to deliver.

She releases Alexander and lands in front of me with her teeth bared and her face contorted. "You will die," she warns. "*You* murdered my children."

"Your children were nothing more than monsters," Amelia spews. "You murdered them the day you turned them into this."

"I saved them," she retorts. "Without me, they would have died."

"I wouldn't have died, Mother," Alexander is standing next to the woman who transformed him years ago. "I was at the circus with my family. You took me from them. *You* did this to me." His perfect clothes are covered in blood, along with his face and hair.

"I was on my way to school," Autumn joins. Her perfect curls are messy and caked with dark blood. "You forced me into your car. You gave me...you gave me to the men before you turned me. They're the ones who nearly killed me. Not my family."

"Me, too," Everly adds. "I was visiting the zoo with my grandmother. Something we did every summer. I was happy being human." She looks at the other two children. "*You* did this to us. You don't deserve to live."

"Enough!" Patrice shouts. "How dare you speak to me in that tone." She makes eye contact with all three of them. "You will be punished."

"No, Mother. *You* will be punished." Alexander transforms into the monster she made.

Patrice matches his energy, transforming into an equally terrifying creature. "Don't flatter yourself, Alexander. I made you. That means you cannot defeat me."

"He's an immortal child, Patrice," Amelia says. "That means he's stronger than you'll ever be."

In a flurry of movement, Patrice moves behind Everly and Autumn, sweeping them into her arms and jumping through the large stained-glass window behind the stage.

"No!" Alexander screams as she disappears with the girls in tow. Amelia wraps her arms around his chest, holding him in place before he runs after them. "Let me go!"

The lycan exit seconds after Patrice, following the psychopath vampire. "They'll find her," I reassure the immortal child vampire.

"No, they won't. She's faster than they are."

"I'll go," Thorne says, following the wolves through the window.

"My sisters," Alexander cries. "She'll kill them." He fights against Amelia, who's barely able to hold him.

"Alexander, stop! You won't be able to fight her alone."

"My sisters!" he continues.

I move in front of him, looking him in the eyes. "Alexander, look at me." His eyes are searching every area of the broken window, staring past me. "Look at me," I repeat, calmly. He slowly turns toward me, tears flowing down his cheeks.

"We'll find them," I whisper.

"Don't make a promise you can't keep, Elsie!" He pulls out of Amelia's grip, moving toward the window.

In a moment straight from a superhero movie, something overtakes my body. Emotion mixed with anger flows to the surface, and I move between Alexander and the window, reaching the spot before he does. Wrapping my arms around him, I pull him to the ground with ease and hold his hands above his head.

"Let me go!" he screams, not able to move against my grip.

"No," I repeat my words from earlier. "I will not let her kill you."

The moment the fight leaves from his eyes, his face returns to the innocent boy from before, and he cries the kind of cry that's reserved for pillows. He cries years' worth of tears, screaming in anger, hurt, and pain.

Watching his pain breaks something deep inside me. I release my hold, pull him to my chest, and wrap my arms around him. "I'm sorry this happened to you, Alexander." Instinct kicks in, and I begin rocking him like I would do my siblings when they were hurt or scared.

Amelia stands guard as I hold him like the child he is. I don't know how much time passes before his sobs begin to soften and his body relaxes in my arms. I gently rub my hands through his hair, offering the love he never received from Patrice.

"The lycan are returning, and I'm continuing to follow her." Thorne pauses. *"If you can hear me, Alexander, I won't let them out of sight."*

Alexander sits up, wiping his tear-stained face. "Does he mean it?"

I nod. "Thorne followed me for three hundred years. He will do everything he can not to lose them."

On cue, the lycan walk through the broken glass. "Topher says they weren't able to keep up with her without being seen by humans. Thorne is still following her," Amelia translates their silent conversation.

Alexander stands and straightens his suit. He bows to the lycan. "Thank you for trying." He runs his fingers through his hair and clears his throat. "I'm ready to go home, Elsie." I don't know when the change came from him calling me Mommy to calling me by my name, but I'm not angry about it.

"I'll come with you," Amelia says, moving to our side. Without explanation, I know she's coming in case Alexander decides to lose his shit. "The lycan will stay behind and clean up." She looks around the room at the destruction. "These poor..." she stops her words, looking at the immortal child next to me. "I'm so sorry, Alexander."

"Thank you," he whispers. "They're better off now." His words sound much wiser than he appears.

The three of us exit the building, running toward the beach house. We arrive minutes later at the empty home. Alexander moves straight to the television, turning it on and allowing the ambient light to fill the room. He sits on the edge of the couch, staring mindlessly at the screen.

"I asked Topher to stop and grab some clothes for him on their way back," Amelia says, standing next to me in the kitchen. The two of us are staring at the immortal child, not sure what to do or how to help him.

"Elsie?" I look up at my name. "May I have some goat's blood?"

"Of course." I grab one from the cooler and take it to him. "Would you like to clean up a little?"

He empties the bottle in one gulp. "I'd like that very much." He turns toward Amelia. "When will the Alpha be here with my clothes?"

I share a look with Amelia. "They'll be at the church for a while," she answers. "I'm sure we can find something around here for you to wear until your clothes arrive."

Alexander stands. "That will be fine." He turns toward me. "Will you help me, Elsie?"

"Yes." I follow him upstairs, directing him to mine and Thorne's bedroom. "There's a shower and supplies inside."

"I'd rather take a bath."

"Ok. Let me get your water going." Moving into the bathroom, I set the water to the perfect temperature, not that it matters for a vampire, but it's something I need to do. The sister in me wants to provide this boy the love he's missed.

Alexander walks into the bathroom. "Will you stay with me?"

His behavior feels *off,* but taking into account that he just murdered his siblings and watched his mother take his sisters, he has the right to be a little *off.* "I'll come back in once you're in the water."

"Thank you." He nods. "Are there bubbles?"

"I'll find some." I leave the boy in the bathroom, moving through several bathrooms on the same floor and finding bubbles not far away.

"I'm in," he says through my mind seconds later.

"I found bubbles," I announce, coming back into the room. Pouring the bubbles into the running water, the tub fills with white foam almost instantly.

Alexander's tiny body is covered in scars. Some look like bite marks. Others look like burns. I close my eyes at the realization that in order for these to remain scars, they were inflicted before he was turned.

"Mother did them," he answers my unasked question after reading my mind. "After she took me, she used me to entertain humans. Some of them liked to bite."

"Oh, Alexander. I'm so sorry," I apologize, fighting the tears from forming in my eyes.

"Why? It's not your fault."

"No, it's not my fault, but I'm sorry for the pain she put you through." I pull the hem of my shirt up, exposing my stomach. "Do you see this?" I point at a long scar on my abdomen. He nods. "The man who took me did it. He stabbed me because he was angry that I was starving." I take a breath, hoping not to fall too deeply into a memory. "He let me bleed for hours."

Alexander looks into my eyes. "Why did he take you?"

"I don't know," I answer truthfully. "We have several theories, but mostly I think he took me because he could."

"Is he still alive?"

"Aye."

"Are you from Scotland?" he asks, noticing my brogue.

"I was. A very long time ago."

"Thank you, Elsie."

"For what?"

He wraps thin arms around his legs. "For being kind to me. It's been a long time since someone has been kind to me."

I've never related to someone more in my life. "You deserve kindness, Alexander. You realize that, don't you?"

"I don't know," he whispers. "I've done…"

"No," I interrupt. "Today is a new day. What you did, you did to survive. You didn't have a choice. That was the person you were. You're not that person anymore, Alex."

He looks up at the shortened version of his name. "My mother used to call me that."

"Would you prefer me to call you Alexander?"

He shakes his head. "My real mother called me Alex."

"You remember her?"

"I do." He wipes a tear. "She was beautiful."

"Where did you live?"

"Chicago," he answers. "I'd like to visit their graves one day." His voice is barely audible.

"When you're ready, we'll go," I promise. "For now, let's get you cleaned up. Maybe one of my T-shirts won't swallow you completely."

"You smell like the lady," Alex says, blowing bubbles off his hand. Chill bumps immediately cover my skin.

"What do you mean?"

The small boy shrugs. "Like fire, I guess."

I slide closer to the edge of the bathtub. "Alex, what did the lady look like?"

Deep blue eyes turn in my direction. "She had hair like yours. I only saw her once, and from very far away. Mother kept my sisters and me away from her. She didn't want her to know we were special."

My mind is a whirlwind of emotion. Dark hair and smelled like fire doesn't exactly narrow down the search. "Was her name Marnie?"

"I don't know. I never heard her name." He sinks below the water, adding a soft pink color to the bubbles. My mind races as my heart aches for this child. His intelligence and ability are the only things sepa-

rating him from the children in chains. I build an imagi-
nary wall around my thoughts and play through the
nightmare he's lived. Watching him blow bubbles
toward the tile wall, I silently vow to protect him with
my life.

back to the crescent city

THE THREE OF us sit in the living area of the beach house, mindlessly staring at the television. Alex has been next to me since getting out of the tub and sliding into an oversized T-shirt. I've kept my thoughts guarded, and I suspect Amelia is doing the same.

The sound of a car pulling under the house draws our attention. Alex sits up quickly. "They're back." He races out the front door, meeting them on the stairwell with Amelia and me behind him. "Did you find them?" he asks the lycan.

"No," Topher answers for the group. The four of them are filthy, wearing rags for clothes, and covered in blood. "I'm sorry, bud."

"The captain?" he asks, turning toward me. "I know you're shielding your thoughts. Have you heard from him?"

"No," I answer truthfully. "You'll be the first to know when I do."

Amelia wraps her arms around Topher, leading us back into the house. "Luna?" I question the young lycanthrope as she passes by. She turns, ignores me, and moves upstairs.

"She's angry," Alex states the obvious. "She feels like you abandoned her at the church." I watch her ascend the stairs without acknowledging the boy's words.

"I'm sorry, Luna." Tears fill my eyes. In the three hundred years I've been on the planet, Luna is the closest thing to a friend I've ever had. She continues to her room without responding. Her blonde hair is caked in dark blood, and her face is swollen and bruised. God, I'm a horrible friend.

"You didn't have a choice, Elsie," Alex interrupts, reading my thoughts again. My shield slipped while thinking about Luna.

"Alex. You're going to have to stop doing that."

"Doing what?" he asks.

"Reading people's thoughts. It's an amazing gift, and you have an amazing talent. But you can't go around invading other people's minds."

He looks down at my words. "I didn't realize I was invading. My apologies."

"Don't apologize," Amelia answers. "It's what helped you survive this long. But you don't need to fight to stay alive any longer. We will protect you."

Alex's face changes from the stoic creature he became when he apologized, to that of a child. "I don't know how to turn it off."

"We'll help you figure it out." Wrapping an arm around his shoulders, I pull him closer. To my surprise, he doesn't pull away.

Topher drops a plastic bag on the table. "I bought some clothes. I hope they fit."

Alex stands, taking the bag into his hands. "Thank you, Alpha."

"You can call me Topher." He ruffles the boy's hair as Alex passes on his way upstairs. Once he's safely inside a bedroom, the lycan speak for the first time.

"We took care of everything at the church," Micah says. His eyes look tired, and the pair of shorts he's wearing are two sizes too small showing every detail.

"What about the bodies?" Amelia asks.

"Most disintegrated," Fynn answers.

"We couldn't do anything with the broken glass, but we cleaned up any clue of what was there." Topher wraps his arm around his wife's shoulders. "What's going to happen with him?" He nods toward the stairs.

"He's staying," I interrupt, suddenly feeling protective.

"No one is trying to get rid of him," Amelia interrupts. "We need to figure out how to help him."

"Elsie?" Thorne rings through my mind.

"Are you okay?" I ask, sounding more like his mom than a lover.

"Aye. Still following Patrice. She stopped to feed." Even through my mind, exhaustion sounds through his voice.

Alex is by my side in an instant. *"Are my sisters alive?"* he asks Thorne.

"Yes. She's forcing them to feed from a man she found in an alley."

"Elsie, what's happening?" Amelia asks.

"It's Thorne. He's still following her."

"Does he know where she's going?" Topher asks.

"Can you tell where she's heading?" I ask, following orders.

"West," he answers. *"She's about to move again. I'll keep in touch."* He goes silent.

"Thorne?" I call through my mind. He doesn't answer.

"What did he say?" Luna asks from the top of the stairs. Her hair is wet, and she's changed into sweatpants and a sweatshirt.

"They're heading west. The only reason he was able to contact me was because she stopped to feed."

Topher pulls a phone out of somewhere on his body and begins calling numbers.

"My sisters?" Alex asks.

"I don't know," I tell him the truth. "Patrice doesn't seem like a thinker. My guess is she's flying by the seat of her pants." I soften my words for the child in front of me.

"There are thousands of places she could be heading," Fynn adds. "West doesn't give us much to go on."

Minutes later, Topher's back in the room. "I called in a favor. When the body or bodies of her meal are discovered, we'll be the first to know. That should give us an idea of where she's heading."

"She's going to replace the children we killed." Alex's words are barely louder than a whisper. "She'll use Autumn to find them."

"What about Everly?" Amelia asks.

"Autumn is older, and she's...special."

"Is she like you?" I ask.

He shakes his tiny head. "No. She's different."

"How is she special, Alexander?" Topher asks.

He looks up at the giant Alpha. "I'm Alex now." He turns toward me. "Autumn can move things."

"Explain what you mean."

"She can make things move by thinking about it," he answers, looking around the room.

"Alex?" Amelia draws his attention. "Does Patrice like to collect special children? Children like you and Autumn?"

He nods. "Yes. My sisters and I are special. Everly hasn't discovered her gift yet, but she's special, too."

"What about the ones that were chained?"

"They weren't special," he answers simply. Sadness fills his voice.

"Alex, you've been with her a while. Where will she go to recruit more children?" Micah asks.

Alex shrugs. "She likes big cities or places where there are a lot of tourists." Topher turns, answering his ringing phone. "She wants a large family."

"Do you think she'll start recruiting soon?" Luna asks, joining the conversation.

"Not until she settles. She likes to have a place to bring them when she...when she turns them."

"The bodies of two men were just discovered outside a casino in Biloxi. Both had bite marks and were drained of blood." Topher slides his phone into the torn pocket of his shorts.

"That has to be her," I announce the obvious.

"When do we leave?" Alex asks, looking around the room.

"We can't just take off and hope that we'll find her," Topher interrupts.

"She's going to New Orleans," Amelia answers.

"What makes you think that?" Micah and Luna ask in unison.

"Because it's New Orleans. Where else could an insane vampire raise a horde of immortal children without being noticed?"

"Oh, I don't know. Anywhere else?" Topher looks tired as he wipes his face. "Why is it always my town?"

"We leave tonight. Thorne is bound to be exhausted. We need to head her off." I move to the stairwell, ready to pack our small bags.

"I can have the plane ready in an hour." Amelia

turns to our hosting lycanthrope. "Can you take us to the airport?"

"Of course," Fynn answers. "I wish I could join you, but my duties are here right now."

"Can I come with you?" Alex's soft voice asks from the middle of the living area. I turn, seeing large tears forming in his eyes.

"Alex, there's no way I would leave you here. Why don't you change into the clothes Topher brought and then come help me pack?" I smile, hoping to offer him reassurance. He nods, grabbing the plastic bag from the table.

"What if he...?" Luna's eyes open wide, asking the question she doesn't want to finish.

"He won't. I'll watch him." I look each of the team in the eyes. "I'll take responsibility for him."

"Elsie, he's a loaded stick of dynamite," Micah says. "We don't know when he'll..."

"When he'll do what?" Alex asks, standing in front of us, wearing his new clothes. His eyes have lost their color, turning into the familiar blackness that his monster form takes.

"Sorry, little man. I've seen what you can do." Micah shifts from foot to foot.

Alex stalks toward the lycanthrope. "I did what I had to do. I'm sure you've done the same." He moves closer to Micah, the top of Alex's head barely reaching his stomach. "My sisters are my priority. If you won't help me, I'll go after them alone." His teeth escape his mouth, and he hisses. "I will not attack any of you unless given no other choice." He looks around the room. "I know what I'm capable of."

"Alex," I call. He ignores my words. "Alexander?" He slowly turns his head toward me. "We all know what you're capable of. No one is going to hurt you, and we're not letting you go after them alone."

His teeth disappear, and his eyes regain their blue hue. "Thank you," he whispers. He moves to my side, lacing his fingers through mine. "Hurry, Elsie." This child is terrifying.

With his words, the team starts moving quickly, gathering up every belonging and evidence of our tenancy. Ten minutes later, we're all standing at the door, ready for whatever lies ahead.

"I'm ready to see Edon," Amelia whispers to Topher once we're piled inside the SUV.

"Who's Edon?" Alex asks from my side.

"Our son," Amelia answers.

"Hybrids can have children?" Alex's words aren't a question.

She laughs. "I was just as surprised as you are, kid."

"That's amazing," he whispers.

"I know," Amelia answers.

Thirty minutes later, we board the jet bound for New Orleans. "This is the first time I've been on a plane," Alex says, rubbing his hands across the leather. "Are they all this pretty?"

Micah laughs deeply. "No. Most smell like a mixture of vomit and feet. This one belongs to Amelia."

Alex turns to the hybrid once more. "You're interesting."

She laughs. "You have no idea."

The minute we're off the ground, Topher and Micah fall asleep, while Luna hasn't said more than ten words since leaving the beach house. Her eyes have lost their sparkle, and sadness covers her face.

"I'm going to go talk to Luna," I whisper for Alex's ears alone. He nods as I stand, moving to the seat across from her. "Hey." She wipes a tear before turning her face away from me. "I'm so sorry. I know an apology isn't going to change anything."

"You're right. An apology doesn't change anything."

"I know what it's like to be left alone."

"How could you?" Luna raises her voice. "Do you know what it's like to be locked in a room where people died?"

"Yes," I whisper. "When Kragen took me, I was locked in the bottom of the ship for over a century. I was surrounded by death for most of those years." I take a deep breath. "I'm not trying to negate your anger and hurt. You have every reason to feel that way. I just wanted to let you know how sorry I am you had to go through it." My words feel more profound than intended.

Luna looks at me with tears streaming down her cheeks. "I'm sorry, Elsie. I didn't mean..."

"I know," I interrupt. "I'm so sorry I couldn't stay longer with you."

She wipes more tears. "I know." She laughs awkwardly. "Hell, it wasn't even a full day. I don't know why I'm being such a baby about it."

"You're not being a baby. You're allowed to feel what you need to." When did I turn into a therapist?

"Acushla?" Thorne's voice is weak.

"Thorne? We're on our way to you." I stand, grabbing Amelia's attention.

"I'm tired. I need to eat. I...I can't keep up much longer. Dammit, I should've eaten today."

"Eat, my love."

"I can't..." His voice is full of sadness. *"I've never drank from a human. I don't know if I can."*

"Thorne?" Luna asks.

"He's not sure he can keep going," Alex answers for me. "He doesn't want to drink from a human."

Tears run down my cheeks, knowing the pain my words are going to bring. *"You're going to have to take a life."*

"Elsie...I can't." His voice trails off.

"Thorne?" He doesn't answer. *"Thorne?"* I stand, moving to the front of the plane and the door.

"No!" Amelia yells as I grip the handle. "You'll kill the lycan if you open it. We're almost to New Orleans."

"How the hell am I going to find him?"

"We'll find him," Alex answers. "I'll help."

three vampires walk into a bar...

FIFTEEN MINUTES LATER, we're on the ground in New Orleans. "Go. We'll work on finding Patrice," Amelia says while we're still taxiing.

"Alex, are you sure you want to come?" I ask.

He doesn't answer. Instead, he laces his fingers through mine as I open the door of the jet. I have no idea how fast we're moving as Alex and I jump. I prepare for a hard landing, when Alex sweeps his arms around me, pulling me to him. We make a soft landing on the runway, while the plane keeps moving.

"How'd you do that?" I ask my tiny friend.

Alex shrugs. "I don't know. I can't fly high, but sometimes I can do stuff like that."

"You're pretty amazing." I ruffle his hair with my hand.

"Thank you, Elsie." He turns a full three-sixty on the tarmac. "There is a lot of energy around here."

"Welcome to New Orleans, kid." Together we run out of the airport, moving faster than human eyes can track.

"Where do you think he'll be?" he asks, as we move to the outskirts of town.

"Thorne?" I call again through our connection, as I've done a hundred times since his last words.

"He's not going to answer," Alex says, sounding older than he appears. "He's exhausted."

"I don't know how to find him." I stop moving. "I need some sort of paranormal tracker."

"I might be able to find him."

"How?"

Alex shrugs. "I can hear their minds." He nods at the large crowds of people passing by.

"I appreciate the offer, but we don't even know if he's in New Orleans. He may still be between here and Alabama."

He smiles. "I mean I can hear further than the people right here. Sometimes I can feel people, too." The look on his face makes me feel like I should already know this.

"Explain."

Alex turns, looking around the street. "Up there." He points at the top floor of a parking garage. He grabs my hand, pulling me to the top before climbing on the railing.

"What are you doing?"

"Just be patient, please." He lifts his arms to the side

and closes his eyes. He stands in silence for several minutes before jumping down. "He's not on that side." He moves to the opposite corner of the garage, copying his movements from before. "I can feel him."

"Where?"

"That way." He points east. "His energy feels weak, like we expected, but he's there."

"Can we get to him?"

"As long as his energy stays constant, I can follow it to find him. I'll need to stop a few times to feel for him, but it should be easy."

I pull him into my arms. "Thank you, Alex." He smiles, grabs my hand, and starts running east.

I've lost track of time as we continue moving in the direction Alex sensed. The fact I'm being led into oblivion by an immortal child vampire who just a few hours earlier was living with a sadistic killer has stayed in the back of mind since leaving the city. Following him out here probably wasn't the smartest decision I've ever made, but we're here now. Either way, I keep my thoughts guarded.

Because of the marshy conditions, we're forced to stay on the main roads, stopping every few minutes to let Alex hone in on Thorne's energy. He's continued leading me east, each time saying the energy feels stronger than before.

"He's that way," Alex announces, pointing into the middle of what looks like a swamp.

"In the water?"

"Yeah."

"Can you swim?" I ask the small boy.

"I don't know. I've never tried." Alex smiles and jumps over the bridge railing, leaving me standing on the side of a busy interstate.

"Alex!" I follow him into the murky water below.

"He's that way," he points and starts swimming like a member of the Olympic swim team. We move through the water like a well-oiled machine, until finally reaching solid ground. "It's getting stronger."

We continue moving at superspeed, only stopping after reaching a small town nestled deep in the marsh. Alex slows down, and I follow his lead. His movement reminds me of a hound dog on a hunt.

My heart jumps into my chest the moment I feel him. *"Thorne?"* I call. "Alex, he's here. I feel him."

"Call him again."

"Thorne, I'm here. Where are you?"

"Elsie," his voice whispers through my mind. I rush toward the energy with Alex on my heels. The feeling leads us to the stilted remains of what looks like an old bait store. *"I'm here."*

We run underneath the building to the edge of the water. Crumpled on the ground is the shell of the man who is usually larger than life. "Thorne!" I yell, falling to his side.

"He needs blood," Alex states the obvious. "The combination of running and no food was more than his body can handle." I look around, not feeling anything nearby. "There's a woman over there," Alex points at a small building with a single light on.

"No," Thorne whispers. "I won't take a life."

"You don't have to drain her." Alex heads across the street to the door of the building. He knocks on the door, and an older woman opens it.

"Hello, little one." She looks behind him, no doubt searching for his adult. "Are you alone?"

"We need your help!" he exclaims. "My dad, he... he's diabetic and needs something to eat." Damn, he's good.

"Oh, baby. Let me get some orange juice. That always helps me." The woman disappears and comes back carrying a bottle of orange liquid. "Where is he?"

"Hide," he whispers for my ears only. I follow directions, slipping behind a pillar of the building. "Over here," he says, running in slow motion back to Thorne's side.

"Oh, he's bad." The woman says, opening the bottle.

I step out of my hiding spot and in front of the woman. "We need your help."

"Where'd you come from?" She tries to hand me the bottle of OJ.

Placing my hands on hers, I pull her closer to me. Her eyes dilate as she looks into mine. "We need your blood."

"You need my blood," she repeats.

"We will only take what we need and no more."

"You'll only take what you need and no more."

The woman kneels, moving in front of Thorne. "Elsie, I can't."

"Yes, you can and will." I gently take the woman's arm, putting it in front of Thorne's mouth. "I'll make sure you don't take too much."

I lick her wrist, numbing it before biting into the vein. The smell of blood makes Thorne sit straighter. I place her wrist to his lips, and he latches on. Soft gulps turn more fierce in seconds as he drinks human blood for the first time.

"Elsie," Alex warns. The woman's heartbeat is slowing down, meaning he has to stop.

"That's enough," I say, pulling the woman's arm away from the hungry vampire. "Alex, take her back to her home, please." He follows directions, leading the woman away slowly.

Thorne wipes tears from his cheeks. "I didn't want to do that."

"You didn't have a choice."

"Is she...?"

"She's fine," I answer his unasked question.

"I couldn't keep up with them."

"You did everything you could."

"I should've eaten. Then I'd have been stronger." He moves to stand.

"Everyone is in New Orleans. Alex was able to sense you and brought me here." I wrap an arm around his chest, pulling him close. "You'll feel better soon."

"We're calling him Alex now?" Thorne laughs softly.

"He said it's what his mother called him. He's a good kid, I think." I smile with my words.

On cue, Alex appears from nowhere. "I helped her get into bed and made sure she had a snack and a glass of juice."

"Thank you," Thorne says. "Elsie tells me you helped find me."

Alex smiles. "I did."

"I'm feeling better. I hate to admit how good her blood tasted."

"You'll be able to go back on goat's blood," Alex offers support like he's an expert.

"They're in New Orleans?" Thorne repeats my words from earlier.

"Aye. We think Patrice might have taken the girls there."

"That would make sense. There are not many places out here to take them with enough food supply." Thorne holds his hand toward Alex, who stares at him confused. "Thank you, Alex."

"You're welcome, Captain." Alex shakes Thorne's hand with a smile. "Do you think you can run?"

"Aye. I feel back to normal, better than normal to be honest." Instead of swimming, the three of us head toward the city, using the back roads, and keeping close to the marshy land. It's not until the lights of the city come into view that we stop to figure out what the hell we're doing.

"Everyone okay?" Thorne asks.

"I'm good," Alex answers first. "Where are we going when we get to the city?"

"That's an excellent question. I don't know where everyone went." I look between the two vampires, noticing their size difference. The top of Alex's head is barely even with Thorne's waist.

"I'd imagine they'll be at the lycan headquarters. That's where I found Topher before." Thorne's words remind me of Luna's babysitting job when I first met her.

"I've never been to New Orleans." A huge smile covers Alex's face as he speaks. "I've read a lot about the city, though. Did you know it's the official birthplace of jazz?"

I huff a laugh. "I'm sure it's everything you've imagined it to be."

We continue running until reaching the French Quarter. I visited New Orleans a few times throughout the years, usually not staying longer than a few days at a time, afraid Kragen would find me if I stayed longer. Entering the French Quarter, the amount of otherworldly energy that hits me in the gut is stronger than I remember.

"Do you feel that?" Alex asks. "Does it always feel like this?"

"Aye. We should keep moving," Thorne answers.

Thorne laces his fingers through one hand, while Alex grabs hold of my other. Together, we appear to be an ordinary family, touring the city of New Orleans. The innocent humans passing by have no idea of the danger we represent.

It doesn't take long before we're standing in front of one of the countless bars in the city. "Is this it?" Alex asks the question I'm thinking.

"Aye. The lycan headquarters. This has been their location for decades." He opens the door, holding it for the two of us. As soon as we walk in, the energy of the room changes, and all eyes turn toward us. The humans in the room are still drinking their beers and continuing their conversations, oblivious to the energy shift around them.

A large man behind the bar stops wiping the glass he's holding and glares at the three of us. "We don't allow kids inside."

"It's a good thing I only look like a kid, then." Alex stares up at the large lycanthrope.

"We're here to see Christopher," Thorne interrupts the tension.

"Wait here," the man sets down the half-clean glass and disappears into an office off the main room.

"He's sweet," I whisper.

Seconds later, Topher bursts through the door with Micah and Luna on his heels. Luna passes the large lycanthrope and reaches us first. She throws her small arms around me, pulling me close. "Oh, thank God. I was so worried."

I pull out of her embrace. "Luna, I'm sor…"

"Stop," she interrupts. "You don't owe me an apology. I knew what I was getting into when I agreed to do it. Sort of…"

"Come into the office," Topher motions toward the door they burst through moments before. All of us pile into the small room as Topher slides behind a heavy desk against a set of bookshelves. "I've got several of my strongest lycan searching for any signs that Patrice is here. Amelia has asked a few of the local vampires to help out as well."

On cue, Erick, the man I met during our last visit to New Orleans, steps into the room, followed by a tall vampire with dark hair.

"There you are, love," Erick says, lifting my hand to his lips. "This is Phillipe. He has agreed to help us find the woman and children."

"Thank you both." I pull my hand away from Erick.

Phillipe's eyes land on Alex. "Is this one of the children?"

I move protectively between him and the immortal child. Alex steps to the side, holding his hand in front of the large vampire. "My name is Alex. I was taken by Patrice in 1920 and turned into a vampire. I was the first of her children and helped her find the rest. I was forced to live with her and do her bidding until Elsie found me." I'm not sure where Alex's verbal diarrhea comes from. He stares at Phillipe a moment before continuing. "I can reassure you, sir, I am no freak. I am in control of my abilities and have never *eaten* anyone."

"How?" Phillipe stares at the immortal child.

Instead of answering, Alex looks around the room. "Who is Celeste?"

"This child reads minds?" Erick asks, knowing the answer. I'm not sure how much information to share with the two men I barely know. I open my mouth to speak, but Alex beats me to it. "Yes, this child reads minds. It's why I'm still alive, and it's why I've never eaten anyone." He glares at Phillipe as he speaks.

"Apologies, young one. You're only the second immortal child I've had the pleasure of meeting. You are quite remarkable." Phillipe bows slightly with his words.

"Thank you." Alex smiles, accepting his answer. He turns back toward me. "Who is Celeste?" he repeats.

"Celeste was Amelia's maker," Topher answers for the group.

"Her maker was like me? A child?"

"Yes," he answers simply. "It's not my story to tell. She's with our son at the moment, but I'm sure she'd be happy to tell you everything when she can."

Alex smiles. "Can I meet Celeste?"

"We might be able to arrange that." Topher turns to the new vampires in the room. "Have you heard rumors of Patrice or the children being in the city?"

"No," Phillipe answers. "However, your phone

message stated that she would've arrived only hours ago. We will be on the lookout."

"I have news of the other situation we discussed." Erick lays a piece of paper on Topher's desk.

"An address?" Topher picks up the paper.

"The last whereabouts of your pirate."

"A pirate?" Alex asks. "There are pirates in New Orleans?"

fran

THORNE, Alex, and I are covered in dirt and mud, and even though I hate to admit it, I'm starving. Running to find Thorne and back to New Orleans has used most of my energy. Topher has us loaded into a different vehicle and is driving across the Quarter to a home that belongs to Amelia. None of us have spoken since we started driving.

The overload of information floating through my brain is almost more than I can keep straight. I have no doubt Alex has heard every bit of it, as I don't have enough energy to hide my thoughts right now.

Topher stops in front of a large home that is the picture-perfect example of New Orleans architecture. Wrought iron gates, adorned with Fleur de Lis, surround the three-story home. The yard looks like a full-time gardener lives here with rose bushes of every color lined next to the fencing. "This is beautiful," I interrupt the silence.

"It's always been one of my favorites." He turns to the back seat. "There's someone inside that Amelia and I want you to meet." God, I don't want to meet anyone. I just want a hot shower and a meal.

"That sounds great," I lie. Alex looks at me as I speak. *"Sometimes you have to pretend,"* I send him a message. He nods and smirks.

Topher leads us into the elaborate mansion, stopping in the foyer. "We're here!" he yells into the house.

Seconds later, an older woman is standing in front of us. She's wearing a vintage dress, and her white hair is perfectly styled and piled on top of her head. Vampire energy flows from her as she turns toward Alex. "Hello, little one. My name is Fran."

Alex holds his hand out to her. "It's a pleasure to meet you, Fran. My name is Alex."

She shakes his hand. "Would you care for something to eat, Alex?"

His eyes open wide. "Yes, please." He turns toward me. "Do you have anything for Elsie and Thorne?"

"I do." She turns toward the two of us. "It's a pleasure to meet you both." She motions to several soft-looking seats in the living area. "Please, have a seat. I'll grab you some blood."

Thorne and I follow Alex into the exquisitely decorated living room. The three of us sit on the sofa, with me sandwiched in the middle, while

Topher heads into a room on the other side of the foyer. Fran returns minutes later with three bottles of bright red liquid. My stomach growls at the sight.

"There's plenty more where that came from. Don't be shy." Fran sits in a matching chair across from us. "Amelia's told me about you." I smile, not sure what to say. She turns her attention to Alex. "You're quite remarkable, young man. I can sense your abilities and strength."

"Is that good?" Alex asks.

"Fran was Celeste's nanny," Topher interrupts, coming back into the room.

"The immortal child, Celeste?" Alex slides forward on the couch, suddenly more interested in the conversation. "The one like me?"

"For many centuries," Fran answers. "I love her like she's my own."

"Where is she?"

"She's living in Mississippi with the love of her life." Fran laces her fingers together as she speaks. Her body language tells me she misses the girl.

"Is she with another immortal child?"

Fran scoffs. "No. She's with the Alpha lycanthrope of North Mississippi, and she's no longer a child."

"How is that possible?" he asks.

"Witchcraft. It came at a great cost for both her and her father." She sighs before turning toward Thorne. "Viktor was your maker."

"Aye. He was a great man. I respected him very much. I'm confused how we never met."

The older vampire smiles. "My job was to care for Celeste. His job was to protect her with his life in business and in love."

"I learned a great deal from him," Thorne answers.

"He was full of information." She huffs a laugh at her words.

"Can I do that?" Alex's words are no louder than a whisper. "Can I use witchcraft to grow?"

Fran and Topher share a look. "That's a conversation for another day," Topher answers.

Surprisingly, Alex doesn't argue. "Topher says I might be able to meet her, to meet Celeste."

Fran smiles. "I don't see why not. I can put in a good word for you."

"Fran is more than just a nanny. She's somewhat of a technological genius." Topher nods his head toward the elderly vampire.

The woman blushes slightly, waving her hand at the lycanthrope. "You flatter me, Christopher."

"I've asked her to look into possible local places Patrice might have taken the girls."

Fran moves across the room, sliding a pocket door under the stairwell. "If you'll follow me, I'll show you my top contenders."

We enter a room that looks like something from a spy movie or television show. Computer screens line the walls, and a control center sits in the middle. Fran begins typing, pulling images up on all the screens. "These are the places that I've narrowed down as possible hideouts."

I stare at the screens, seeing different buildings, most looking abandoned. "How many is that?"

"Forty-two," she answers.

"How the hell are we supposed to check forty-two buildings?" I ask.

"I have a pack of lycan—" Topher starts.

"No," I interrupt. You saw how effective that was in Alabama." My words come out more harshly than intended.

"What are you not telling us?" Alex asks, staring at the elderly vampire in silence, no doubt, reading her thoughts. He turns toward a screen on the far wall. "This is where she thinks they'll most likely be."

Fran wrinkles her forehead. "I was getting to that part, young man." She moves closer to Alex, staring him in the eyes.

"Yes," he answers. She repeats the motion, and Alex answers again. "I've had it since I was changed."

"I'll be damned," Fran exclaims, clapping her hands loudly. "I always knew it was a possibility but have never seen it until now." She moves closer to Alex. "You're special, aren't you?"

"What are you talking about?" Thorne speaks for the first time since arriving.

"I'm talking about the vampire council and why immortal children are outlawed."

"They're outlawed because of their inability to control their emotions," Topher answers.

Fran shrugs. "Maybe. I've always had other theories behind the law."

"Because Alex can hear other people's thoughts?" I ask, confused.

"That, among other things." She types quickly on the keyboard, pulling up what looks like ancient writing from an even older looking book. "I took the liberty to upload both Harrison's and Viktor's libraries into one source a few months back."

"Harrison?" I ask. "The one who nearly killed Amelia?"

"The very same." She zooms in on the document.

"That's Sanskrit," Alex announces, staring at the screen.

Fran turns toward the child. "Can you read Sanskrit?"

He shakes his head. "No, but I recognize a few of the characters."

"There's not much mentioned, but I remember reading this not too long ago." She pushes a button on the keyboard, and the unfamiliar language translates into English. She highlights a passage. "How about now? Can you read that to us, Alex?"

"*A child inflicted with the blood of a vetala may hold power in their body.*" He turns toward the rest of us. "What is a vetala?"

"They were believed to be spirits inhabiting the

bodies of the dead," Fran answers. "It's a fancy way of saying vampire." She types a few more things, pulling up an old black-and-white photograph. "This is a picture of what was believed to be an immortal child from the late 1800s."

I stare at the image of a beautiful young girl. An oversized bow holds her perfectly styled ringlets in place. She's smiling, displaying two tiny pointed teeth hanging over her bottom lip. The caption under her picture reads, "Telekinesis."

Fran pulls up another picture—this one of an older boy. The photograph looks to be from around the same time period. The caption under his picture reads, "Telepathy."

"Like me," Alex says from behind.

"I found these pictures, among several others, hidden deep in some government archives." She looks around the room. "Don't ask."

"What are you saying?" Topher asks.

"I'm saying that there have been records of immortal children that are like Alex throughout time. Children that have special abilities."

"Amelia and I had that discussion. We're thinking the same."

"I couldn't read minds until...until she turned me." Alex's voice is full of sadness.

Fran shrugs. "Maybe it was something you always had, but when you turned, the ability was enhanced or brought to the surface."

"My sisters?" His eyes are wide as he looks at me.

"Do your sisters have abilities?" Fran asks.

"Autumn does. She has telekinesis. We haven't discovered what Everly can do, yet."

"These are the girls your *mother* took with her?"

He nods. "The rest are gone."

"Were they...special?" she asks.

"No," he whispers. "They were nothing but killing machines. That's what she called them." Tears form in Alex's eyes with his words.

Without a word, Fran walks to the immortal child and wraps her arms around his tiny body. "My goodness, you remind me so much of my Celeste. She was strong and wise beyond her physical age. She's going to love you when she meets you." Alex pulls back, wiping his cheeks.

"Thank you, Miss Fran."

She huffs a laugh. "You're already sounding like a Southerner."

"She's going to try to find more," Alex adds. "More special children like me and my sisters."

"We're not going to let that happen," Topher answers. "Fran, can you pull up those locations again?"

She types a few seconds on the keyboard, and the locations pop back to the monitors. "Alex is correct. This is the one I think has the highest probability of her being there." She enlarges the screen, showing what looks like a warehouse.

"What do you think?" Thorne asks Alex as the boy stares at the building.

He shrugs. "I don't know. Patrice picked the places we stayed at random. The one thing they had in common was they were all isolated."

"This building certainly fits that criterion. It's on the other side of the river and barely standing." Fran huffs. "It's where I'd hole up if I were trying to do the same."

"What are we waiting for?" Alex asks the group.

"We can't just go in there with guns blazing," Fran answers. "If she is in that building, instinct tells me she's not alone. She had help from someone." My mind instantly flashes back to the sulfur smell in my room at the church. I haven't shared that information with anyone. Other than hoping to hide it from my mind, I don't have a good reason as to why.

"She's going to hurt them." Sadness sounds through Alex's voice. "Without me to choose the next children, she'll force Autumn and Everly to do it. If they choose wrong..." he doesn't finish his sentence. He doesn't have to.

"Did you choose Autumn and Everly?" Fran asks the immortal child.

"Yes."

"Did you know they were special when you chose them?"

He shakes his head. "Maybe?"

"Can you explain that?" Fran persists.

"I don't know. The way they thought was different. I'm not sure how to explain it." He sighs. "Most people think in words or images. If they think about a red apple, and they see some sort of apple. It will vary in color, size, and stuff like that. Autumn and Everly were different."

"How did they think?" I ask, coaxing him on.

He turns toward me. "Like you."

Every eye in the room turns in my direction. "How do I think, Alex?"

He shrugs. "Think about an apple." I do as he suggests, picturing the bright red apple in my mind. "Now, do something with the apple."

"I'm not sure what you mean."

"Take a bite from the apple, rotate it." He shrugs. "Do something specific."

I close my eyes, envisioning the juicy red fruit. Lifting my hand to the apple, I pull it toward my mouth, feeling the smoothness of the skin, and take a bite. The sensation of fruity sweetness fills my palate. I haven't had an apple in over three hundred years, but the memory of the flavors satisfies my taste buds.

My eyes open to everyone staring at me in anticipation. "What happened?" Thorne asks.

"I tasted the apple." The sweetness is still in my throat. I swallow self-consciously, not sure what to think. "Is that not normal?"

"No," Alex answers.

"What does that mean?" Topher asks the question I want to know the answer to.

"I think it means you're like me."

I scoff. "Alex, I mean no offense, but there has to be more than that to determine if someone is special."

He shrugs. "I'm sure there is, but that's the way I do it. Elsie, you have a gift. I can tell."

I look into each set of eyes staring at me. "I don't have a gift. That's ridiculous."

"You're stronger than you should be, Elsie." Thorne's words remind me of Amelia's on the beach.

"You all don't believe that, do you?" No one responds.

......

We make plans to meet everyone at the lycan bar in four hours. Alex, Thorne, and I need to clean up, and Fran graciously offers her home for us to do just that.

Since arriving, Alex has had three bottles of blood, while Thorne and I have had two. It's not the worst thing I've had to drink, but it's certainly not the best. The room Fran directed us to is ornately decorated and screams vampire vibes. After making sure Alex was situated and has everything he needed, Thorne and I do the same.

Thorne's energy has been off since arriving at the house. After taking a shower and finding clothes that fit, he's been staring into the empty fireplace for long enough that I'm concerned.

I move behind him, wrapping my arms around his waist. "What's going on?"

He squeezes my hand, pulling it to his lips. "I don't know what you mean."

"Something's bothering you." I move in front of him, pulling his attention toward me. "Talk to me, my love."

"I'm sorry," he says, tears filling his eyes.

"Why are you sorry?"

He pulls away, moving toward a window on the opposite side of the room. "I somehow feel like this is all my fault."

I stare at the man who pursued me for three hundred years. "How the hell is this your fault?"

"I should've never let him take you," he repeats his words from weeks ago.

"Thorne, I..."

"No," he interrupts. "I just stood there and watched as he took you from the deck of my ship. I was the captain. It was my ship. Instead of fighting him, I allowed him to take you."

"You didn't *allow* him to do anything. No one allows Kragen to do anything. I don't blame you. I blame him."

"You should blame me." He runs a hand through his hair. "I do." I don't know what to say. "What if what Alex says about you is right?"

"That I'm somehow special?" I scrunch my forehead, not sure where he's going with this.

"Aye." He makes eye contact with me. "What if that's the reason *he* took you?"

"You think Kragen took me because I'm a freak?"

"You're not a freak, and nothing else makes sense."

I sigh. "Kragen admitted to taking me because your crew killed, or he thought they killed, Eudora."

"Aye, maybe that was part of it. But I can tell you one thing. If you were killed by a group of humans, I would've destroyed every damn one of them, leaving nothing behind."

"What are you saying?"

He turns, facing me. "Kragen knows more about you than he's letting on. It's why he's obsessed with you. You have something he wants."

whatever...

ALEX KNOCKS on our door exactly three hours later. "I know you're in there," he whispers through the lock.

Thorne and I have been wrapped in each other's arms since his admission. Neither of us is in the mood for anything more. *"Come in,"* I think loudly.

The door opens, revealing a version of Alex I've never seen before. He's wearing a pair of blue jeans and a button-down plaid shirt. He looks modern and even more adorable than before. "Look at you," I exclaim. "You look perfect."

"Do you mean it? Fran insisted that I put it on. She said I needed to look *up-to-date*."

"I agree," Thorne adds. "You look great, little man."

Alex smiles. "Fran's waiting on us." We follow him down the stairs to find her waiting in the foyer. Instead of the antiquated dress she was wearing earlier, she's sporting a pair of slim-fitting slacks and a soft knit shirt.

"Y'all ready?" she smiles as she speaks. "I called an Uber already." She pulls her phone from her pocket. "And...it's here!"

Ten minutes later, we walk into the now-familiar lycan bar, feeling the energy shift the moment we enter. We don't stop to ask questions, instead, following Fran straight into Topher's office. He's sitting behind his desk with Amelia in his lap, surrounded by the now-familiar faces of the people who have become my friends.

"Who is this modernly dressed young man?" Luna asks with a smile.

"It's me, silly," Alex answers, returning her smile.

"Fran!" Amelia is on her feet and hugging the vampire before I register movement. "It's so good to see you."

"You, too. You're looking great."

Topher stands, turning into the Alpha. "Fran, would you share your theory with everyone?"

She shrugs. "It's not so much a theory as a hunch." She pulls a photograph out of her bag. "I feel like this is a strong contender for Patrice's hiding place."

"I recognize that building." Amelia takes the photograph from her. "Isn't this place off of the docks?"

"It is."

"What makes you think that's where she is?" Micah speaks for the first time.

"Deductive reasoning."

Amelia looks around the room. "What are we waiting on?"

"We're waiting for backup," Fran quips.

Micah scoffs. "We have an Alpha, a future Alpha, a lycanthrope, a hybrid, three vampires, and an immortal child. I don't think we need backup."

"Alex isn't going," I interrupt his rally call.

"Elsie? I'm going," he argues. *"They're my sisters,"* he tells me silently.

"What if she hurts you or, worse, takes you back to that life?"

"I'm willing to risk it. I appreciate your concern, but I have to try to save them." He looks at his feet. *"It's my fault they're there in the first place."*

I stare at the small vampire before giving in. "Okay," I say aloud.

"That was interesting to watch," Fran announces, sitting on the edge of Topher's desk. "You two were just communicating, weren't you?"

"Aye," I answer for both of us.

"Is that something you do regularly?"

I shrug. "Just with Alex and Thorne."

She turns toward the captain. "You can communicate with Elsie, even though you share no blood bond?"

"Aye." He looks around the room as he asks.

Fran shrugs. "Maybe both of you are *special.*"

"I'm not special," Thorne scoffs.

"Why else would you be able to communicate with each other telepathically?" She persists.

"I assumed it was because of the love we share." Thorne's words bring chill bumps to the surface.

"That's sweet, but no. That's not the reason, and it's not normal. You two have a gift, and I think it's obvious that Patrice was collecting children with the same gift."

I stare at the older vampire. "I'm not like Alex. I can't hear people's thoughts. I can't move things like Autumn. I'm just a regular vampire." The irony of my words isn't lost on me.

"Aye, me, neither," Thorne agrees.

"We'll discuss you two later. Our goal is to find Alex's sisters before something happens to them," Fran reprimands.

"Is that a common thing? Immortal children having abilities?" Luna asks, changing the subject.

"Not any more common than a human child having abilities," Fran answers. "From my research, it seems that human children who were gifted, their abilities become enhanced when they become a vampire."

"You think the boy always had the ability to read minds?" Micah asks, nodding toward Alex.

"Maybe, or it could be something he would have never noticed had he remained human."

"How would Patrice have known Alex had a gift?" Luna asks.

Fran shrugs. "Maybe it was the luck of the draw. She chose the perfect child. Maybe she could sense something in him but wasn't sure what. There are a million possible reasons." She turns toward Alex. "Nothing personal, little man."

"I know," he whispers.

"When Patrice realized Alex's talent, she tried to find more?" Micah puts the puzzle pieces together.

"That bitch planned the entire thing," Amelia says, moving to the middle of the room. "No wonder she welcomed you into the group so readily." She nods toward me. "She planned the whole damn thing, down to the death of the chained children."

"Patrice wanted us to kill the children?" Alex looks around our small group. "She wouldn't do that, would she?" Alex wipes tears from his eyes.

"I'm sorry, Alex. I think she would." I pull him close. "I don't think she was alone," I whisper.

"Elijah?" Thorne asks.

I shake my head slowly. "I smelled sulfur at the church."

"Shit!" Thorne slams his hand down on the desk. "You just now thought to say something?" His words are angry—a side of him I haven't witnessed before.

"What does that mean?" Fran asks, looking between the two of us.

"Kragen," Amelia answers.

"Or Marnie," I interrupt.

Fran crosses her arms across her chest. "I hear the names you're saying, but I have no clue who these people are. Who are Kragen and Marnie, and why would they be helping Patrice?"

"Kragen is the pirate who took me from Thorne's ship three hundred years ago. Marnie is his daughter." I refuse to look at Thorne as I speak.

"And?" Fran persists. "What does that have to do with all of this?"

"Kragen is a sadistic asshole, and his daughter is half goddess," Thorne answers like his words are common knowledge.

Fran stares at our group, no doubt letting Thorne's words sink in. "Is that the plot of a fantasy book, or are you being serious?"

Amelia scoffs. "I'm afraid it's real. The sulfur smell is associated with the two of them." She makes eye contact with me. "And Elsie."

"Who was at the church before me, Alex?" I turn to the small boy.

"I never saw anyone at the church, but there was someone at the house that smelled like you. She had dark hair and eyes."

"What was her name?" Thorne insists.

Alex shrugs. "I don't know. I only saw her once." He looks at his hand. "She was a vampire. That's all I know."

Fran sits on the edge of Topher's desk. "It looks like there's more at play here than we thought." Short arms cross in front of her chest. "We need to find the girls and Patrice. The rest will fall in place from there."

"Agreed," I add. "Stopping Patrice is the first priority. We can't allow her to do this to more children. Kragen and Marnie or whoever the hell is helping her will be next."

"Elsie's right." Fran turns toward Amelia. "We could always call the council."

Topher sighs. "Do we want to involve the council? We all remember that whole fiasco."

"No," Amelia answers simply. "I say we go to the warehouse and see what we find."

"Are we just going to pull up in front like some sort of paranormal X-men?" Luna asks. "I mean, I'm okay with that, but we need costumes." She smiles, helping relax the tension in the room slightly.

Twenty minutes later, we're sitting in front of the building from Fran's picture. I send my energy through the dilapidated structure, feeling nothing human or inhuman. I have no doubt that everyone in this vehicle has already done the same.

"I feel nothing," Amelia says, confirming my suspicion.

"Aye, neither do I," Thorne agrees.

"We should still investigate. Be prepared for anything." Fran leads us to the loading dock. A rusted chain is all that's holding the double steel doors closed. It disintegrates as soon as she touches it, releasing its hold. "Well, that was easy."

The heavy doors slide open with a grunt, welcoming us into a large room that seems to be the entire building. Windows line the back wall, over-looking the Mississippi River. "This place has been empty for as long as I can remember," Topher says, moving to a closed door on the right. He pulls it open, revealing another empty room.

"I don't smell anything," Luna says, lifting her nose high in the sky. "At least nothing paranormal. There's a faint smell of humans, but even that is old."

"She's not here," Alex confirms. "I don't smell her or my sisters. Where's the next place to visit?" He moves to the other side of the building, looking through what remains of a broken window.

Fran shrugs. "I thought this was it. I'm as surprised as everyone else."

I turn, realizing Alex is no longer by the window. In fact, he's not in the building. "Alex?" My voice echoes off the brick walls. *"Alex?"*

"Outside," he answers. *"By the river."*

I find him on the banks of the Mississippi, standing with his arms out to his sides, allowing the breeze to lift his dark hair from his head. "Is everything okay?"

"I feel her." His voice is barely loud enough to hear over the wind.

I follow his line of sight, seeing nothing but brown water leading to the open sea. "Out there?"

He nods ahead. "She's that way."

Thorne moves to my side. "What's happening?"

"I feel Patrice," Alex answers.

"Are you sure? There's nothing out there but water."

Alex turns toward Thorne, his face saying more than words could ever speak. "I know what she feels like." He nods toward the open water. "She's out there." Seconds later, Fran and Amelia are standing next to me, with the lycan running toward us.

"She's that way." Alex points once everyone is outside.

"There's nothing out there except open sea," Topher answers.

"There's nothing that says they have to be on land." Amelia's words hit me in the gut.

"Kragen," I whisper into the wind. With the insanity of the past few days, I forgot about an important detail from the church and Patrice. "Oh, my, God."

"What?" Thorne questions me.

"Patrice. She knew my name. When we were at the church, she called me Elsbeth Abernathy. Kragen is the only way she would've known."

"Shit."

"What would Patrice gain by working with Kragen?" Amelia asks. "It doesn't make sense."

"It makes perfect sense." Fran moves in front of us. "The two of them share an acquired taste." She looks me in the eyes. "It seems your pirate enjoys collecting people with abilities, too."

I scoff. "That's ridiculous. In my years on that ship, I never met anyone with any abilities other than cruelty. The only ability I have is survival." Anger fills me for no apparent reason.

"Whether you choose to believe it or not, you have an ability." Amelia moves next to Fran. "I sensed it the first moment we met. You are strong, both mentally and physically, along with something else I can't quite put my finger on."

I scoff at the hybrid. "That's nothing more than what my father called stubbornness. It doesn't mean I'm special or have an ability."

Amelia shakes her head and shifts into the six-foot bright-red wolf I've seen several times. Without giving me time to think, she's on top of me, pinning me to the ground. "What the hell are you doing?" I ask the woman who I thought was my friend.

Thorne moves to my aide as the lycan jump between us. "No," Topher warns my lover. Thorne bares his teeth, as all three lycan work to hold him in place.

"Let me go," he warns. "I will kill you all."

"Stay back, Thorne. Amelia's not going to hurt her."

Amelia begins to growl. The sound starts low in her chest as she slices a claw across my chest, bringing blood to the surface. What the hell? "Amelia? What are you doing? I...I thought we were friends. I don't want to hurt you."

"Elsie!" Alex yells from behind me. I turn, seeing Fran wrap her arms protectively around him, pulling him away from whatever this is.

"Stay back!"

"You have to fight!" Thorne's voice echoes through my mind. *"Fight her, dammit!"*

I pull my dominant arm free of her hold, hitting her square in the chest. She barely budges but moves enough for me to free my other arm. Using both, I push her chest, knocking her to the side and freeing my body. Amelia turns and stands on her hind feet. Holy shit, she's double my height and terrifying.

"What are you doing?" I repeat.

The wolf claws at me again, this time making contact with my cheek, slicing my skin, and leaving a trail of blood behind.

"Stop!" Thorne yells. "Let me go, dammit!"

Something inside me takes over. I stare at the giant wolf in front of me and allow the anger that's filled me my entire life to surface. The power is nearly overwhelming. Without warning, I leap through the air, wrapping my arm around her throat, and hold her in place.

To my surprise, I'm easily holding the giant wolf in place with nothing more than my body. I bare my teeth ready to rip her head from her body when she shifts back into human form in an instant. The change in size throws off my balance and knocks me to the ground next to her.

She stands, ready to continue the fight if needed. Both of us stare at each other, breathing harder than if we'd run a race.

"What the hell was that?" I scream.

"Amelia killed the oldest vampire in the world

while in wolf form," Topher's words are no louder than a whisper.

"And?" I spew while still panting.

"You could've killed her just now."

The lycan release their hold on Thorne who rushes to my side. "Are you okay?"

I nod, turning back to the redheaded woman. "I'm not that strong."

"Yes, you are," she argues.

I scoff. "I just got the upper hand. It was nothing more than luck."

"And you could've easily killed me."

Every member of our group is standing in awe of the fight that just happened, even me. I'm not stronger than Amelia. That was a fluke. Wasn't it?

"That was fun," Luna claps her hands, breaking the silence.

"Fran's right. You have abilities." Micah speaks for the first time. "You're special."

"While you were with Kragen, did anything happen?" Fran asks.

"There's not enough time in the day to tell you everything that happened while I was with that bastard. You're going to have to be more specific." My words sound angry.

"Did you ever *feel* strong? Maybe break something you shouldn't have been able to, or overpower someone stronger than you?" she continues, seemingly unfazed by my temper tantrum.

I think back to the day I escaped and the young boy, Elliot, who helped me. "Yes," I whisper. "I killed two vampires at once when I was escaping."

"Were they older?"

"Yes." I make eye contact with each one in our group. "It doesn't mean anything."

"It means everything. You're stronger than you should be." Fran shrugs with her words.

Thorne turns toward the group. "I think that's why he took her in the first place. Why he took her from my ship."

"Maybe he and Patrice met somehow, and the two of them discussed their discoveries," Fran adds.

"That's why Elsie smelled sulfur at the church," Luna joins the conversation.

I look around the group, mindlessly talking about me like I'm nowhere to be found. Alex makes eye contact with me. *"I'm sorry, Elsie."*

"Aye, me, too."

I move to the center of the newly formed circle. "I can't do this." I turn, leaving the group standing on the banks of the Mississippi.

a plan

I'M in the French Quarter within minutes. I slow down, matching the speed of the humans around me. I could kill ten of them before anyone was aware of my movement. Hell, probably before anyone noticed the bodies. Why would I think something so horrible? *What's wrong with you, Elsie?* Amelia's right. You have a ginormous chip on your shoulder. It's time to figure out why.

The fight with Amelia and the revelation of Kragen's reasoning for taking me weigh heavily on my mind. Through the years, I've speculated why he took me. I've imagined every scenario possible, but this? This wasn't anything I could've ever imagined.

Amelia's wrong. I'm not stronger than I should be. Even if I am, there's no way Kragen could've known. Questions flow through my mind, as I continue moving, finally stopping on Bourbon Street and in front of a familiar door.

I take a deep breath before entering the dark tavern. Without question, I move toward a private booth in the corner, looking for the British vampire who owns the bar.

Erick stands as I approach. "Good afternoon, Elsbeth Abernathy. What brings you to my humble establishment?" He looks behind me, searching for other members of my party.

"I'm not sure," I answer honestly.

He motions to the empty bench in front of him. "Please, join me." I follow directions, sliding into the seat across from him.

"Would you care for something to drink?" He raises a slim hand in the air.

"No, thank you." I slide to my escape. "I'm sorry. To be honest, I don't know why I came here."

Erick places a hand on top of mine. "Stay for a bit, love."

I nod, sliding back into the seat. "I had to get away."

He laughs. "I have days like that. Particularly with Phillipe. He...how do the young ones say it? ...gets on my nerves, occasionally."

His words make me smile. "Yeah, I get that."

"What have your friends done to warrant your escape?" He lifts a slim wineglass to his lips, taking a small sip of the red contents.

"They didn't do anything. It's me."

Erick smiles. "What did you do to warrant your escape?"

I sigh before answering. "Amelia and Fran think I'm *special*."

"In what way?"

"Like Alex. They say I'm stronger than I should be." I find a small piece of fuzz on the table to play with while talking.

"What gave them that idea?"

I shrug. "Amelia attacked me in wolf form, and I was able to fight her off and get the upper hand."

"I see. Why did she attack you?" he asks, taking another sip from his glass.

"To prove a point."

He leans back, resting his rigid back against the seat. "Amelia attacked you to prove that you were strong?"

"Aye."

"I'm gathering, she was correct?"

"Aye," I repeat.

A deep chuckle leaves his lips. "In the few years I've known Amelia, I've never known her to do anything without purpose. She is wise beyond her years and very well respected in our community."

"You think I'm special, too?"

"I've had no opportunity to judge your strength, however, I sense something in you."

"Have you met others that you *sensed* something in?"

"Throughout the years, yes, on occasion."

I look up at his words. "Recently?"

"Other than you and the child, no."

"He's special."

Erick nods in agreement. "Is this why you came to visit today?"

I copy his movement, resting my back on the seat. "I had to get away from Patrice, Kragen, and generally everything."

"I met him many years ago."

I sit up straight. "You didn't mention that before."

"It wasn't relevant to our conversation at the time."

"When?"

Erick shrugs. "Five or six decades ago. He came through looking for someone."

"Me?" I scoff.

"He didn't tell me a name, and I didn't ask." He sits straighter, taking another sip. "He's special, too."

I stare at the vampire in front of me. "What are you saying?"

"I sensed something in your maker, too. I believe it's what helped him to discover you in the first place. You know what they say, birds of a feather..."

"How do you know this?"

He takes another sip from his glass. "Call it a hunch."

"Is he like me?"

"That, I don't know, my dear. When you discover what his ability is, feel free to share."

"Patrice?"

"I've never met her, however, if the boy was her creation, she's connected to your pirate somehow, whether through shared interests or innate talent." Erick smiles as he speaks. "It was a pleasure to visit with you again, love. I do hope you'll have a brilliant evening." His words are a dismissal as he toasts the empty air in front of him with his glass. "Please tell Amelia I miss her company and expect a visit soon."

I stand. "Thank you, Erick Chapman." I don't know what I'm thanking him for. All he did was confirm everyone's suspicions and raise a few more questions.

"My pleasure, Elsbeth Abernathy."

I leave the bar, not sure what the hell just happened. Erick oozes of charm, but I feel like I was just put in my place without a finger lifted or his tone raised.

I'm back on the busy street in minutes, mixing with the unsuspecting humans. I feel the twinge of familiar energy not far from the bar. *"Alex?"* I ask through my mind. *"Are you following me?"* I'm met with silence. I continue moving when the sensation hits me again. *"Alex, I feel you."* I stop, searching for his energy. *"There's no point in staying quiet, I know you're here. I'm okay."*

"I'm sorry, Elsie," he says a few seconds later.

"It's not your fault. It's not anyone's fault." I sigh through our connection. *"I'll wait here for you."*

Seconds later, bright blue eyes are in front of me. He

doesn't speak, just wraps his arms around my waist. "Don't leave me."

I pull away from his embrace. "I'm not leaving you, Alex. What makes you think that?"

He shrugs, wiping a tear. "You left everyone."

"I needed to get away for a minute. I'll never leave you or Thorne." I pull him close again, hugging him tight.

"Good, because I'm not far behind Alex," Thorne's words echo through my mind, making me laugh out loud.

"You can't get rid of us," Alex says, smiling.

"I don't want to."

Thorne is in front of us in a blink of an eye. "Are you okay, acushla?"

"Aye. I'm sorry I left."

"Don't be." He laces his fingers through mine.

"I talked with Erick." I mindlessly rub my thumb across his. "He met Kragen decades ago, and thinks Kragen is special."

"Like us special?" Alex asks.

"Aye, like *us*." Adding me to that feels foreign to my thoughts.

"I knew it. That's why he wanted you," Thorne fills in the blank.

"That leaves me with the question of why all the games? Why pretend he wanted me to kill him? Why pretend you killed his wife? Why let me escape and run for two hundred years? What the hell is he doing?"

"I don't feel like the whole Eudora and Marnie thing was a lie." He looks around the area. "To be honest, I'm a little surprised neither of them has popped up during all of this."

My stomach knots, thinking about all of the drama going on in our lives right now.

"Alex? When you said you could feel Patrice earlier in the water, do you think she was actually in the water?"

His tiny shoulders raise. "I don't know. I could just feel her."

"Then I should go to them," I answer with resolve. "It's me that Kragen wants. If Amelia is right, I'm the only one who can defeat him."

"What if she's wrong?" Thorne asks. "What if this is all part of Kragen's games? Hell, he had you on his ship not long ago. If he wanted you for anything other than to torture or kill, he would've done something then. None of this makes sense."

"Kragen thrives off of doing the unexpected. He's a sick bastard, and I'm tired of playing his games."

"I won't let you go in there alone, acushla. Don't ask me to let you go to him twice. I made that mistake once, I won't make it again." Anger pours off Thorne.

"I'm not asking for your permission." My words are harsh, and I immediately regret speaking them out loud.

Alex moves between us. "No."

"Alex, I have to do this."

"We're not going to let you do this alone," Alex continues. "Thorne may not be saying it out loud, but he's thinking it."

"Aye," Thorne agrees. "I love you, acushla. Allow me to help you. You don't have to be everyone's savior."

"I'm coming, too." Alex laces his fingers through mine.

I can't prevent the tears from flowing. "What if something happens to either of you?"

"It won't," Alex says simply. "Besides, we're going to have help." He slides over, revealing a small horde of lycan and two vampires. The group that has quickly become my friends.

"Don't say what you're thinking," Alex warns. "Let us help."

"Thank you," I whisper, fighting my inner demons.

"We have a plan," Amelia answers for the group as they approach.

We follow her to a narrow door and up a narrow spiral staircase into a beautifully decorated loft apartment.

"This is nice," Luna announces. "Vampires have the best digs." She sits on the floor next to the oversized television. Micah slides next to her.

"Thank you," Amelia answers. "This is where Topher and I fell in love." Everyone stands awkwardly quiet after her admission.

"Well, then," Fran interrupts the silence. "Why

don't we get a plan together and figure out how to defeat this pirate and Patrice?"

Amelia sits on the large sectional sofa with a spiral-bound notebook in her hand. "I find it easier to take notes." She draws a line down the center of the page. "What do we know about Patrice?"

"She collects special children," Alex answers. "And she used me to get rid of the ones that weren't."

"She dresses like a modern-day soccer mom, and we're pretty sure she's in cahoots with Kragen," I add to the list.

"Do we know how old she is?" Fran asks.

"No. Elijah said she was turned into a vampire while visiting Ghana. He didn't know how it happened." Amelia speaks while writing.

"Elijah also said their makers were friends, and they paired them together," Micah speaks for the first time.

"Yes!" Amelia adds his words to the list.

"We know her maker wasn't Kragen." I look around the room. "Any ideas on who her maker might be?"

"Honestly, I don't think it matters." Fran shifts in her seat. "What matters is her connection to Kragen." She turns to Alex. "Did Patrice take you with her often?"

He shakes his small head. "Only to find new children or food."

"The question is, what is the connection between Kragen and Patrice, and are they working together?" Fran continues.

"Erick thinks Kragen has abilities." I turn my focus to Amelia. "He wanted me to let you know that he misses your company, and he expects a visit soon."

Amelia laughs. "Erick thinks Kragen has an ability?"

"Aye," I answer.

Alex's energy changes instantly. He stands, moving toward a window overlooking the street. His breathing picks up as he spots something outside.

"What is it, Alex?" I ask, moving to his side.

"There's someone outside. Someone like us."

"A vampire?" I ask. He shakes his head.

"Someone with abilities?" Amelia asks, joining us at the window.

"There." He points at a boy around his age, standing next to what I assume are his parents. "He's human."

"There are humans with special abilities. That's been proven for many years." Fran joins us.

Alex turns toward me. "Patrice is following him."

"She's outside? Are you sure?" I ask.

"No, but she's nearby."

I move to the door at vampire speed, only to run into a petite hybrid. "We need to follow her, not kill her." Amelia stops me. "She'll sense you and run. She needs to continue to think she's smarter than us. The only way to find the girls and stop Kragen is by you and Alex staying away from her."

"We can't let her get that boy. You know what she'll do to him," I retort.

"I'll go," Fran says. "She won't recognize my energy. To her, I'll appear as an aging, useless, New Orleans vampire." She moves through the door. "I'll report back soon."

fresh blood

FRAN MOVES out of the house at vampire speed. Amelia's right, Patrice will recognize my energy, but I'm not a fan of not being in control.

"Anyone want to play a game while we wait?" Luna breaks the silence.

Alex moves beside me, squeezing my hand. "Fran found her already. She's talking to me."

"How is she doing that?"

He shrugs. "She's thinking really loudly."

"Can you talk to her?"

"I tried. I don't think she hears me."

I move toward the window overlooking the street, searching for anything that might provide answers. The young boy Patrice was stalking is still on Bourbon Street, a block further down. I turn toward the audience. "I'm going down there." I hold my hands up proactively. "No one panic. I'm not going to do anything dumb. I just want to try to talk to him."

"I'll come with you," Alex says, lacing his fingers through mine.

"Me, too." Thorne joins, making us look like a young family as we exit the loft.

"There they are." I nod toward the family a few blocks away. "How can we do this without looking like stalkers?"

Alex pulls a plastic dinosaur from his pocket. "I found this earlier. We can use it." We close the distance, practically bumping into the family.

"Hey!" Alex says to the boy. "Did you drop this? I found it back there?" He points behind us.

The boy stares at the tiny toy. "No, but it's super cool."

"Yeah, I thought so, too," Alex continues. "My name is Alex. What's yours?"

"Brayden," he answers. "Mom?" he looks up to his mother. "This is Alex."

"I see that." She smiles before turning back toward the poster she and her husband are studying.

"They're busy," Brayden answers. He stares at Alex, looking him in the eyes longer than usual. "You feel weird."

Alex laughs. "What?"

Brayden shrugs. "I don't know how to explain it. You just feel weird."

"Do you think he's special?" Thorne asks the two of us.

Brayden looks at Thorne. "What did you say?"

"I think that's our answer," I smirk with my silent words.

"Come on, Bray," his mother urges, pulling him away from us. "We need to get back to the hotel before the riffraff appear out here."

I laugh. "I hear there are vampires that roam around the streets of New Orleans."

"Vampires?" the mother asks. "That would be cool to see. I love a good vampire story."

"That makes one of us," I answer.

"It was nice meeting you, Alex," Brayden adds. "I hope you find the owner of the dinosaur."

We watch the trio move further down Bourbon Street, not sure what to do. If Patrice has her eyes on him, he and his family don't stand a chance. "Are you sure Patrice was after him?" I ask Alex.

"Yes. I could feel and hear her. Usually, she keeps her thoughts hidden, like you. But she was open."

"She's hoping that boy could read her mind," Thorne answers. "What would be the point of that?"

Looking around, I don't feel any paranormal energies other than the ones in the loft. "Maybe she doesn't use her shield since she thinks Alex isn't nearby."

Alex pulls his hand away from me. "I don't intrude on people's thoughts." He scrunches his face as he speaks.

"What?" I ask, confused.

"You just thought that."

"Alex, I did think that, but I didn't mean anything by it." I place my hand on his shoulder. "I'm sorry. I didn't mean to upset you."

"It's fine." He scoffs. "Next time you want to think mean things, put up your shield."

I laugh. "I thought it was, and I wasn't thinking mean things."

He turns toward the family, disappearing down the street. "Oh! I think I know Brayden's ability." He runs, catching up with the family seconds later. Thorne and I are inches behind.

"Hey, Brayden." Alex hands the dinosaur to the boy. "Since I can't find the owner, I thought you might want it."

"Sure," the boy smiles, taking the small toy.

Alex turns toward me. "Mommy, where's that shield you were talking about?"

I'm not sure what he's doing, but I focus on adding strength to the shield that protects him from reading my every thought. I encase my thoughts, placing an invisible shell between him and me. "It's up, son." I laugh awkwardly with my words, trying not to look like a lunatic to the young family.

"Dad?" He looks at Thorne, who nods in response.

I don't know what Alex is doing, but I test the shield, thinking a particularly sexual thought about the man I love.

Alex turns toward me, with his eyes wide open. "Really?" he whispers. *"I need to wash my eyeballs."* He turns back to the boy. *"Brayden overpowered your shield."*

"Shit."

"What hotel are you staying in?" Alex asks the young boy. "Maybe we could meet up and go swimming or something."

Brayden looks at his mom. "Is that okay?"

"Sure, honey." She turns toward me. "We're staying in the Windsor Court. It's not far from here."

"I know where that is," Thorne adds. "How about tomorrow?"

"We had plans to go to the zoo tomorrow. Maybe you could meet us there?" Brayden's mother asks.

"That sounds great." I grab Alex's hand, pulling him away from his new friend. "We'll see you after lunch."

"Bye, Alex." Brayden waves. "See you tomorrow."

It's not until we're at the entrance of the loft apartment that I speak words out loud. "What was that, Alex?"

"Brayden made your shield not work. That's why I could hear Patrice."

Everyone meets us at the door as we enter. "What happened?" Luna asks with a smile.

"Alex thinks Brayden is able to break down shields," I answer, not really sure what I just said.

"Explain," Amelia demands, moving closer.

Alex spends the next few minutes telling the group

his theory, ending with our meetup at the zoo tomorrow.

"What would be the advantage of that ability?" Topher asks.

"If that boy has the ability to break down barriers as a human, imagine what he could do as a vampire." Micah wraps his arm around Luna's shoulders, making me smile. "I can't even begin to imagine the possibilities."

"Is anyone opposed to disbanding our group for the evening?" Amelia wraps her arms around Topher as she speaks. "I feel like we're treading water at the moment, and I could use some family time." She turns toward Thorne and me. "Why don't you two stay here in the loft? No one is living here at the moment."

"What about me?" Alex asks.

"I would love for you to come with me for the evening and introduce you to our son, Edon." She smiles as she speaks. "Celeste left a bunch of games that have been begging to be played with since she left. I'm sure she wouldn't mind sharing them with you."

Alex smiles. "I'd like that." He turns toward me. "Is it okay if I go with Amelia and the Alpha?"

"Of course." I wrap my arm around his shoulder, pulling him in for a hug. "I'll see you tomorrow." Amelia winks as they leave the loft.

I wait until the door latches behind them, and their energy disappears before turning toward my captain.

His curly hair is a mess of frizz, making him even sexier than usual. "Looks like we're alone."

"Aye," he whispers. "It's been a while since we've been alone."

I stalk closer. "Aye, I can't even remember the last time we weren't surrounded by immortal children, lycan, or other vampires."

"What are you suggesting, acushla?"

Moving in front of him, I run the back of my hand against his cheek. "I'm not suggesting anything." I move my hands down to the hem of the T-shirt he's wearing, slowly and methodically pulling it closer to his head and revealing the rippled chest I've longed to run my fingers over.

Thorne's breathing picks up as I slide the hem over his head, leaving the pair of jeans hanging tightly on his hips. "God, you're gorgeous." He raises his hands, reaching for my waist. "No, I'm in control." I place his hands back at his sides and move my hands to his belt. Slowly, I unlatch the heavy buckle, leaving the leather hanging on each side. Unbuttoning the metal clasp, I take my time pulling the zipper down, making sure each metal click echoes off through the loft.

"Are you trying to kill me, woman?" He smiles, licking his lips.

"Maybe," I tease. With his jeans loose, I pull them open, allowing them to slide down his legs and leaving the part of him I want the most, standing at attention. Thorne raises his hands, trying to touch me, and again,

I force them back to his sides, reminding him who's in charge. I lower to my knees, kissing his torso as I descend.

I slowly work my thumb over the tip of his cock, teasing him until he begins to move with me. Sliding my hand to his balls, I place my mouth where my hand was moments earlier. Slowly, I push my tongue against the head of his cock while massaging him with my hands.

Seconds later, his hands grasp the sides of my head as he gently moves me to take him in further. I follow his lead, relinquishing some of my control, and fill my mouth with nearly every inch of him. Thorne sighs in response as he begins to move in and out, matching the pace of my hands and tongue. "Elsie," he breathes.

He tries to pull back, keeping himself from release, and I refuse to let go. I begin to rub faster, placing one hand at the base of him and the other on his balls, massaging at the same tempo as my tongue moves on him. Thorne gives in and begins moving in rhythm, pushing further into my mouth.

Seconds later, his breath catches as he releases into my mouth. "Oh, God. That was...perfect." He sighs, lifting his pants back to his hips.

"You're welcome." I smile. Seconds later, Thorne has me in his arms, carrying me toward a door on the other side of the room. "What are you doing?"

"Returning the favor." He kicks open the door, nearly taking it off the hinges. He gently lays me down on white bedding. I sit up, reaching for my shirt. "No. This time, I'm in charge."

Letting his pants fall to the floor, he grabs my legs, pulling me toward the end of the bed. Moving on top of me, he straddles my hips with his own and slowly lifts the hem of my shirt, pulling it off with one quick move. Slowly and seductively, he pulls one strap of my bra loose, then the other, freeing my breasts from their bondage. "You're the one who's gorgeous."

The intensity of his stare alone is nearly more than I can handle. Reaching for my leggings, he pulls the waistband, releasing them and my underwear in one quick tug. I'm lying on the bed completely naked and more turned on than I can remember.

I reach for him, only to have my hands pushed into the bedding. "No. I'm in charge, remember?" He smiles as he speaks, flashing the smile I haven't seen in a few weeks.

Sliding his hips back, he lifts my legs, placing them on his shoulders. He lowers his head, finding the exact spot on the first try. The moment his tongue touches me, a shock passes through my body, and I gasp on contact. He slowly kisses the softest part of me, finding my favorite part with his tongue. Alternating between sucking and licking, he brings me to near orgasm in seconds.

"Not so fast," he scolds as he brings me to the rim.

"I'm okay with fast," I pant.

Thorne laughs as he enters me with his fingers,

lifting them into the perfect position. "Look at me, acushla."

Lifting onto my elbows, I watch as his fingers touch the perfect spot, joined by his tongue on my clit. The combination of the two is more than I can handle, bringing me to the brink of orgasm in seconds. My legs shake uncontrollably as he continues his assault.

"Come for me, my love. Come on my hand," he whispers, and I do just that. The sensation is almost more than I can handle as my body lifts from the bed, and I cry out.

I collapse on the bed in a puddle of ecstasy as Thorne sits back on his heels "You are so beautiful, acushla."

"You make me beautiful."

We spend the rest of the day and into the next, making up for lost time.

a trip to the zoo

THE SUN HAS BEEN high in the sky several hours before Thorne and I pull away from each other's arms. I feel his eyes on me as I move toward the shower.

"Need some company in there?" he asks.

"As much as I'd like to say yes, we need to get ready for our trip to the zoo."

Thorne flops onto his back with a sigh. "I've never been a fan of zoos. Not a fan of seeing the animals in cages."

The warmth of the water feels perfect on my skin. I take a minute to review everything we've learned since this adventure began. To be honest, it's been a whirlwind of confusion. I'm tempted to take Thorne and Alex and run away, somewhere we can't be found. Doing that would throw me back into the loop I've spent the past two hundred years in. Nope. Elsbeth Abernathy is done running.

I turn off the water and find Thorne lying on top of the sheets, naked. "I thought I'd try to distract you one more time."

I laugh. "It's tempting. You're tempting, but I suspect we will have company before too much longer. I don't want to scar Alex any more than he already is." Pulling the towel off, I pop his leg with a loud crack.

"Ow, okay, woman. I'm getting up." He stands, moving in front of me. "I love you, acushla." He covers my lips with his own, gently forming the connection between us.

I pull away, refusing the temptation to look down. "I love you, too, Captain."

He moves into the shower, and I search for something to wear. The closet is full of clothes that don't belong to me. Sorting through the rows of items, I find a pair of pants that should be the right length, along with a T-shirt folded on the top shelf. I slip on the outfit just as Alex and Luna's energy hits me. I open the door to find the immortal child wearing a pair of shorts and matching shirt. "Good morning, Elsie!" He throws his arms around my waist.

"I'm sorry it's so early. I was only able to hold him off a few hours." Luna ruffles Alex's hair as she speaks.

"Your timing is perfect. We're almost ready." On cue, Thorne enters the room.

"Thorne," Alex says, running toward him, copying his movement from earlier.

"Hey, bud. Are you okay?"

"Yeah, I just missed you guys."

"Well, you're in luck because we're all going to the zoo," I answer. "Where is everyone else?"

"They're going to meet us there," Luna answers.

"The couple said they'd be there after lunch." I glance at a clock on the wall. "If we leave soon, we'll have time to scope everything out before they get there."

Thorne throws a bottle of goat's blood at me. "You might want to eat first."

I try handing the blood to Alex, who pushes it away. "I already ate. It's your turn."

Three sets of eyes stare at me as I loosen the top, lifting it to my lips. Without thinking, I empty the bottle in one gulp. My eyes water at the taste, but it soothes the rumbles in my stomach.

"Let's go!" Alex takes the empty bottle, setting it on the large bar in the kitchen area. "I've never been to a zoo before."

I pull him to a stop. "You've really never been to a zoo?"

He shrugs. "My parents never went to one, and the zoo wasn't the top priority on Patrice's list of things to do."

I laugh at his wording. His personality has changed over the past few days. He's more relaxed, and I like it. "Today is your day."

The four of us catch a streetcar to the zoo, unloading exactly fifteen minutes later. I sense energy the moment we enter. "Fran's with them," Alex says, sensing my thoughts.

Moving to where the energy is the strongest, we find Amelia and Topher kneeling in front of a stroller, with Fran and Micah looking on. "There they are," Alex says with a smile.

"Looks like you two got some well-needed rest," Fran says with a wink as we approach.

"Yeah, we did," Thorne answers.

"What happened yesterday?" I ask Fran. "Were you able to find Patrice?"

"I followed her as far as I could. Her trail ran cold around the warehouse."

"The same warehouse we searched?"

"I sent several men to check it out this morning. There were no signs of anyone being there," Topher preempts my next question.

"She couldn't have just disappeared," I state the obvious.

"I followed her trail to the water." Fran moves closer to the stroller.

Alex looks at me. "I told you she was in the water."

"Yeah, but that doesn't make sense. Unless she's on a ship—"

"Or an island," Thorne interrupts.

"There aren't any islands large enough to hide anything larger than a lizard close to the city," Topher adds.

"Alex!" a young voice calls from behind. "You came."

"Hey, Brayden. Of course, we came." He moves toward the human boy, patting him on the shoulder. Alex's calm and cool demeanor amazes me.

"Hello," his mother greets us. "I didn't expect you to bring other people."

"I'm Fran." She moves in front of the family, shaking their hands. "I hope you don't mind that we tagged along. My daughters and their spouses love the zoo. We'll go separate ways, so we don't have a huge crowd to deal with." She laughs as she speaks.

"Of course, we don't mind," the woman answers. "It's a pleasure to meet you all." She looks at each person in our group. "You certainly have beautiful daughters."

Fran laughs. "I do. It's all in the genes."

I stare in awe at the elderly vampire. Hidden behind her weak facade, she's a force to be reckoned with. "*Mom*, we'll meet y'all later?"

"Sounds good, *honey*," Fran answers.

Thorne, Alex, and I follow the family toward the beginning of the zoo. Brayden and Alex immediately run ahead, staying close enough to see. I know without asking that Alex is hoping to discover more of his ability.

"So, how long are y'all visiting the city?" Thorne asks, putting on a strong Southern accent.

"We're heading home tomorrow," the father answers. "I'm afraid I don't know your name."

Thorne holds his hand out, shaking the humans. "Thorne, and this is my wife, Elsie."

"Michael, and this is my wife, June." He looks at the two boys, staying ahead of us. "Looks like they've made friends."

"Alex is our little social butterfly," I answer. *"Don't get too far ahead,"* I send a warning.

"We're good."

We spend the next hour visiting every animal on display. The energy of my pretend family is nearby, offering support if needed. We move to the back portion of the zoo, to the edges of the Mississippi River while the boys disappear behind a hedge of bushes.

"This is such a beautiful area," June says, over-looking the murky water.

"Yes, it is," I agree.

"Where are the boys?" Michael asks, looking around. "Brayden?" he calls.

"Alex!" I copy. Neither boy answers. *"Alex!"* I'm met with silence.

I turn, meeting Thorne's eyes. *"I'm sure they're around here somewhere."* He reassures me through our connection. "We'll find them," he says out loud as he and Michael leave the two of us alone.

"Elsie!" Alex's voice calls through my mind. *"Can you hear me?"*

"Aye. Where are you?"

"Patrice is here!"

"I can't feel your energy. Where are you?" I turn, searching for his familiar feeling.

"Brayden and I are hiding."

"Dammit, Alex. She'll find you."

"No, she won't. Brayden doesn't just pull down our barriers, he's a shield, too."

I turn toward the unsuspecting mother, looking her in her eyes. "June, I need you to come with me and not ask any questions." Her eyes dilate as she repeats my words. I wrap my hand around hers, pulling her closer to the energy of my family. *"Thorne?"*

"I heard. We're on our way."

Seconds later, I'm standing in front of two lycan, a vampire, a hybrid, and a baby that I don't know how to classify. "What's happened?" Amelia says the moment we approach.

"Patrice is here," I answer.

"How do you know?" Fran asks.

"Alex senses her. He says the boy is a shield and is hiding their energy from her."

"That's useful," Luna adds.

"She must have followed them here," Thorne says as he and Michael join our group. Michael's eyes match his wife's as they stand emotionless beside us.

"I'll protect them," Fran says, nodding toward the parents and Edon. "Go, find that bitch."

"Split up," Thorne orders. "She can't be far."

Amelia and Topher move toward the city, while

Micah and Luna stay inside the zoo grounds. Thorne and I head back toward the water. "What are we looking for?" Thorne asks.

"I don't know. A boat maybe?" We comb the edge of the river, searching for an unmanned boat that would've brought Patrice to shore. Other than the ferry that brings people up and down the river, there are no boats docked anywhere nearby.

"You don't think she'd swim?"

"I doubt it. She doesn't seem like the kind that would want to get her hair wet." I stop moving, standing still. "Why don't I feel her?"

Thorne copies my movement. "Aye, I don't feel her either. In fact, I don't feel anyone."

"What?" I send my energy out, searching for the familiar energies of the lycan and Fran, finding nothing. "What the hell?"

I catch a glimpse of dark hair moving through the zoo faster than human speed. I don't feel the vampire, but there's no denying that it's Patrice. Grabbing Thorne's arm, I pull him behind an ancient oak tree, hiding us from view. The woman moves closer, and my suspicion is correct. It's Patrice. Shit.

"That's her. She'll sense us," Thorne says.

We watch as she continues moving, walking past our hiding spot. *"She didn't feel us,"* I state the obvious.

"How is that possible?" he asks once she's moved on.

"Brayden. Alex said he's a shield."

Thorne laughs. "Yeah, I heard, but there's no way he would be able to shield the entire zoo, is there?"

We move from our hiding spot, following behind the insane vampire. "Apparently there is. We can't let her out of sight. We have to follow her."

"Remember, we'll lose Brayden's shield the further we move from him." Thorne's reminder rings through my mind.

We follow Patrice through the zoo, back to the river and a small dock slightly upriver. "There's her boat." I nod toward a small vessel docked along the pier.

"Elsie," Alex says through my mind. *"You're getting too close. She's going to sense you."*

"We can't let her escape. It's the only way to find your sisters."

"No," he answers. *"She'll kill both of you."*

"We don't have a choice."

"Yes, we do." I turn, finding the two boys standing behind us. "Keep him safe. She won't kill me." Before I have time to react, Alex is gone, following Patrice.

"Hello, Mother," he says, stopping behind her.

"Alex! No!" Without words, Patrice grabs him and has him inside the boat seconds later.

"Stay back, Elsie!" he warns. *"You have to keep Brayden safe. I'll be okay. I'll let you know where we go. We have no choice,"* he repeats my words from earlier.

"Alex," I lose the battle to keep my sadness from sounding through my voice.

"What's going on?" Brayden asks. "Where did Alex go? Where are my mom and dad?"

"Alex will be back soon. He had to take a trip." Thorne wraps an arm around the human boy. "I'll take you to your parents." He looks at me. *"Don't do anything you'll regret, Elsie. Alex is smart. He knows what he's doing."*

I wipe a tear, thinking of the things she could do to him. *"Stay in contact with me, Alex."*

"I will." His voice already sounds weaker. *"The lady from the church is here. She smells like you..."* his voice trails off.

"Smells like me? Alex? Alex!"

Thorne and I share a look just as Fran appears moments later, pushing a stroller and dragging two humans with her. Their pupils return to their normal size as they recognize their son.

"Brayden?" Michael asks, looking around. "How did we get back here? Where's Alex?"

"He took a trip," the boy answers, repeating Thorne's words.

"How did we get back here?" June asks.

"We just walked over here," Fran answers. "Thank you for your conversation. It was a pleasure to get to know you two. In fact, I'd like to offer you a place to stay for the night."

"Oh, no. Thank you, but we're heading home tomorrow," June answers.

"I'm sorry, June. We can't allow that to happen." I

move closer to the family. "Brayden is in danger. If you leave New Orleans with him, we can't guarantee his safety."

"Danger from what?" the father asks.

"A member of our community," Amelia says from behind. We turn, finding her standing in front of three large wolves.

"Oh, my God!" June screams, pulling Brayden to her side.

"We're here to help you. To help him," I say, nodding toward her son. "He's special."

"What do you mean?" Michael asks.

"He has an unusual ability, which will draw others to him. Others, who don't have your son's or your best interest in mind. There is a woman after him now," Fran answers. "We're not your enemy."

"What are those?" June asks, nodding toward the wolves.

"Lycan," Amelia answers. "And they're vampires." She nods in our direction.

"I knew it," Brayden says. "I *knew* you all were something."

lighthouse of horrors

"JUNE, we need you, Michael, and Brayden to come with us." Amelia moves closer as the lycan shift back into human form. "It's not safe for Brayden to be out here."

"What the hell do you mean?" Michael spews. "This is the first time I've ever felt unsafe while being in New Orleans."

"Believe me, sir. We're not the danger." Topher moves closer.

June pulls a phone from her purse. "I'm calling the cops."

"Don't do that, June," Fran says, moving closer to the young family. She steps in front of the mother, placing a hand on her arm and looking her in the eyes. "Put your phone away. The police won't help you." June follows the directions of Fran's calming voice.

Fran smiles. "Good. You and Michael go back to your hotel room."

"Not without Brayden," Michael interrupts.

"Brayden's going to stay with us for a few days."

"Fran, are you sure this is a good idea?" Amelia whispers.

"No, but they're not going to let him go willingly."

Brayden steps between his parents and the team of paranormal creatures. "Why am I in danger?"

"You have a gift, Brayden. A gift that someone wants very badly. Alex has a gift, too," Fran continues.

"What gift?"

"You heard Thorne speak in his mind yesterday, and you have the ability to raise and lower shields," I answer honestly, trying not to waste any time.

"What does that mean?"

"It means you're special, and if your ability is enhanced by becoming one of us, there is no limit to your ability."

"You people are insane," Michael continues. "You can't take our son."

Brayden turns toward his parents. "No, Dad. They're right."

"What?" he continues. "You can't be serious."

"You know I've always been weird. These people are telling the truth. I can sense it."

"Brayden, you're eight years old. You don't have the mental fortitude to make a decision like this. We...*I* won't allow it," Michael continues.

"Then you have one option." Brayden stands straighter as he speaks. "You can come with me and let these people protect me, or you can go home and let these people protect me. Either way, I'm staying with them until the danger has passed."

"Like hell you are. You're coming—" Michael starts.

I move in front of him, interrupting his words, while Fran does the same to June. "Michael, we are not going to hurt your son."

"You are not going to hurt my son," he repeats.

"He's already been discovered by the woman who took Alex, and there is no doubt that she will come after Brayden, too."

Michael repeats my words, his pupils dilated, while Fran convinces June. When we're finished, they resemble zombies, waiting for their next meal.

"What did you do to them?" Brayden asks.

"It's called compulsion," I answer truthfully. "We're simply..."

"Making them think something different," he answers.

"Yes."

Brayden looks back at his parents. "I can do that, too." Fran and I share a look.

"We need to get you somewhere safe," Micah says as he and Luna move to our sides.

Brayden turns toward his parents. "Mom, Dad. We're going with them now." Michael and June nod like good little zombies and begin following our scantily dressed crowd out of the zoo.

"Alex?" I call through our connection, praying he'll respond. I'm met with silence on the other end. My mind reels over who the woman who smells like sulfur is. Anger fills me at the thought of Patrice or this woman hurting the boy I've grown to love.

Ten minutes later, Topher pulls our mode of transportation to a stop in front of a typical French Quarter home. Decorative metal fencing lines the perfectly manicured yard. Topher pushes a button, forcing the fence open and revealing an oversized garage.

"Your family can stay here until the threat is over," Amelia says, climbing out of the SUV.

We usher the family inside, through the secured entrance. The house is beautifully decorated and, like all of the ones we've been inside since being here, reminds me of a decorator magazine. "Your rooms are this way," Fran leads them upstairs.

"What the hell are we going to do with them?" Luna whisper-yells. "They're human in case no one noticed!"

"We couldn't leave Brayden out there," Amelia answers. "Have you heard from Alex?" She looks at me as she asks.

"Not since the zoo."

"Dammit. What was he thinking?" Luna asks. "I can't decide if he was being brave or stupid."

"He was thinking that someone needed to follow her, and he's the one she was least likely to kill." Anger fills my voice, thinking about the boy who sacrificed his safety for us.

Topher lays a large map on the dining room table. "I've been thinking." He moves to one side of the paper. "Alex said Patrice was in the water. Aside from being on a ship, which the Coast Guard would've found by now, she has to be on land somewhere." He points to a tiny dot halfway between the bay and the Gulf. "This is the only place large enough to hold anything. It's a lighthouse that was built during the Civil War and used to keep Union soldiers from moving into the city."

I move to his side. "You think this is where she is?"

Topher shrugs. "It makes sense." He looks around the room. "That's where I'd go."

"We can't just take a boat and demand that she gives us the kids back." Luna crosses her arms in front of her chest.

"Luna's right. We need a plan," I agree.

Fran sets a laptop on top of the map. "These are the original blueprints for the lighthouse. The house next to the lighthouse was built to house the keeper and his family. There'll be a large room on the bottom floor and bedrooms on these floors." She points at two rooms above the main room. "If she's there, Patrice will most likely have the children in the bedrooms."

"Patrice is strong, but with the children's help, we can overtake her." Micah crosses his arms in front of his chest.

"You all are forgetting something important. We

can't get close without her recognizing our energy," I add to the conversation.

"Not if you take me," a young voice says from the landing of the stairs. "Sorry, I was eavesdropping. Mom says it's a bad habit."

"Brayden, we can't take you. You're human, and…"

"Is Alex there?"

I nod. "We think so."

"Then I'm willing to risk it." He nods his head toward Luna. "She can protect me."

Luna laughs. "Although I look tough, I'm young and no match for Patrice. You'd be the one she'd be after."

"How would you be able to hide us?" I ask, ignoring Luna's words.

Brayden shrugs. "I don't know. Like I did at the zoo, I guess."

"Do you know how you do that?"

"I imagine a big clear shell and place it on top of whatever I don't want to hear, or I guess, what I don't want to hear me."

"Is that what you did at the zoo?" Micah asks.

"Not on purpose. Sometimes it happens without me realizing it."

"Can you do it now?" Topher asks the young boy.

Brayden closes his eyes, and the lycan and vampire energy disappears in an instant. It's like I'm standing alone in the middle of a silent room.

"Holy shit," Amelia whispers. "I don't feel any of

you. Even Topher's energy is gone. We could leave him on the boat—"

"No," I interrupt. "We will not put him at risk."

"You, Thorne, and I can go into the lighthouse, the lycan can stay on the boat to protect the boy," she continues.

"You can't be serious. What if this were Edon?" My words are harsh, causing Amelia to recoil.

"I want to go," Brayden continues. "If I come close to dying, one of you can turn me into a vampire or a wolf, if it works like that."

I huff a laugh. "That's not a solution, Brayden."

"Elsie!" Alex's faint voice calls through our connection. *"Thorne? Can you guys hear me?"*

"Alex is talking." I hush the crowd.

"We're at a lighthouse in the middle of the water."

"We know where you are. We're coming, Alex." I turn toward the group. "You were right. She took him to the lighthouse."

"Keep him talking," Amelia says. "Fran?"

"I'll stay with Edon and Brayden's parents. I always miss the excitement." Fran looks annoyed.

"Alex, we're on our way."

"Elsie, the woman is strong. She's stronger than Patrice."

"Who is she?"

Alex pauses before answering. *"Autumn says her name is Samirah."*

"Bitch!" I yell out loud.

"What are you not telling us?" Topher asks.

"Samirah's there, too," Thorne fills in the blank.

Fran looks around the room. "Who is Samirah? I feel like y'all are dropping names like raindrops at this point."

Thorne and I share a look. "Samirah was a friend of mine," Thorne says without looking up. "She's from Savannah. I helped her and a few others out of a bind a few years back. They returned the favor by helping us retrieve Elsie from Kragen."

"Why is it a bad thing that she's with Patrice?" Fran continues.

"Samirah betrayed us," I add. "Turns out she was working with Kragen the entire time. The only reason she'd be there is because of him. That son of a bitch has his hands in everything. Seems like nothing's changed. She's still working with him." I resist the urge to glare at Thorne.

"Am I the only one thinking clearly?" Luna raises her hand from the side of the table. "We still don't have a plan. If Samirah's there, you're going to need us to get off the damn boat."

"Dammit." I slam my hand on the table, knocking a piece of antique wood to the floor. "We'll have the boat leave with Brayden after we get there. By that time, it won't matter

if we have a shield or not." Amelia takes control of the situation. "When we get inside, we don't leave either of them alive."

We load the SUV, leaving Fran in charge of Edon and Brayden's family. "I'll have a boat waiting for you at the dock by the Riverwalk," her voice echoes through the speakers as we pull away from the curb. "Make sure Brayden puts the shield up before you board the boat. We'll wait for him at the docks when the boat returns."

"Thank you, Fran. We'll keep in touch." Topher hangs up the phone. "That's only a mile or so away. As soon as we get there, can you put up your shield?" Topher asks the human boy.

"Yes, sir."

The Alpha pulls the SUV to a stop in the middle of the road, blocking traffic in the already congested area. We unload, running toward the dock. I wrap my arm around Brayden, helping him keep up with the rest of us. "Put the shield up," I remind him as we run.

"Already done," Brayden answers.

Just as Fran promised, a center console fishing boat is docked at the pier. We load without slowing down just as an older man steps out from behind the wheel. "Howdy, folks. Seems you're in a hurry." He laughs.

"Whatever she promised you, I'll double it if you can get us to the lighthouse quickly." Amelia moves in front of the man.

"That's not necessary," he laughs. "I have to follow all the maritime rules."

"Triple," Amelia offers.

The man smiles. "Y'all might want to sit down and put a life jacket on the boy." He moves us out of the marina slowly, then pushes the boat to its limit once we're clear. "Hang on."

"This is fun!" Brayden exclaims as we bounce along the rough water of the Mississippi River.

"Don't let the shield down," Amelia warns from the other side.

He nods.

"It's right up there," our captain says as we fly through the water. He's gone from wanting to obey the rules to a wild man behind the wheel.

"We're almost there, Alex," I send through my mind.

"You're going to have to swim," he answers.

"We can't. Brayden's with us."

"You brought him? Why?"

"He's our shield."

"Patrice will hear the boat." Disappointment sounds through his voice.

The glow of the lighthouse is visible, even during the day. "We need to slow down!" I yell toward our captain. "We want to surprise the people we're coming to visit."

The man slows the boat down to a no-wake speed as our trek toward the lighthouse slows to a crawl. "Everyone quiet," I whisper. "Brayden, whatever happens, don't let that shield down." Nodding toward the small door under the center console. "Climb inside and hide. Don't come out until you're back at the marina and not for anyone except Fran. Do you understand?"

"Yes, ma'am." He climbs through the door, hiding underneath a large tarp.

"Go straight to the marina." Amelia warns the captain. "A woman will meet you with your money and will take the boy."

He silently brings the boat to a stop along a narrow dock leading to the rocky terrain of the lighthouse. The six of us exit the boat, moving toward the tall building.

Brayden's shield is still in place as the boat silently moves away from the dock and back toward the city. I can't feel any energy other than my own, which means the shield is still in range. We're almost to the entrance when his shield releases, sending a rush of energy straight into my body. I've gone from feeling nothing to being overwhelmed by energy in less than a breath.

The door opens, and Patrice exits with hands propped on her hips. "Well, hello there. I wondered when you'd show up." She looks at our group. "Oh, you brought friends!"

have you checked the children?

"WHERE ARE THE CHILDREN, BITCH?" I don't have time for niceties or games.

"What children?" Patrice answers. "There are no children here."

"Cut the bullshit, Patty," Amelia spews. "We know you have Alex, Everly, and Autumn."

Patrice laughs, sending chills down my spine. "Oh, you mean *those* children. You should've been more specific."

"Alex. Are you inside?" I'm met with silence. *"Alex?"*

"Are you okay, dear?" Patrice continues. "You looked a little confused."

"What did you do to them?"

"Them?" She crosses her arms across her designer spandex-clothed body. "Oh, the children. I keep forgetting the reason for your visit." She laughs again. "They're around here somewhere."

"Give us the children, and we won't kill you," Amelia says, filling me with anxiety. If Patrice lives, Alex and the girls will never be safe.

"You smell like the dog you fuck." Her words are full of hatred "Shifter, I believe you're confused. You hold no power here. In fact, you hold no power anywhere." Patrice moves vampire speed inside the lighthouse, returning in the blink of an eye with Everly gripped tightly in her arms. Everly's eyes grow in realization of who we are.

"Are you okay?" I ask the terrified girl. She nods her head, while her eyes tell a different story.

"Of course, she's okay. She's been well-fed since being here, haven't you, girl?"

"Yes, Mother."

"Where are Alex and Autumn?" Topher interrupts the insanity.

"Shut up, wolf. You are beneath the air required to speak to you."

"You just did," Topher retorts, making me smirk.

Patrice puts her hands on the girl's shoulders, pushing her away from her body. "Make them leave," she whispers into Everly's ear.

"Please don't make me, Mother."

Patrice turns the young vampire toward her. "You know what will happen if you don't. Do you need a reminder?"

"No," Everly sobs.

"Good." The evil mother turns her immortal child back toward our group. "Make them leave."

"I'm sorry," Everly whispers as she stares at the lycan behind me. She closes her eyes just as Micah's scream pierces my ear drum. I turn, finding him lying on the rocks, curled into the fetal position, and holding his head in pain.

"Make it stop!" he screams.

"Good, girl. Now to the others," Patrice says calmly.

"Everly?" I question the young girl. She ignores my words, turning her attention toward Luna. Her eyes close, and seconds later, Luna is on the rocks next to Micah, both writhing in pain. Topher shifts, hovering over the two lycan, protecting them with his wolf body. Whatever Everly did to Micah and Luna is affecting him, too. He keeps shaking his head and fighting to keep his footing on the rocks.

"Stop!" Amelia demands.

"You know, for the longest time, I didn't believe this one had any ability." Patrice pulls her hands from Everly's shoulders. "What a surprise it was to discover just how wrong I was." She laughs dramatically. "It's not often I admit when I'm wrong. Consider yourselves lucky."

I shift my attention toward the young girl. "Everly, don't do this," I warn. "Whatever you're doing, let them go."

"I can't," she whispers with tears flowing down her cheeks. "She'll kill them."

"You're killing them!"

"She'll kill Alexander and Autumn."

"Find the children, I'll stay out here," Thorne speaks through my mind.

"What about the lycan?"

"Amelia and I can handle it. Get to the kids."

I don't wait to be told twice. Thorne steps between Everly and the lycan as Amelia shifts into wolf form. Banking on Patrice's distraction, I move at vampire speed inside the lighthouse.

The room I enter is nothing more than an empty shell. The smell of mold fills my nose as I search for Alex's familiar energy. "Alex!" I call through the space. I don't think twice about shouting my announcement. If Samirah is here, there is no doubt she's aware that we're here.

"Alex!" I call again. My voice echoing off the concrete walls.

"Elsie," Alex whispers through my mind. His voice sounds weak and barely audible.

"Where are you?"

"Under."

"Under what?" Alex doesn't answer. *"Alex!"* Shit. What did that bitch do to them? I change tactics. "Samirah? Where are you, you crazy bitch? I know you're here. What happened? Did you get tired of Kragen? He's a hard pill to swallow." My words taunt her, hoping to draw her from her hiding spot.

"Do you know how many young girls he took

advantage of? How many innocent lives he stole, drained, and abused?" I continue my taunts, working my way up the spiral staircase toward the living quarters. "I can't imagine what it's like to be you, willingly giving your body to a monster like him. You're just one of hundreds, hell, thousands of others." I stop walking. "Oh, wow. You might want to get checked for diseases. Oh, wait. Vampires can't get STD's, can they?" I continue moving. "Either way, the lack of self-esteem you must hold deep inside. You know, I've heard that never really goes away. Whatever sort of person you were before being turned is intensified after you're turned. You must have been one hell of a human."

Samirah's energy overwhelms me as she rushes in front of me. "You know nothing of me or my life." Anger fills her words.

"Sure, I do." I continue my verbal assault. I look her up and down, realizing she's wearing the same sort of dress Kragen forced me to wear so many years ago. I can't hold the laugh inside. "Look at you. He's dressed you like one of his little wenches. One of his toys." I look around at what's left of the lighthouse. "Let me guess. Kragen sent you to do his dirty work? He never was one to get his hands dirty. At least in that way."

"I should've killed you when I had the chance."

"Don't fool yourself, Samirah. You never had the chance to kill me. In fact, you don't have one now. Where are the children?"

"The children are none of your concern," she retorts.

"That's where you're wrong. They are every bit of my concern." I step closer to the woman. "You're nothing but a plaything to him. When he's bored of you, he'll throw you away like I witnessed him do so many times before. You're an idiot if you think anything more."

"Kragen loves me."

I laugh. "The only person Kragen loves is himself. I was with him for nearly a century. I know him. He'll discard you like the trash that you are." I move even closer, sending my energy throughout the room and filling every open space.

"You're jealous."

My laugh echoes off the brick walls. "No. Jealousy is not an emotion I'm feeling at the moment."

It's Samirah's turn to laugh. "You're weak. That goat's blood you're drinking makes you a weakling, just like it did Thorne." She looks behind me. "Where is he, by the way? I was hoping to see him again." She licks her lips. "He was always so *delectable*. Tell me. Does he still whimper just before he comes?"

I don't hesitate. The back of my hand slaps across her cheek, shoving her hard into the staircase wall.

"That almost hurt." She holds her cheek, smiling. "Seems like I've touched a nerve." She stands straighter, removing her hand from her face.

"Where are the children?" I return to my mission.

"Didn't you and Patrice just have this same conversation? I'm beginning to see why Kragen got rid of you in the first place."

"I'm done with you." I move in the blink of an eye behind Samirah, wrapping my elbow around her neck. "It's time for you to die."

Samirah shoves her head backward into mine, slamming our skulls together with such force, that the impact forces me to loosen my grip. She's across the room in a heartbeat and standing on a half-destroyed chest of drawers. "You know, Thorne and I fucked for years. I was just one of *many* he enjoyed the company of while he was seeking solace from your disappearance. Your captain isn't the saint you think he is."

I refuse to listen to the ramblings of a crazy woman. Or in this case, a crazy vampire. "Where are the children?" I repeat for the last time.

Samirah leaps from the chest of drawers, landing on top of me, and knocking me to what remains of the wooden floor. She wraps her legs around my waist, holding my arms above my head with hers. "I'm older than you, bitch. You don't stand a chance."

I take a deep breath, searching for the strength that's reared its head a few times in the past. My ability, as Amelia and Fran believe. Deep in the recesses of my mind, I find it. Imagining the tiny ball of strength spreading throughout my entire body, I close my eyes, allowing it to take control. Before when I've used the *ability,* it was just something that happened. Now, I feel it. The surge of power rushes me.

"Just because you're old, doesn't mean you're strong." I lift my arms easily, throwing her petite body off mine and across the room. Samirah slams into the metal railing of the stairs, sending a high-pitched ring throughout the lighthouse. She stands, shaking her head and reminding me of a cartoon character.

I'm in front of her a heartbeat later. "I asked you a question." Lifting my foot, I roundhouse kick her in the stomach, knocking her into the concrete wall once more. "I won't ask again."

She struggles to stand, wiping blood from the back of her skull. "Bitch," she mutters under her breath. "How are you so strong?"

"Because Patrice isn't the only one who collects *special* humans." I move faster than she can track, slamming her head into the wall and leaving a head-sized dent. "I'm guessing that's why Kragen sent you here in the first place."

"Kragen didn't send me, you stupid whore." Samirah pulls away from the wall, staggering as she attempts to stand still.

"What's with all the name-calling?" I tease before hitting her once more. The blow is more than her weakened body can handle. She hits the wall and slides to the floor in a crumpled pile. "If you think Kragen doesn't have his hand in this entire situation, you're dumber than I thought."

Samirah's face transforms into a creature from nightmares. She flies off the wall, moving straight toward me. The world slows down, giving me the ability to see every detail of the situation. The roar of the waves stops, the whisper of the wind goes silent, and my body focuses on nothing but Samirah. Without any thought, I grab her throat mid-flight, wrapping my fingers around her throat tightly until her body and head are no longer connected. She falls to the floor in a sickening thud and immediately begins to disappear.

I wipe her blood on my already-stained pants. "Told you I wouldn't ask again."

Turning back toward the stairs, I take in every inch of the narrow lighthouse. I don't know what's going on outside, and I don't take the time to figure it out.

"Alex! Autumn!" My voice echoes through the building. "Make a sound, do something to let me know where you are!"

Dammit, I don't feel his energy anywhere. I run the length of the staircase, looking in every nook and cranny along the way. Other than remnants of broken furniture and rusted metal, the lighthouse is empty, which means the children are not inside.

I move outside not sure what's waiting for me. Patrice and Everly are standing in the same spot as before, but the image in front of me is terrifying. Luna and Micah are still in human form, lying on the rocks with Topher lying on top of them. All three of them are convulsing from whatever Everly is doing to them.

My eyes are drawn to Thorne. He and Amelia are fighting each other while Patrice cheers them on. Thorne is exhausted and filthy, while Amelia is covered in blood.

"Thorne! What's going on?"

"Not in control," he breathes through our connection.

Not in control? What does that mean? My eyes turn back to Everly.

"Everly?" I yell toward the young girl. Tears are streaming down her cheeks, as she stands victim to her crazy kidnapper. "Are you doing this?"

"Why don't you show her, my dear," Patrice says with a sick smile. "Show Mommy what you're capable of."

"Don't make me, Mother," Everly begs. "I'm not strong enough."

"Do it, or they die."

I step in front of the duo, blocking Everly from the pain she's causing my friends. "Leave her alone, Patrice."

"Oh, for God's sake. Why must I do everything myself? If you release them, your brother and sister will die. Do you understand me, Everly?" The immortal vampire doesn't respond as she wipes a tear from her cheek. "You just can't find good help these days."

Patrice turns her attention toward me before landing on top of me, knocking me to the sharp rocks below. Feeling the strength return, I stand, straightening my torn shirt. "My patience is running thin, *Mother*. Where are the Alex and Autumn?"

Instead of answering, Patrice runs toward me faster than my eyes can track. Like before, the world around me slows. The cries of my friends are nothing more than faint echoes as the fight behind me moves in slow motion. In front of me, Patrice is running toward me with her teeth bared and death in her eyes. I don't wait for her arrival.

Leaping through the air, I land behind her, wrap my arm around her throat, and twist until there's nothing left holding her head and body together. Patrice's body collapses to the rocks below, followed by her head. "You're right. It is hard to find good help these days."

The moment Patrice is dead, Everly releases whatever control she has over the lycan and vampires. Amelia and Thorne stop fighting, both collapsing to the rocky terrain as Topher moves toward his wife, still in wolf form. Luna and Micah sit up, working to catch their breath.

"I'm sorry," Everly whispers. "I didn't mean to hurt anyone."

Everly collapses into my arms the moment I reach her side. "It's okay," I console her. "No one blames you."

Thorne joins us. He's covered in blood, and his clothes are practically nonexistent. "Are you okay?" he asks, out of breath.

"Yes. Samirah's...gone." Thorne nods in understanding. "I can't find Alex and Autumn."

"They're underneath," Everly mumbles the words into my filthy shirt.

I pull away, looking her in the eyes. "Underneath where, Everly?"

She points to the solid rock underneath our feet. "Underneath," she repeats.

"I'll go," Thorne pants.

"No. You'll never make it. You're too weak and need to heal." I look around the rock at my friends who are recovering from the battle they just fought. "It has to be me."

I move to the edge of the water. Other than the piece of land I'm standing on, there's nothing else in sight, God, I hate this. Memories of being dragged behind Kragen's ship flash through my mind. *Relax, Elsie. You can do this.*

"Give me ten minutes. I'll be healed enough to do it." Thorne moves to my side.

"Alex and Autumn may not have ten minutes." I turn toward the immortal child, who's leaning against the door of the lighthouse with tears streaming down her cheeks. The pain on her face gives me the strength I need. "Take care of her." I nod toward Everly. "She's terrified."

Thorne turns his head toward the girl, and I take advantage of his distraction, diving into the water below. The moment I make contact with the murky water, flashbacks of my time with Kragen threaten to overtake me. I've worked for two centuries to block those memories from surfacing, and I'll be damned if I allow them in now.

"Alex?" I call, changing the direction of my thoughts.

I swim deeper into the water, staying next to the solid rock that's provided the base for the lighthouse for a century.

Both Alex and Everly said under, which makes no sense. The rock will go to the sea floor. Unless...

I push away from the rock, focusing my eyes on every crack, every crevice, searching for an opening. Maybe there's a cave or something. *"Alex?"* I call again, still receiving no answer.

Swimming super speed, I work my way around the rock. I'm almost around when I spot what looks like a narrow crack close to the sea floor. Approaching it, I realize there's barely enough room to squeeze through. Dammit, this has to be it. This is the only possibility.

Turning sideways, I slip an arm and leg through, shimmying my way through. Once inside, the darkness of the cave is nearly overwhelming. Through the murky water, the walls of the cave are barely visible.

I send my energy through the space, searching for any energy and receiving nothing in return. Dammit, where are they? I continue swimming until hitting what feels like the back wall of the cave. Running my hands along the stone, I search for anything that doesn't belong. Kicking through the water, my foot rubs against something not made of stone. Something soft yet solid.

Swimming closer, I find Autumn. Her tiny body is chained in silver, and her eyes are closed. Large welts cover her face, left by the chain that holds her in place. I don't hesitate. The chain burns my hand but doesn't debilitate me as I rip it away, rushing the immortal child toward the cave entrance.

Squeezing both of us through the narrow opening, I kick toward the surface, jumping from the water to the rock in one move. "Oh, my God. You found them," Amelia exclaims, taking the small child from my arms.

"She was chained," I say, moving back to the edge of the rock.

"Alex?" Thorne asks, moving to my side.

"I'm going back." I jump without another word and return to the small hole underneath the lighthouse. I move quickly to the spot where I found Autumn, finding nothing. The cave is empty. What the hell? *"Alex!"* I call through our connection.

I search every inch three times, hoping somehow I missed his tiny body. Why would she separate them? Fear overtakes me, thinking of the young boy I've grown attached to. Could he be dead?

Seconds later, I'm back on the surface. Amelia has Autumn cradled in her arms, rocking her. Everly is next to the two of them, with Luna's arms wrapped around her.

"She's not waking up," Everly cries.

"She's a vampire. Give her body a moment to accli-mate," Amelia reassures her.

"Alex?" Topher asks.

"He's not down there." My voice is no louder than a whisper. "I searched the entire cave. Autumn was alone."

"That's not possible. Mother took them together." Everly stands, moving toward the edge of the water.

"The woman took him," Autumn's weak voice says.

"Autumn!" Everly wraps her arms around her sister.

"What woman, Autumn?" I ask, moving to her side.

"The goddess," Autumn answers before closing her eyes again.

this can't end well

THE SIX OF us stare at each other, not sure if we heard Autumn correctly.

"The goddess?" Amelia repeats. "Are you sure, Autumn?"

She helps the immortal child sit up, coughing water as she moves. "Yes. The goddess." She coughs again, this time spewing gallons from her body. "She's the one who took us down there. She left me and took Alexander."

"Eudora?" Amelia asks our group.

"Anything's possible at this point." I turn back toward Autumn. "Was there anyone with the goddess? Another woman perhaps?"

"No," she answers. "She was alone."

I cross my arms in front of my chest. "Is anyone else confused? This entire thing is a load of shit. I don't know who's going where or when, or who the bad guy is. It seems to be changing rapidly."

"I think we can all agree that Kragen is the bad guy." Thorne moves to my side. His wounds are mostly healed, and he stands straighter than earlier. "Patrice was a close second."

Amelia helps Autumn to her feet. "Can you tell us what the goddess looked like?" she asks the young girl.

"She was beautiful. Her hair was the color of sand, and her eyes were the color of emeralds."

"That certainly sounds like Eudora. What would she want with Alex?" Thorne asks the group.

"His ability?" Luna answers. "It could be very valuable."

"Yeah, but Eudora's a goddess. The ability to read minds is nothing in her world," Micah answers. "There's more to it than the obvious."

"Because of me," I say as reality hits me. "She's holding him until I do what she wants."

"Don't take this the wrong way, Elsie, but what would a goddess want from you?" Luna's words are harsh.

"She wants her to kill Kragen," Thorne fills in the blanks.

"Are we back to that again?" Luna continues. "What the hell is it with you and Kragen? Do you two have some sort of love connection?"

As soon as the words leave her mouth, Thorne is on top of the young lycanthrope with teeth bared. Topher doesn't waste a second and shifts back into wolf form. He snarls at the vampire, protecting the member of his pack.

"Stop!" I shout, moving to the center of the shit show that's about to begin. "This isn't going to solve anything." I make eye contact with Amelia, who moves closer to her husband. I do the same for Thorne.

"What the hell was that?" Luna asks. "I'm here to help, and you try to kill me?"

Thorne's teeth return back to normal. "I'm sorry, Luna."

"Yeah, well sorry's not going to fix the fact that you just tried to eat me."

"Everyone needs to calm down. We'll be no help to Alex if we're fighting each other." Amelia rubs a wound healing on her arm from her fight with Thorne as she speaks. "If Elsie's right and Eudora took Alex to convince her to kill Kragen, then we need to figure out our next step."

"I'm next stepped out," Luna announces, sitting heavily on a large rock.

"We can't leave him," Everly says, tears filling her eyes. "We can't leave Alexander alone with her."

"Yeah, I know," Luna answers. "I'm just hangry."

"What does that mean?" Everly asks.

"It means I need to eat." Luna stands, pulling Everly with her. "I have no intentions of leaving Alex with Eudora." She sighs and props her hands on her hips. "Do we even know where to find Eudora?"

"She left a message for you," Autumn says, moving toward her sister.

"Patrice?" I ask.

Autumn's tiny head shakes back and forth. "No, the goddess."

"What's the message?" Thorne asks.

The young girl closes her eyes before speaking. "If you want the boy, you know what you must do." Autumn wipes large tears from her eyes. "She's going to kill him if you don't do what she wants."

I wrap an arm around her shoulder. "I'm not going to allow that." I turn toward the paranormal team. "I won't allow her to kill him."

"I think I speak for everyone when I say, we won't allow that either." Amelia props her hands on her hips, copying Luna's stance. "Let's go kill the bastard."

"No," I interrupt. "This is something I have to do alone."

"Elsie—" Thorne starts.

"I'm sorry, Thorne. I have to do this alone. She has Alex. I won't allow something to happen to you or anyone else for that matter." I turn back toward the group. "I'm the only one who can do this."

"The boat is on its way to pick us up." Amelia slides a phone back into her pocket. "We'll discuss this further at the house."

I nod, knowing I have no intentions of discussing anything. Discussing is all we've done. It's time for action.

On cue, the roar of an engine echoes off the concrete walls of the lighthouse. Topher carries Autumn, while Thorne carries Everly. We load the boat in silence.

"You folks look like you've been in a fight," the captain announces with an awkward laugh. "Everyone okay?"

"We're good," Micah smiles. "Just ready to get back to land."

"I can understand that." He turns toward Amelia. "The boy is with the woman who paid me."

"Good. Thank you for taking care of him," I answer for the group.

We pull back into the Riverwalk and to the dock we departed from earlier. "Oh, I almost forgot," our captain says as we unload. "The woman asked me to let you know that the SUV is parked in lot G." He shrugs. "I'm guessing y'all will know what that means."

"We do, thank you again," Luna answers. We move in slow motion into the parking lot area, searching for G.

......

Several hours have passed since being back at the house. Thorne hasn't spoken much since returning. Angry energy pours from him, and if the tables were turned, I'd feel the same.

"You know I have to do this alone," I announce as he exits the shower. He's wearing nothing but a towel, hung low on his hips. I focus on keeping my attention on his face.

"No, I don't know that." He pulls the towel off, revealing every inch of him while he dries his extremities. "Why are you always doing this?"

I clear my throat before responding. "Doing what?"

"This!" He throws his arms to the side. "You insist on doing everything alone. You're going to burst in there with guns blaring and get yourself killed. Kragen has been building a crew, and we have no way of knowing how many people you're going to come in contact with."

"Thorne, you have to..."

"No, Elsie. I don't have to do anything except protect you." Tears fill his eyes, and guilt fills me at the sight.

"I'm sorry, Thorne."

"I spent two hundred years searching for you, and now that I've found you, you're...you're..."

"What? Being stupid? Crazy? What label do you want to put on me?"

"I'm not labeling you." He wipes a tear from his cheek. "You're asking me to lose you again and again and again." Thorne slips on a pair of loose-fitting sweatpants before sitting heavily on the bed. "I can't keep doing this."

Tears well in my eyes. "I understand." My words are no louder than a whisper.

"I don't think you do, Elsie. I'm not telling you

goodbye. I'm telling you I love you, and I need you to lower those walls you keep bound around your heart." He moves in front of me. "I'm not Kragen. I'm not the men on his ship." His voice trails off as he moves until there's barely space between us. "I'm Captain Hawthorne Rex. The man who fell in love with the strongest woman he'd ever met." Warm fingers slide along my cheek. "You're still the strongest woman I've ever met, but you can't ask me to stand by and allow you to walk into the unknown alone. *I'm* not strong enough."

Tears slide down my cheeks. "What if something happens?"

"Then we'll be together." His voice has softened, as he wipes my cheek dry. "I don't want to be here if you're not. I don't want to live my life without you. We're going together, Elsie."

"Okay," I whisper.

Thorne pulls me close, wrapping his arms around my waist and lifting me off the floor. I wrap my legs around his waist, feeling every inch of him through my thin leggings. "We don't have time," I pant between kisses.

"I'll be quick," he answers, backing me up against the ornately wallpapered wall behind us. "Get these off." He pulls at the fabric separating the two of us.

I follow directions as he lowers my feet to the floor, allowing me to lose the pants while never losing contact with his mouth. Seconds later, my legs are back in position as he backs us into the wall. Strong hands grab my ass, pulling the softest part of me closer to the hardest part of him.

He doesn't waste a moment. The moment he enters me, my breath catches in my throat. The sensation of being filled completely is nearly enough to bring me over the edge right there. Thorne pushes deeper, his speed intensifying as the two of us make up for our years apart, make up for the pain that we've shared, and the pain we're about to experience. His tongue pushes into my mouth, matching the intensity of his thrusts.

"Acushla," he sighs just as he pushes deep inside, holding himself as his entire body shudders. The connection pushes me over the edge, causing us to climax in unison. The sensation brings tears to my eyes. Not tears of pain, but tears of complete and utter love for the man who became a vampire to find me. The man who's been at my side since I was the sickly nineteen-year-old, taking care of her younger siblings. The man who's willing to fight by my side, even if it means his death.

"I love you," I whisper into his ear. "I love you for who you are and everything that you've done and will do."

"I love you, too."

Pulling my legs from his body, I lower myself to the floor, never taking my eyes off Thorne's. "It's time."

"Aye," he agrees. "It is."

We take a few minutes to dress, each finding clothes that are easy to move in, not sure what the future holds. We move downstairs, finding the rest of our crew, along with Fran and baby Edon.

"The girls are resting upstairs," Fran announces as we join them.

"Brayden?" I ask anyone who will answer.

"Locked in one of the guest bedrooms on the third floor," she answers. "I didn't want the temptation around the girls."

"Thorne is going with me," I announce.

My new friends share a look. "Yeah, we figured," Luna answers.

"Topher and I need to stay here with Edon," Amelia adds. Sadness fills her voice.

"I wouldn't have let you come anyway." I turn toward Luna and Micah. "Before you two say anything, you're not invited, either."

Luna looks at the wooden floorboards. "Elsie, I'm sorry for being a bitch earlier."

I pull her into a hug, allowing her fragrance to fill my nostrils. "Luna, you're my only friend. I didn't think you were being a bitch. You're tired. Hell, we're all tired."

"Where's Kragen?" I ask the Alpha.

Topher closes his eyes. "The bayou."

"That's a large area," Thorne interrupts. "Can you narrow it down slightly?"

"I've got the GPS in the SUV set for you. It'll be

easier to get there in a vehicle and draw less attention." Topher hands the keys to Thorne.

Amelia hugs me, pulling me tight. "Be safe. I'm sorry about earlier." She moves in front of Thorne. "Sorry about the fight. Everly's power is stronger than anything I've ever experienced." She nods upstairs to where the girls are.

"Aye. I've never felt control like that before. It was a little...off-putting."

"Thank you for everything. In case we—" I start.

"No. We're not going to think like that," Luna interrupts. "You guys are going to do what needs to be done and get Alex back. Kragen has lived past his prime, anyway."

......

Thirty minutes later, we turn onto a road that gives *end of the world* vibes. Tall ancient oak trees that have withstood hundreds of storms through the years line the path. Their twisted branches stretch and turn in all directions as they beckon us into the unknown.

"This looks like the perfect place for a pirate," Thorne says as we continue. "It's also the perfect place to figure out what we're going to do when we get there. We haven't talked about a plan."

I shrug. "I have no idea what we're going to find when we get there, which makes it impossible to form a plan. Right now, the plan is simple—kill him."

"Aye." His voice is barely audible.

The sensation of vampire energy comes from nowhere and hits me like a brick wall. Thorne slams on the brakes, obviously feeling it too. "What the hell?"

We step out of the SUV, searching through the trees for the source. "Do you recognize the energy?" Thorne asks.

"Somewhat. But I'm not sure who it belongs to." I move behind the SUV, and the feeling grows. "It's worse back here." The energy feels both young and old at the same time. I raise the lift gate of the SUV, and the energy nearly overtakes me. A hand-sewn quilt covers the floor. Underneath are two very suspicious bumps. Pulling the quilt back, two tiny heads pop out, each smiling a toothy grin.

"What the hell? Girls, why are you here?" Thorne scolds.

"We want to save Alex," Everly answers. "He's our brother."

"We're not going to save Alex. We're..." I walk away, not sure how to explain what we're doing. "Where we're going, it's not safe for either of you."

"We want to help," Autumn answers with large tears filling her eyes.

Thorne pulls the quilt completely away. Both girls are wearing modern clothing and are cleaner than earlier. "We appreciate your offer, but we're not willing to put either of you in that kind of danger." I cross my arms in front of my chest as I speak, hoping to appear more threatening to the immortal children.

"Whatever you're doing, we can help." Autumn slides out of the back of the SUV, clearly not intimidated. "We have abilities."

"Aye, I know. The man we're going to see will want you for those abilities."

"How'd we get this far from the house without recognizing your energies?" Thorne interrupts, asking an excellent question.

Everly smiles. "I borrowed the boy's ability and hid us."

"Brayden's ability?" I ask. "How?"

She shrugs. "I don't know. I just did."

"Can you borrow anyone else's ability?"

Everly turns toward her sister. She stares at the doe-eyed girl for a few seconds before turning back to the SUV. Seconds later, the SUV is lifted from the gravel road, hanging in the air several feet.

"Holy shit. Did you do that?" I ask, knowing the answer.

"I guess," Everly answers before putting our vehicle back on the ground.

"Maybe they *could* help." Thorne's words are no louder than a whisper.

"We could!" Autumn enthusiastically answers for the two of them.

"You're asking us to take you into an environment

where you could die. Do you realize this is not a game?" I turn into the stern parent.

"Will this help get Alex back?" Everly asks.

Thorne and I share a look before I answer. "It could, but there's a chance all of us could die trying."

"Then you have to let us help. We'll stay out of your way and use our abilities from a safe spot," Autumn argues.

"There are no safe spots." I prop my hands on my hips. "Thorne and I may not survive. If that happens, you will be taken captive, and...and you'll wish you were dead." I don't go into detail.

The girls turn toward each other locked in a silent conversation. "We're coming," Autumn answers. "It's no use arguing with us. You won't win. We'll just follow you."

"Dammit," I sigh. "One condition." The girls nod. "If something happens to Thorne or me, you run. You run faster than you've ever run in your lives, and you don't turn around for anyone or anything until you're safe with Fran or Amelia. Do you understand?" I can't believe I'm considering this.

"We understand," they answer in unison.

the swamp of death

"THE GPS SAYS we'll be there in ten minutes," I announce as if I'm the only one who knows how to read it.

"Aye, we should walk from here," Thorne agrees.

"We're surrounded by a swamp," Autumn adds. "Are you sure this is where he is?"

"Not the exact location, but in this vicinity...and he's a pirate, so this is the perfect environment for him." Thorne pulls the SUV to a stop along the edge of the narrow road.

"A pirate?" Everly asks.

I sigh before answering. "Kragen is the pirate who took me from Thorne's ship nearly three hundred years ago. He's an ancient vampire and a monster. I've spent two centuries running from him."

"If you've been running from him, why are we trying

to find him? Especially if he doesn't have Alex. This seems dumb." Autumn's simplified version of the insanity that is my life makes me laugh as I climb out of the SUV.

"You're right," I answer. "The goddess and Kragen were married a long time ago."

"The goddess?" Everly asks. "The goddess was married to a vampire?"

"Aye. They had a child. Her name is Marnie."

Autumn stops walking. "There is someone out there that's half vampire and half goddess? What does that make her?"

Thorne scoffs. "Terrifying."

"What does that have to do with Alex?" Everly continues.

"Eudora took Alex to force me to kill the pirate. He's my maker, and I'm the only one strong enough, which means I'm the only one who can kill him." Even saying the words out loud, it's still confusing.

"That's dumb," Autumn continues. "Why doesn't the goddess just kill the pirate herself?"

"Because if she does, their daughter will die, too," Thorne answers.

Everly moves in front of the three of us. "So, you're supposed to kill the pirate, and if you do, we get Alex back?"

"Aye. That's it in a nutshell."

"What makes this pirate so hard to kill?" Autumn asks.

"He's nearly one thousand years old and is collecting vampires to be his crew," I answer.

"Ah..." Autumn shrugs. "Two immortal child vampires are stronger than twenty regular vampires. Especially young ones."

"I don't want you two to fight. You will use your abilities and stay away from the fighting. Do you understand?"

The girls shrug at the same time. "We'll see," Autumn answers for the both of them.

We continue walking until the road begins to disappear into a swamp ahead of us. "We're going to have to swim from here." Thorne reaches down, lifting Autumn above his head and propping her on his shoulders. I do the same for Everly, and the four of us work our way through the murky water.

We're several miles in when the faint smell of sulfur surrounds me, stopping me in my tracks.

"What is it?" Thorne asks.

"I smell him."

He nods, before moving again. The water has gotten deep enough that even on my shoulders, Everly's feet are fully submerged.

"Can you do what you did earlier with Brayden's power?" I ask the girl on my shoulders.

"Already did," she answers. "I did it as soon as we entered the swamp."

"Smart girl." I turn toward Thorne. "With Everly's shield up, we're going in blind."

"Or human," Autumn adds.

The smell of sulfur fills my nose once more, telling me we're moving in the right direction. I lose track of time as we stomp our way further into the muck. Something large slides into the water from a patch of dry land. The thought of what could be near my feet is almost as terrifying as what we're searching for. I've never realized how much I depend on my ability to sense energy until I'm denied access.

"I see something," Everly announces from my shoulders. "It looks like a house."

"There are some people that live out here in the swamp. Can you see it well enough to make out any details?"

"Looks old and made of wood," she answers.

"Do you see anyone there?" Thorne asks.

"I don't know. It's too far away."

We keep moving toward the building in the distance. With Everly's vampire eyes, it's still several miles ahead.

"I see someone," Autumn whispers. "They're on the porch." She stares into the distance. "A man is sitting in a rocking chair."

"Is he human?" Thorne asks.

"I can't tell."

"I can let the shield down," Everly suggests. "Just long enough to figure out what he is."

"Do it," I answer. "Only for a second." The young girl takes a deep breath and energy floods me. Not only do I feel Kragen, but he's not alone. "Put it back!" I shout.

"Bastard," Thorne whispers.

"Aye. There were others."

"That felt yucky," Autumn whispers from Thorne's shoulders.

"Kragen *is* yucky," I answer. "Everly, keep the shield up. The only chance we have is for them not to feel us. We have to get as close as possible to figure out our next step."

We continue moving toward the house and the awaiting enemy with the shield securely in place. We're less than a hundred yards from the building when Everly makes a strange sound from my shoulders.

"What's going on?"

"Something feels like it's poking at me," she answers, resting her head in her hands.

"Poking?"

"Yeah. Like a knife stabbing at my brain."

"Someone's trying to get through the shield," Thorne whispers.

"The closer we get, the more it hurts," Everly whispers.

Thorne moves next to a large cypress tree. "Climb up," he directs Autumn. "This is as close as you two are getting."

I follow him, pushing Everly behind her sister. "What about the shield?" she asks.

"Hold it over us as long as you can. Don't release

yourselves from it. If you're going to lose control of the shield, keep it over the two of you, and let us go. Do you understand?" I answer.

"I think so." Everly's voice sounds exhausted.

"Yours and Autumn's safety comes first."

The girls climb the tree, hiding in the recesses of its branches. Once I'm sure they're in a safe spot, we continue moving toward impending doom or freedom. The irony of me not killing Kragen when I had the chance, to now being forced to do the deed by the Goddess of the Sea, isn't lost on me. Instead of taking his life on his ship, Thorne and I are stomping our way through a swamp to his front door.

The house is still twenty feet ahead when I feel Everly's shield lift and a swoosh of energy flow in. *"Here we go,"* Thorne says through my mind. We don't waste any more time. Without the protection, we leap from the murky water to the porch of the house seconds later, finding the porch empty. The vampire who was outside earlier is gone, but his energy still lingers.

Thorne rips the door off its hinges, and we enter full speed, finding it empty. No furniture, no people, no vampires...no nothing.

"Where are they?" Thorne asks.

"Kragen's close. I sense him."

Back on the porch, I turn a full three hundred and sixty degrees, searching for the source. A few hundred yards away I spot something that fills me with dread. The bow of a pirate ship looms in the distance. It's not as large as the one he abandoned in North Carolina but a ship, nonetheless.

"*Do you see it?*" I ask, nodding toward the dark wood.

"*Holy shit.*"

"*How does he plan on getting it out of here? We're in a swamp for God's sake.*"

"*Does Kragen need a plan?*" Thorne stares at the ship. "*There's no point in hiding. He knows we're here. Let's go say hello, shall we?*"

"No need," a familiar voice says as Kragen lands on the porch in front of us. He's wearing a pair of cargo shorts, a tank top, and flip-flops. I hold in the laugh that's trying to escape.

He looks me up and down with a disapproving smirk. "It seems you've let yourself go a bit, my dear. You look as if you've tromped through a swamp." He laughs at his joke. "Although I'm not unhappy to see you, I will say I'm surprised to see you so soon. I imagined we'd continue our little cat and mouse game for a hundred more years or so."

"Believe me, it wasn't by choice."

"*Don't tell him the truth,*" Thorne warns.

"If you didn't already figure it out, Captain, I can hear your communications with each other." Kragen crosses his arms across his chest. His laugh echoes off the nearby trees. "Surprise!" He stares at us. "What, you two thought you were the only special ones?" He shrugs, turning toward me. "Until Elsbeth, I thought I was the only one."

"That's why you took me? Because I was special? Why all the bullshit excuses?"

I want to slap the smile off his face. "Entertainment?" he answers with a shrug.

"Torturing me, allowing others to torture me, holding me captive for a century, chasing me for *two* centuries, and terrorizing me was *fun?* I knew you were a sick son of a bitch but not to this extent."

"I'm just full of surprises." He turns toward Thorne. "If I'd have realized you had a gift, I could've had a pair. Imagine the fun that would have presented."

I move closer to the pirate. "You're going to die."

"That sounds familiar," he teases. "Shall we play this game again?"

"Samirah's not here to save you this time," Thorne adds. "She's dead."

"Aww, what a pity. Although, I'm not sure what's worse. You thinking she saved me, or you thinking I care if she's dead."

"Have you ever cared about anyone?" I spew.

"Once," he answers, looking at Thorne. "Until your men killed her. Imagine my surprise when I found such a gifted young girl on the ship. In fact, Captain, you should thank Elsbeth. If it weren't for her, I would've sunk your entire ship and taken them all as my crew. She saved you and your men."

"I didn't kill Eudora," Thorne answers.

"No, your men did, which makes you responsible."

"She's still alive, you insufferable asshole!" I shout.

Kragen stares at me like I've spoken a language he's never heard before. "Lies! If she were alive, she'd come to me."

"How can you be this dumb? She's the one who sent me here to kill you."

"Lies. Shut up, bitch."

I've struck a nerve and continue my attack. "She wants you dead so badly that she's followed me through two different cities to ensure I complete the task."

I've never seen Kragen so flustered. His demeanor changes, and he lowers his arms. "You're lying."

"She hates you so much that she pretended to die and is forcing me to kill you." I continue my assault.

Kragen doesn't hesitate. He moves toward me at full speed, wrapping his hands around my neck and pushing me off the porch into the water below. His hands are still tight as he holds me against the slimy bottom of the swamp. *"I should've killed you the day I took you from that ship."* His words echo through my mind.

"You weren't strong enough then, and you're not strong enough now." I reach inside, pulling the ability that started this shit show in the first place, and wrap my hands around his. Slowly, I pull his fingers away from my throat, pushing my hands between his hand and my neck. *"Get the fuck off me. You don't control me anymore."*

Slipping my arms closer to his head, I twist my body, freeing myself from his hold. I breach the surface, leaping to a cypress tree nearby. "I knew there was more to you," Kragen says, landing on a different branch. "It only took three hundred years for you to discover it. Join me, Elsbeth. We can rule together."

"You're joking, right?" I can barely keep my smile at bay.

Thorne leaps from the porch, landing on the branch next to me. "In case you're confused, asshole, Elsie won't be joining you."

"Tsk, tsk, tsk. What a shame. We could've been great together, my dear."

Without warning, I leap off my tree, landing beside Kragen. "I'd rather die."

"That can be arranged." Kragen moves faster than I can track, wrapping an arm around my waist and lifting us into the sky above.

"Elsie!" Thorne shouts as we fly over the tops of the trees and the swamp below.

"We're not doing this again!" I shout, rotating my body to face his.

"That's going to be a bitch of a fall," Kragen says moments before I free my arm from his grip.

"I'd rather recover from the fall than smell your putrid breath one more second." Pulling my arm back, I punch his jaw hard enough to dislocate the bones and tendons holding it in place. Blood covers me, as his wound pours dark red liquid. I take advantage of the distraction and follow the first punch with another, hitting him on the other side, completely separating the bones in his jaw.

The assault causes Kragen to loosen his grip, hurling me toward the murky water below. I'm a few hundred feet up. Kragen's right. The impact is going to hurt like a bitch. I rotate, putting my feet toward the ground in hopes I'll be able to land standing up. With the rate of speed I'm moving, there's no way this is going to work.

"Elsie. Your legs will shatter," Thorne's words echo through my mind. He's telling me something I already know, but I don't have any better ideas.

Pulling my legs to my chest, I brace for landing when something grabs me from the air, moving me away from the water. Seconds later, I'm standing on the porch of the house without a clue of what happened.

"Are you okay?" Everly's weak voice asks. She's standing beside me with a wide smile covering her face.

"Holy shit. You can fly?"

The tiny girl shrugs. "I guess. I saw the pirate do it, so I borrowed the skill."

"Thank y..." My words are cut short by Kragen landing beside Everly.

"Who is this lovely, talented creature?" He picks up one of her small braids in his hand, rubbing it between his fingers.

I pull her from his side. "Leave her alone."

My stomach curls at the look on his face. It's a look I

remember from the bottom of his ship. "How did you learn to fly?" He ignores my threat.

"Don't answer," I interrupt.

"That was quite rude, *Elsbeth*. I believe I'm talking to the girl." He smirks. "Are you a bit jealous?"

"Fuck you," Everly spews as Thorne lands on the other side of her.

"I see you've picked up Elsbeth's intellectual vocabulary. She's developed quite a filthy mouth over the years." Being around Kragen makes me physically sick. My stomach turns being this close to him.

"I'm going to guess the reason I didn't feel the child earlier means there's more to her than just flying." Kragen takes a step forward.

"Stay where you are," I warn.

"Or what? You're strong but not strong enough to defeat me. It's my blood that runs through your veins. I'm the one who made you. You can't kill me." He turns his attention toward Thorne, and my stomach drops. "You see, my dear. I know you." He licks his lips. "I know your weaknesses." Kragen moves faster than my eyes can see, knocking into Thorne and pulling him into the water below. Seconds later, they lift from the water, with Thorne wrapped tightly in Kragen's arms.

"Stop!" Everly shouts from below. The two vampires freeze mid-flight. "Put him down!"

Kragen turns in our direction, landing the two of them on the wooden planks of the porch. "Why am I doing this?" he asks.

Everly turns her back to the men, pointing at the tree where the girls were hiding. Seconds later, Autumn lands on the porch next to the rest of us and runs toward me.

"How are you doing this?" Kragen repeats. His hands are frozen to his sides, seemingly tied by an invisible force.

"My sister has a very special gift," Autumn speaks for the two of them.

Kragen looks between the girls. "You're doing this?" A wicked smile covers his face. "Come with me, young one. We could rule the world. Two of the most powerful creatures on earth, together would be invincible."

"Shut up," I spew. "There's nothing powerful about you. You were a weak man who turned into a weak vampire."

Thorne steps protectively close to Everly as the ancient vampire stares her down. "I can offer more than Elsbeth ever could. You will be safe with me, forever. Protected from the ones that mean to do you harm. Come with me, my dear." He reaches his hand toward the immortal child.

Everly glances between me and Thorne. "You hurt Elsie. She's not the only one you've hurt. I can feel them. Their pain calls to me." Her eyes turn solid black. "You don't deserve to live."

Kragen's laugh fills the swamp. "Many have spoken those words before, young one, yet here I am, in the flesh." He turns toward me. "You've uttered those words a few times over the centuries, *Elsie*." He mocks my name with his tone.

Everly moves to the railing of the porch, breaking off a small piece of wood. "Everly?" I question as she passes the pirate vampire.

"I'm okay."

Placing the piece of wood in Kragen's hand, she backs away slowly. "Stake yourself through the heart."

Kragen looks at the small girl with a mixture of wonder and awe. "Have you gone mad?"

Autumn joins her sister, and the two girls hold hands, staring at the man who I've spent most of my life running from. Autumn lifts her free hand into the air, forcing Kragen off the porch and hovering over the water.

Whatever Everly's doing to his mind is causing him distress. His body is shaking, fighting the mind control sent by the tiny vampire in charge of his movements. The wooden stake is still held tightly in his hand, as he fights to keep his body under his control.

"Did you hear me, Pirate?" Everly teases. "Kill. Yourself."

Autumn rotates her wrists, and the pirate rotates in unison.

"Kill. Yourself." Everly repeats. Her words are softer as she focuses all of her energy on Kragen.

Thorne and I flank the small girl, placing a hand on her shoulder, offering our energy as Autumn continues to rotate Kragen's out-of-control body. I focus on the strength held deep inside and send every bit of it into Everly. "Kill. Yourself," I add to their chant.

The look on Kragen's face is one I've dreamed about for three hundred years. Black fills in the whites of his eyes, as he fights against the invisible force pushing against him. A faint voice echoes in my mind, one I vaguely remember from centuries ago. *"Burn him,"* the voice whispers. *"Burn him, Elsie. You have the power within you."*

Pulling my energy back from Everly, I focus on the voice in my head. The small voice reminds me of my sister Bonnie. What is happening? Am I losing my mind? I glance at Everly and Autumn, confused if it's them I'm hearing.

"Elsie, burn him!" I don't second guess. Focusing on the monster floating in front of me, I imagine his body bursting into flames. The energy flowing through me overwhelms me as I fight to regain control.

"Burn," I whisper, turning my attention fully onto Kragen. "Burn, you son of a bitch."

Kragen's skin begins to glow as small cracks form on the surface. His eyes search for the source, and his hands are still held tightly to his sides. "What is this?"

"It's redemption," Thorne answers for our group. "You're going to die now, Kragen. We've decided." His skin splits as his body tears open, revealing what looks like hot lava underneath. The stake in his hand moves slowly from his side and in front of him, dangerously close to his heart.

"Burn," I repeat. On command, his skin comes to life and begins to melt from his body, revealing something from nightmares.

"Do it now!" Everly shouts as a burst of energy flows from her tiny body and into Kragen. He loses control as the stake slowly slides into his heart and an ear-piercing scream escapes his lips.

Tears fill my eyes as the man who made me—the man who killed my brother—the man who tortured, raped, abused, and beat me for years turns into ash before my eyes.

Autumn continues holding him in the air until there's nothing left to hold. She releases her hand, dropping his charred clothes into the murky water below. Everly collapses from exhaustion. Her eyes are closed, and her cheeks appear sunken in.

"Everly? Is she okay?" Autumn asks.

Thorne scoops her into his arms. "She's exhausted. Killing Kragen took all of her energy." Neither of them asks about the fire, and I'm grateful. I don't have an explanation for myself, let alone anyone else.

Lifting Autumn into my arms, I hug her tight. "Thank you," I cry and squeeze the tiny hand of the passed-out girl in Thorne's arms. "Thank you, both."

"Can we go get Alex now?" Autumn whispers, wiping tears.

I have no idea where to begin looking for Alex. I don't share that information with the immortal child in my arms. "That's exactly what I intend on doing," I answer, completely unsure how to make that happen.

"Where is Kragen's crew?" Thorne asks, cradling Everly to his chest. "I sense more energy but can't determine how many or where."

"Aye. I feel vampire energy, but it's weak." I glance at Everly. "Do you think she's still shielding us?"

He shrugs. "It's possible. I don't think we've discovered the limit of what she's capable of."

"I don't feel anything special," Autumn adds. "There are vampires, but they're not any danger to us."

"How do you know?" I ask.

"If they were, we'd be dead." Her words are simple and straightforward. "Alex is our first priority. As soon as we tell the goddess that he's dead, she'll give us our brother back, right?"

Thorne and I share a knowing look. "Aye. Let's get back to the city." Thorne leaps from the porch to the top of a large tree with Everly wrapped in his arms. I do the same with Autumn, leaping from tree to tree until we reach the dirt road that leads to the abandoned vehicle.

Less than an hour later, we pull in front of the home we left only a few hours ago. Everly's been awake since being back on the road. Several bottles of goat's blood later, her energy is slowly beginning to return to normal.

"There's someone new inside," Autumn announces as we pull to a stop in front of the house. "I don't recognize the energy."

"I feel it too." I turn toward Thorne, not sure what awaits us.

"If they're in Fran's house with the baby and Amelia, they won't be a threat." Thorne exits the SUV, opening the door for the girls to follow.

The visitor's energy is strong, ancient feeling as we approach the door. I reach for the handle, just as the door opens, revealing someone who looks so much like Amelia they could be twins. Long red curls hang down her back and bright blue eyes stare into mine. "You must be Elsbeth," she says with a bright smile. Kneeling, she brings herself face-to-face with the immortal children. "Hello, girls. I'm Celeste."

the demigod from hell...literally

"CELESTE?" I question the young girl. "Amelia's maker?"

"That's me!" She smiles warmly, making me instantly feel at ease. She looks past me, moving toward Thorne. Tears fill her wide eyes. "My father was your maker. I smell him."

"Aye." Without another word, she wraps her arms around him, pulling him close. Thorne allows her to take in his scent without pulling away.

Several minutes pass before she releases her grip. "Thank you. It's not often I get a chance to be this close to him." She wipes a stray tear. "There are only a few vampires who carry his blood. He never forced anyone to become what we are. You are one of only a few."

"Aye," Thorne laughs awkwardly. "It took many years to convince him. He was a great man."

"That, he was. I'm sorry to stop you. Please, go in."

Entering the foyer, I'm not shocked to find every one of our newfound family waiting for us. Amelia wraps her arms around me the moment we shut the door. "Tell me everything," she demands, leading us into the living area.

Fran moves toward the girls the moment we enter. "Everly? Autumn? What were you two thinking? Do you know how dangerous..."

"Without them, we wouldn't have made it," I interrupt her scolding. "They made things...easier." We spend the next few minutes describing the death of the man who has terrorized me since I was human. I don't include information about the fire, and thankfully, no one mentions it.

My words still don't feel real. I expect to find him looming in the corner with an evil smile and telling me how this was all part of his master plan and surprise— he's still alive.

"How did you do it?" Everly interrupts my thoughts. The room quiets down as she speaks. "How did you do it?" she repeats, staring at Celeste.

"Do what?" Celeste asks.

"How did you grow? I know what you are. I can feel it. Why don't you look like us?"

Celeste smiles. "Magic. I researched and sought practitioners who were able to help me. I traveled many miles and spent a lot of money to find the right person."

"But you found them," Everly answers.

"I did." Celeste looks down as she speaks. "It wasn't without *discomfort*."

"Can we grow up?" Autumn asks.

"My becoming an adult came with a huge sacrifice," Celeste continues. She looks around the room, making eye contact with Amelia. "Along with causing the death of my father, I am no longer immortal."

"Like a human?" Everly asks.

Celeste nods. "I can die—I *will* die. There's more." She pauses. "If I take a life, I regain my immortality but will become a child again and remain that way the rest of my existence."

"Was it worth it?" Everly whispers.

"Yes." Celeste smiles. "Without question, yes. I'm in love with a lycanthrope, and we're going to be married soon. We'll grow old together and die as mortals. I've lived a very long and fruitful life and met some amazing people along the way. So, for me, it was worth it."

Everly stands from the couch. "We're going to find our brother and do the same."

"Do what?" I ask, not sure what she's declaring.

Autumn stands by her sister's side. "We want to be like Celeste. We want to be grown-ups."

"I don't think it's that easy," I intercede. "You don't just declare to be grown, and it happens."

Celeste moves closer to the girls. "If that's what you want, I'll get you in touch with the people who helped me."

"There was more than one?" Autumn asks.

"Yes. That's a story for another day." She turns toward me. "Where is their brother?"

"Eudora has him."

Celeste looks around the room. "Is Eudora a vampire?"

"Worse," Amelia answers. "Eudora is the Goddess of the Sea."

"They're real?" she answers, excitement covering her face.

"She's kind of a bitch," I answer, matching her enthusiasm.

"Do we have any idea where she would take the boy?" Celeste moves toward a tall bookshelf.

"Anywhere," I answer.

"He can find him." Everly points at Thorne.

The look on Thorne's face is a mixture of confusion and amusement. "I'm afraid I don't know where to look any more than you do. I'm sorry, little one."

"Yes, you do," she persists. "It's your ability."

Thorne wrinkles his forehead. "You have an ability other than talking to Elsie in her mind. You can find people."

He laughs. "If that were the case, I'd have found Elsie years ago."

"But you found her?" she persists.

"Aye, but it took two hundred years."

Everly refuses to back down. "If you lean into your ability, you can help us find Alexander, or I can borrow your power. But you have to use it first."

"What do you mean borrow his power?" Celeste joins the conversation.

"It's what I do. I can make people do things and borrow other people's abilities." Everly has gone from being the immortal child with no ability, to an ability that seems to have no limits.

"Show me," Celeste says.

Everly stands, facing Amelia's twin. She closes her eyes, and Celeste follows suit. "Do a cartwheel," Everly whispers. Celeste moves to the center of the room and completes a perfect cartwheel. "Hop on one foot," Everly continues, and Celeste follows directions.

"Why am I doing this?" Celeste asks between jumps.

"Because I told you to."

"How is this possible?"

Everly shrugs. "It just happened."

"That's enough," Fran interrupts the show. Everly stops on demand.

"How did you do that? I'm much older than you, yet I had no control over my actions."

"I didn't have any ability until the lighthouse." She shrugs as she speaks.

"Do you have an ability?" Celeste asks Autumn. The immortal child doesn't answer. Instead, she raises her hand, lifting Celeste into the air a few feet before lowering her feet to the ground.

"Damn," Celeste whispers.

"Thorne has the ability to *find* people?" Topher repeats Everly's statement from earlier.

Everly nods. "I can borrow his ability, and we can find Alex."

"Where's Alex?" a sleepy voice says from the top of the stairs.

"Brayden. What are you doing awake?" Fran rushes to his side. "Your parents are still sleeping."

"I heard voices. Lots of voices." Brayden looks at the amount of people in the living area. "What's going on?"

"Nothing that concerns you," Fran says, turning him around.

"I can feel them." His voice is weak.

Celeste rushes up the stairs and is standing in front of the boy a heartbeat later. "You're human?"

Brayden scrunches his face. "I am."

"Show her what you can do, Brayden," I coach him from below. He yawns widely before the ease of his shield surrounds us.

The look on Celeste's face makes me smile. She turns back, looking at the rest of us. "What just happened?"

"Brayden is a shield, among other things," I announce.

"Holy shit." She covers her mouth after cursing in front of the kids. "What else can you do?"

The human boy shrugs. "I don't really know. Where's my mom?"

"I'll take you to her." Fran pulls the boy down the hallway toward his parents.

"Does their brother have an ability?" Celeste asks, back at my side.

"Telepathy." I turn toward Thorne. "And he was able to locate Thorne earlier."

"Damn. I got cheated. I don't have an ability." Celeste smiles as she speaks.

Amelia laughs loudly. "Anyone who's ever met you knows you have an ability. It may not be superhuman, but you have the ability to show love to whoever you meet. You are kind, strong, and brilliant."

"Awe, thanks, Mom," Celeste answers with a laugh.

"The girls are right. We have to find Alex, which means finding Eudora," Luna interrupts.

"What about Marnie?" Micah speaks for the first time. "She's bound to know where her mother is."

"Why do I feel so lost?" Celeste asks. "Who is Marnie?"

"Kragen and Eudora's daughter," Amelia answers, like it's common knowledge.

"Do you think she's still in this area?" I ask, already knowing the answer.

Everly turns toward Thorne. "Use your ability."

"I don't know how," he answers.

The young vampire moves in front of him, wrapping her tiny hands around his. "Close your eyes," she demands. Thorne follows instructions. "Picture Alex in your mind." The energy in the room rises a few levels as

Everly wraps her arms around Thorne's waist, pulling him closer. The silence in the room becomes deafening as minutes pass before she pulls away, sucking in a deep breath. "I'm seeing a ship. It looks old but new at the same time. It looks like a ship that a pirate would live on." Everly looks around the room. "Does that make sense?"

Luna, Micah, Thorne, and I make eye contact. The only pirate ship that we know to be fully operational and complete is in the possession of the lycan of Charleston, formerly owned by Kragen. "It makes perfect sense," Micah answers. "Except, there's no way in hell she has it. It's under lock and key in Charleston."

The energy in the room shifts, and everyone in the room feels it. "Someone's here," Everly whispers just as the doorbell buzz echoes through the house.

"I'll get it," Fran says, moving toward the closed door. "Hello. May I help you?" she says as the rest of us move behind her.

"Well, hello!" a familiar blonde girl answers. She looks behind Fran at the group of paranormal creatures who've surrounded the older vampire. "Perfect. It seems I've found most of you in one spot."

I step in front of Fran. "What do you want, Marnie?"

"May I come in?"

Fran moves to my side. "Of course." She motions to the living area.

Marnie sits in the same spot I occupied moments

earlier. "This is quite a room full, isn't it?" She claps her hands like she's at a performance.

"What do you want?" I refuse to be friendly.

Marnie turns her attention toward Everly and Autumn. "Hello, girls."

"Don't talk to them," Amelia interrupts. The girls move to my side, wrapping their small arms around my waist.

"You smell like the fire," Everly whispers. "Just like Samirah and..." she looks up at me. "Elsie."

Marnie laughs. "Yeah, it's my curse. I guess you can never get rid of your parents, no matter how hard you try."

"Cut the bullshit, Marnie. Why are you here?" I spew.

"I can assure you, there is no bullshit to cut. I'm here on behalf of my mother."

"Kragen's dead." My words are short and to the point. "I did what she asked. Where's Alex?"

"No, you didn't." Marnie stands, moving toward the fireplace. "You didn't kill him at all." She turns her attention toward Everly. "He killed himself, didn't he, young one?"

"Semantics, Marnie." The irony of using Kragen's words is almost comedic at this point. "Kragen's dead. What difference does it make how it happened?"

The energy shifts again, as Marnie transforms into something from a mythology encyclopedia. Her body lifts off the floor, rising nearly to the ceiling. Her once blonde hair lengthens to her knees, turning the crimson color of dried blood. Long arms lift to her sides, as seaweed extends from each finger, covering the room in green slime within seconds. Marnie's eyes open, losing the beautiful shade of green they were moments earlier, and replacing it with bright white light. Her jaw stretches wide, forcing her mouth open wider than humanly possible. The scream that leaves her body breaks every window, pottery, and glass in the house simultaneously.

"Give me the children." Her words vibrate through the room. "They belong to us."

I slide the girls behind my back, hiding them from whatever the hell is happening in front of us. "They don't belong to anyone," I argue.

"Fran?" a soft voice says from above. "Who's that? She feels weird." Fran runs up the stairs, hiding Brayden from the chaos below.

Amelia steps beside me, linking her arm through mine. "You are not welcome in this home. Leave now!" Celeste does the same on my other side.

"Isn't that cute? A trio of vampires."

"Quartet," Thorne says, joining our group.

"Fuck you, Marnie," Amelia spews as she transforms into the giant wolf I've seen several times before. Topher, Micah, and Luna do the same, joining our small line.

Marnie's laugh echoes through the room. "You

fools. You have no idea who you're talking to. I am a demigod. You can't win."

"You heard her," I continue. "You are not welcome here."

"Not without the children."

Celeste steps away from my side, transforming into what can only be described as a monster. Her angelic face is disfigured and demonic. Dark eyes replace the blue, and her skin is darker than before. She's absolutely terrifying.

I join her, turning into my own version of a monster as the immortal children run upstairs at vampire speed. Fran joins us, and the eight of us face a demigod—half vampire, half goddess—fully fucked.

Marnie lifts higher toward the ceiling, pulling the seaweed with her. The eight of us spread out, surrounding the creature in front of us. "Give me the children," she repeats. Her voice vibrating through the room.

"Over my dead body," I spew.

"That can happily be arranged." Marnie flicks her finger, pulling a long strand of seaweed from the wall with it. Before my eyes track movement, she's wrapped it around Micah and Luna, forcing them to the floor with a heavy thud.

Topher doesn't hesitate. He's in the air, heading straight for Marnie's throat seconds later. She knocks him to the side with barely any movement, throwing him into the foyer.

Amelia is next to jump toward the creature. She leaps with her teeth barred and lands on Marnie's chest. Swiping a large paw, she tears into Marnie's body, leaving claw marks in her wake.

"Bitch!" Marnie screams as a piece of seaweed wraps around Amelia's body, throwing her to the ground. "Give me the children, and I will allow you to live. If you want a fight, I'm game. However, none of you will survive."

Luna and Micah continue fighting the bindings holding them in place, unable to free themselves from her grip.

"Get the children out of here," Thorne sends through our connection. *"I love you...always."*

Barely giving me time to understand his words, he leaps through the air, wrapping his arms and legs around the demigod. "No!" I shout as my ability takes over. I fly through the air, landing on the wall behind Marnie, wrapping my arm around her throat. It takes every bit of my strength to hold on.

"Don't bite her!" Everly shouts through my mind. *"Her blood will kill you instantly."* I have no idea if Everly is correct, but I've learned not to question the immortal child and her abilities.

"Everly, don't come down here, but we need your help."

Marnie pulls Thorne from her side, throwing him across the room. His body hits the wall hard, leaving a human-sized dent in the wood. He slides down, seemingly unconscious.

I continue pulling her neck, keeping her from moving any further. "Let go of me," she warns.

In a moment from an epic fantasy movie, Celeste steps forward holding what looks like a Viking-era sword. I have no idea where she found it, but I'm okay with it. She moves faster than eyes can track, slicing her way through the seaweed extensions. The instant they're separated from the demigod, they wither, turning into dust.

Micah and Luna are instantly on their feet, each staggering slightly as they stalk closer to the fight.

Celeste continues her assault, moving closer to Marnie until barely any space separates them. She lifts into the air, looking the creature in the eyes. "Leave. Or I will kill you."

Marnie's mouth opens, releasing another ear-piercing scream as she twists, pulling from my grip and throwing me off of the wall behind her. I land across the room, jumping to my feet in an instant.

"Where's our brother?" Everly calls from the top of the stairs. The immortal children are standing hand in hand with their eyes locked on Marnie.

The demigod lowers to the ground, keeping her arms to her sides. "Come with me, and I'll show you."

"Okay," Everly and Autumn answer in unison.

"No!" I scream just as a whirlwind of action ensues all at once. Luna rushes up the stairs, standing in front of the girls protectively as the rest of us rush toward Marnie.

She sweeps her arms into the air, forming what looks like a large bubble that encases everyone except Luna and the girls. "They have decided," Marnie's voice booms through the room. She snaps her fingers, filling the bubble with water.

Each of us begins tearing at the magic that surrounds us. I use my teeth, while the lycan use their claws. Nothing works. The lycan can't breathe.

"Oh, my, God. Luna," Celeste's voice echoes through the water, staring through the wall of our cell. "Luna."

Marnie stalks up the stairs, heading right toward the immortal children and their lycanthrope protector. "Luna!" I scream as the pale wolf stands on her hind legs, biting at the creature with everything that she has.

The room turns slow motion, and I watch in horror as Marnie slices through Luna's small body like she's cutting butter. "No!" I scream while fighting against the restraints. Luna shifts into human form as she falls down the stairs, landing in a pool of blood on the landing.

"We'll be okay," Everly says in my mind as she and Autumn are wrapped in Marnie's arms and dragged through the door seconds later.

"They can't breathe!" Amelia says, drawing my attention back to the lycan and our trap. Topher and Micah are fighting less than earlier, telling me they're running out of oxygen. We continue fighting against the bubble, unable to make a tear through it.

"Topher!" Amelia cries. Her voice has lost the strength she always carries with her. "You're going to be okay, baby."

I focus all of my attention on the human boy who's upstairs, hidden in his room. *"Brayden! We need your help. If you can hear me, we need you to come downstairs."* Micah has begun to convulse under the water, returning to human form as Amelia wraps her arms around Topher, blowing air into his mouth.

"Brayden!" I call again. *"The wolves are going to die."*

Dark hair at the top of the stairs grabs my attention as the human boy peers around the corner. He moves slowly down the stairs, stopping to look at what remains of Luna.

"You have to cut the bubble." He looks up, realizing what's going on. *"Find a knife,"* I demand.

Topher's body shifts into human form as he and Micah have no fight left in them. Brayden disappears through a swinging door, returning seconds later, holding what looks like a butcher knife.

"That's it. Cut it!"

Brayden lifts the knife above his head, bringing it down on our prison. The bubble explodes, releasing the gallons of water and throwing the small boy backward.

Amelia grabs Topher as Celeste grabs Micah. The two of them work in tandem, fighting to help the lycan breathe. Both work as if it's something they've done hundreds of times before.

I run to Brayden, lifting his soaking wet body off the floor. "Are you all right?"

He coughs a few times. "I think so. What happened?"

"It's a long story." I wrap my arms around him, carrying him away from the trauma that surrounds us.

A deep cough grabs my attention. I turn to see Topher sitting up and breathing. Seconds pass before Micah does the same. Both men seem confused and weak, but they're alive.

"You saved them," I whisper to Brayden. "*You* did that."

not a happily ever after

SEVERAL MINUTES PASS before the room calms down enough that I'm able to release my hold on Brayden and move toward my only friend, Luna—or what's left of her. Her face looks as angelic as always. Her normally vibrant bright green eyes are open, and her pupils are fixed and dilated. Her heartbeat stopped quickly, and she died instantly. Even being armed with that information doesn't help the sorrow I feel toward the young lycanthrope. "I'm so sorry, my friend." I can't hold in the tears.

A cold hand lands on my shoulder. "She was a warrior," Thorne says, squeezing my skin gently.

"Yeah, she was." I watch as he gently lifts what's left of her into his arms, cradling her to his chest. I follow them downstairs and to the dining room table where he lays her body.

Fran and Celeste move to my side, and the three of

us stand in awe of the tiny woman. "She died for nothing," I whisper. "Marnie took the girls, anyway."

"The girls will be okay for a short while. Luna is our priority right now." Celeste's words sound much older than she appears. "She will be honored by the lycan community here in her hometown. She deserves that."

"Aye, she does." Thorne wipes a tear.

Topher and Amelia join our group. He's weak and moving slowly, but it's clear he's healing. "She will be held in the highest honors," he says, wiping a tear.

Micah appears from nowhere. Like Topher, he's weak and looks exhausted. "My sweet Luna," he whispers, bending down and kissing her on her perfect cheek. "I never got the chance to make you my mate." Chill bumps cover my skin at his words. I'd seen cute interactions between them, but never realized they were at the mate part.

"I'm sorry, Micah. I feel responsible for this. If I would've..."

"No," Amelia interrupts. "You can't take responsibility for this. Luna knew what the dangers were. She made the decision to try to help the girls. That was heroic. She was no match for Marnie, but she tried." She looks at me. "You don't get to own this."

Her words strike a chord, and I nod. "How can we help?" I ask Topher, her Alpha. He doesn't respond. Instead, he gathers her into his arms as the lycan leave the house full of vampires.

Amelia wraps an arm around my waist. "Lycan have

strict burial traditions that vampires are not allowed to attend."

"I understand." I don't want to understand, but I do.

We spend the next few hours cleaning up what's left of the house. Every window is shattered, and glass is everywhere, but with vampire speed, the five of us make decent time. I took Brayden upstairs immediately after he released us from the bubble, locking him inside the room with his parents. Whatever compulsion Fran used on them is magically still working. With the insanity of what happened downstairs, I don't know how.

"I'll get the windows replaced tomorrow," Fran announces as Thorne drags the last trash bag to the road. "Such a shame. Some of these windows were as old as the city."

"What's next?" I ask once every task is completed.

"We find the children and kill Marnie and Eudora," Thorne announces.

"Why do I get the feeling that's going to be easier said than done?" I lower my head into my hands.

......

Fran works her magic, compelling Brayden's parents into forgetting everything that's happened after meeting us on Bourbon Street. She doesn't bother trying to wipe Brayden's memory. His ability would prevent it.

After leaving the "bed-and-breakfast" they booked, the three of them set off on their way home, completely oblivious to the shattered windows and insanity of our lives.

"Do you think Marnie and Eudora will go after him?" I ask, nodding toward the Uber leaving the house.

"Yes," the rest of the vampires answer in unison.

"He's more powerful than all of them," Amelia adds.

......

Thorne and I wait a few days before heading to what is now known as home—Charleston. The events of the past few weeks play through my mind in rapid succession.

With Kragen gone, the thing I've spent my life running from is gone. The irony of the situation is, I don't know who I am without him in my life. What kind of fuckery is that?

"What are you thinking?" Thorne asks as we sit on the porch of a colonial-style home, right in the center of downtown.

"I'm thinking I have to save them."

"Yeah. We will."

My phone rings, startling me back to reality. *"Hello?"*

"Elsie, it's Amelia."

I don't respond. God, I suck at dealing with trauma.

"There was an accident with Brayden's family," she continues.

I slide forward in the rocking chair I've been sitting in for hours. *"What happened?"*

"Car wreck. His parents are dead, and he's in the hospital. It's only a matter of time until he dies as well."

"What...what does that mean?"

"It means he's going to die," she answers simply.

"I hate to say it, but maybe that's for the best." I instantly feel horrible about my words. He's just a kid. He doesn't deserve to die.

"Yeah. We have another idea."

"No," I answer before giving her a chance to explain. *"His choice will be taken away. You can't do that to him."* My stomach knots, thinking about Brayden becoming a vampire.

"I know. I swore never to do that to someone. It's Celeste's idea. She thinks he's the only link to find the children."

Tears fill my eyes. She's right. Without him, we'll never locate Eudora, Marnie, or the immortal children. Brayden's powers will be limitless. We need him, but at what cost? *"You're talking about taking a child's life to find other children who shouldn't exist."*

"You're preaching to the choir, Elsie. Fran, Celeste, and I have spent the past few hours discussing the pros and cons, each time ending in a stalemate."

I laugh. *"It's all cons. There are no fucking pros to this whatsoever."*

The phone makes a strange sound, and a different voice comes online. *"Elsie, it's Celeste. I know how horrible it sounds, but after everything's done and Alex and the girls are found, I'll make sure they go to the same people I did. They'll spend the rest of their immortal life as adults."*

"Brayden never had the chance to be a kid."

"He's going to die, Elsie. He won't have that chance, anyway. Why not save him and use his powers to save the others?"

I don't know what to say. There is no logical argument against what they're about to do. Yes, he might help us save the others but at what cost? *"It's already done, isn't it?"*

Celeste is quiet for a few minutes. *"Tonight. We've got a plan to get him out of the hospital and back here."*

"If you've already made the decision, why call me?"

"You deserved to know," Amelia answers for the two of them.

I hang up without responding and wipe the tears from my cheeks. "I'm sorry, acushla. I think they're right. It's the only way to find the others." Thorne stands, pulls me to his front, and wraps his arms around my waist. We stand, wrapped in each other's arms for longer than necessary.

"Excuse me," a voice says from the front gate. We pull away from each other, expecting to see a tourist hoping for a quick tour of the historic home.

"Can I help you?" Thorne asks, straightening his now-wrinkled shirt.

"I have a certified letter for a Miss Elsbeth Abernathy." He holds a sealed letter where I can see it. "Are you Elsbeth?" he asks, staring at me.

"Aye, I am."

He holds the letter through the wrought iron gate. "If you'll sign saying you received it, I'll be on my way."

I scribble my signature, thanking the deliverer. "Who's it from?" Thorne asks once we're back on the piazza.

"The law firm where you settled Francis's estate." I open the envelope, finding a single tri-folded piece of paper, and read the words aloud.

Miss Abernathy,

My name is Abigail Orcutt. We had the pleasure of meeting while you were settling the estate of Francis Hawthorne. As part of my internship, I spent quite a bit of time in the archives of our firm. Reading through old client files has proven helpful in several situations, one of them being yours. I took the liberty of researching the connection between you and Aaron Abernathy further after our meeting and discovered information that could be vital for you and your lifestyle.

I pull the letter away from my face. My lifestyle? Does this woman know that I'm a vampire?

"What is it?" Thorne asks.

"I'm not sure," I answer truthfully before continuing.

Aaron Abernathy left a book and specific instructions for it to be delivered to his sister, Elsbeth Abernathy, should she ever be found. The book was safely bound and has been hidden in the basement of the city library ever since, with no hope of locating her...until now.

Aaron was one of New Orleans's most powerful warlocks, and the book left for you is his grimoire. One that can only be uncovered and used by you. I look forward to hearing from you soon.

Sincerely,
Abigail Orcutt

"Holy shit." I set the letter on a table nearby. Thorne

stares at me expectantly. I huff a laugh, not sure what to think of the newest development in the shit show of my life.

"What does that mean?" he asks, looking as confused as I feel.

"My family has vampires, lycan, and now witches."

"Oh, my," he whispers, making me laugh. "What's a grimoire? I've never been around witches or warlocks."

"His book of spells, along with instructions."

"This could help us find the children." Thorne takes the words out of my mouth.

"And helping us defeat Eudora and Marnie," I add.

He offers me his arm, leading me through the courtyard and onto the busy street. Together we walk at a human pace toward downtown Charleston, and hopefully, the answers we need.

**Please consider leaving an honest review for "Voyage of Fury and Fate". Your reviews help me get noticed on the Zon.

Leave a review here.

Read book 3! "Voyage of Magic and Malice."

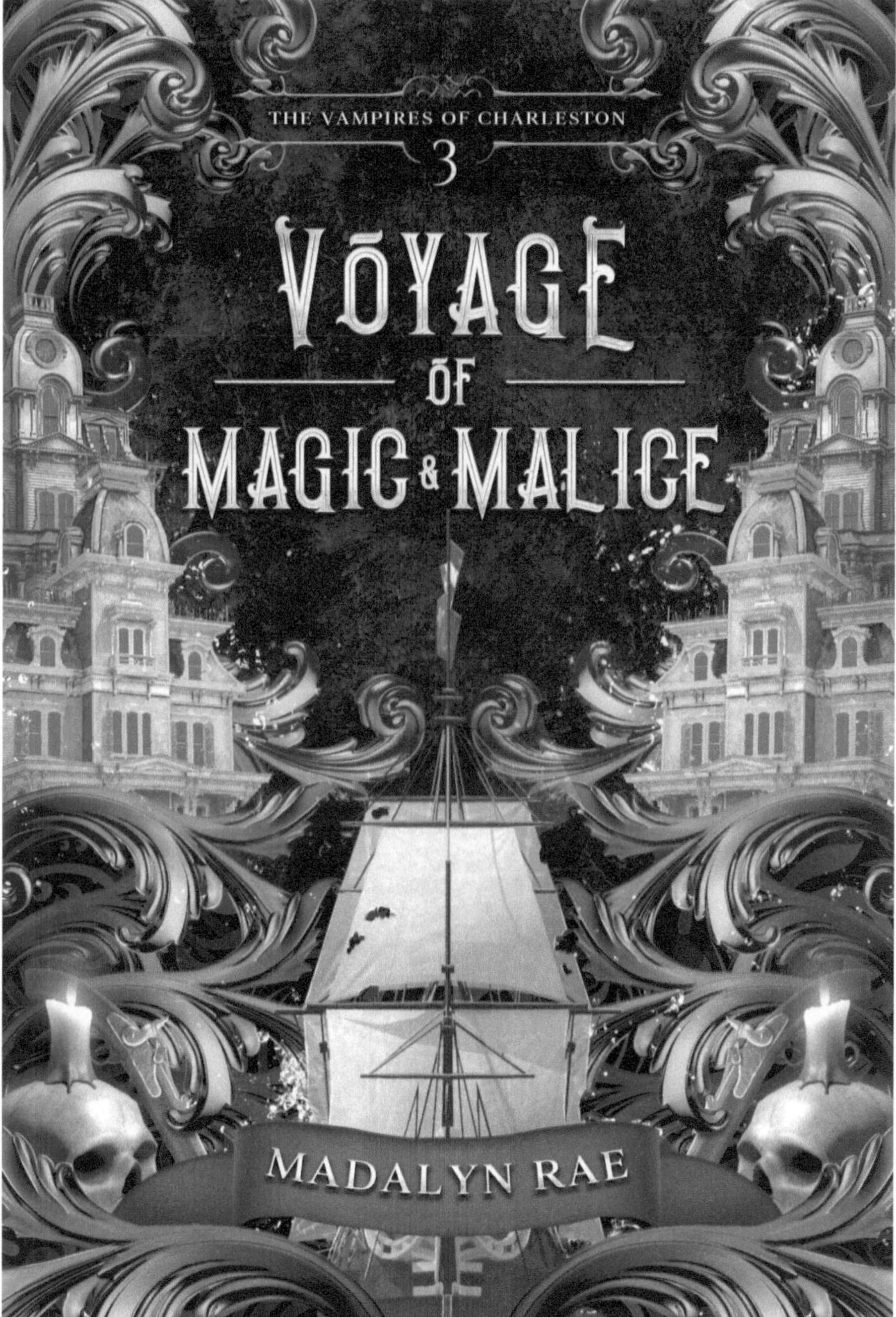

THE VAMPIRES OF CHARLESTON
3
VOYAGE
OF
MAGIC & MALICE
MADALYN RAE

Madalyn Rae is the pen name for an author who loves telling a story. As a teacher of tiny humans during the day and author by night, she hopes she's able to draw you into her world of fantasy, make-believe, and love, even for a brief moment.

She lives on the Gulf Coast's beautiful white, sandy beaches, with her two loyal yet mildly obnoxious dogs, Whiskey and Tippi. She's the mother of two amazing adult children and a son-in-love.

When not teaching or pretending to write, Madalyn is immersed in the world of music. Whether playing an instrument or singing a song, she is privileged to know that music is the true magic of the universe.

The Elementals Series

Birth of the Phoenix-Adria's Novella-Prequel

Phoenix of the Sea- Book 1

Guardian of the Sea- Murphy's Novella

Ashes of the Wind- Book 2

Embers of the Flame-Keegan's Novella

Fire of the Sky-Book 3

The Elementals Collection-Box Set

The Elementals Collection